Echoes of Love

GINA ARDITO

The following is a work of fiction. Any resemblance to actual persons, living or dead, is purely coincidental.

PROLOGUE
Simion, Amatia
April, 1805

"It isn't fair. Why must you go to St. Petersburg?"

Chesna Dubrow's open resentment stirred guilt in Pietor's heart. Not enough guilt, however, to fully tamp his excitement over the coming trip. Poor Chesna, seated on the stone bench at the curve of the drive, chewed on her lower lip. Her question needed no answer. She already knew about the heated arguments between him and his father. She always heard and often smoothed their ragged debates into a reasonable compromise. But not this time.

He averted his gaze from the unshed tears that glistened in her lake-blue eyes. Instead, he focused on the baggage atop the coach. Three trunks' worth of personal belongings. With more to follow, once he was settled. Clearly, his father predicted a prolonged absence for him. Beneath the rising sun, Amatia's royal coat of arms gleamed gold and crimson on the carriage door, a vivid reminder of his responsibilities. Regardless of his illegitimate status, despite the fact that Amatian law forbade Pietor from ever inheriting anything from his father, Prince Milos had insisted his son receive the traditional education of Amatian royalty.

"Everything will change now." The raw pain in her voice cut through him like shards of glass.

He knelt beside her and clasped her trembling hands in his. "I *will* come back," he vowed.

1

Chesna shook her head, and a lock of tawny hair fell across her face. "You will forget me."

He laughed. How could he possibly forget her? He'd as soon forget the glory of a sunrise on the lake or the feel of warm spring grass on his bare feet. Could a man look upon a painted masterpiece, and then forget the beauty in each brush stroke? No. He wouldn't forget his sweet Chess. "Not in a thousand lifetimes, my dove," he said aloud.

At his statement, her gaze dropped to the ground. "I wish I might go with you."

He poked a finger in her shoulder. "*You* are not permitted to attend university."

Her head shot up, and she folded her arms across her chest. "I would make a very good student. Better than you, I daresay."

"Yes, you would," he admitted with a wry grin. "And imagine how much worse it will be for me when I do not have your work to copy from."

"You mock me?" She sniffed back tears.

"Never, Chess." He rose and paced before her. His brain, anxious to begin the exciting new journey, waged war with his heart, held captive by his sweet, gentle dove. "But I have no choice in this matter. My father complains I've tarried too long already."

The tears fell now, leaving silver streaks on her porcelain cheeks. "Go, then. Go to your university. I shall stay here in Simion. And in a short time, you'll be so involved with your studies, your new friends, and the beautiful women of St. Petersburg, you'll forget all about me."

"Listen to me." He kissed her palm, and then curled her fingers to capture the spot. "No one else will touch my heart. I leave it here with you. Until I return."

"*If* you return." She swiped her closed fist across one cheek. "I've heard the ladies in St. Petersburg are beautiful. They dress in splendid gowns with rich furs and sparkling jewels. They paint their faces and flirt outrageously with handsome young men. Even the married noblewomen take lovers."

Pietor frowned. "No woman, married or nay, could ever sway my heart from you. I will write you every day, tell you everything I do and see. And when I've completed my education to my father's satisfaction, I will rush home to you."

She grabbed his hands inside her own. Her moist eyes glittered in the early morning light. "Swear it!"

His gaze remained locked on hers as he vowed, "I swear upon the soul of my late mother, I will return to you. I will not forget you. I will not forget my promise to you."

"And I swear upon the soul of *my* late mother," she replied, "I will wait for you."

Pietor pulled her into his arms and held her close for one long moment—a moment that might have to last them years. He inhaled the honeysuckle scent of her hair, rubbed a silken tress between his fingertips one final time, as if his skin might absorb her memory.

Finally, he pulled away and stepped inside the waiting carriage.

As the horses lurched forward, he leaned out the window, and repeated his vow with all the ferocity stored in his heart. "I *will* return to you, Chesna Dubrow."

1

Simion, Amatia
June, 1812

Queen Jasia was dead. The vibrant, happy lady from Lithuania had lost her life—and that of her daughter—in the rigors of childbirth.

Chesna Dubrow, royal governess, paced outside her father's bedchamber, waiting for his appearance. Each step she took, each second that ticked by, weighed down her shoulders with sorrow. As the door locks tumbled to open, she averted her eyes, a habit ingrained from years ago.

"Chesna?"

Only after her father addressed her did she turn in his direction. She'd obviously come at the most inopportune time. He had tied a purple robe around his slender frame, but the skin of his throat and upper chest peeked out through the neckline. His silver hair stuck out in several directions, his cheeks flushed with exertion, and scarlet tinged his lips.

"I'm sorry, Papa," she said, head bowed. "I wouldn't have disturbed you if—"

"I know, my sweet. What is it? The queen?"

Grief lodged in her throat, and she nodded.

Judging by the shadow that crossed his eyes, he understood what she could not say. He quickly crossed himself. "May God grant her peace. The babe?"

"Dead with her," she replied harshly.

Pulling his bedchamber door closed, he jerked his head to beckon her away. "When?" he asked as he strode down the vast hallway with her on his heels.

Before her eyes, the man who'd entertained his latest lightskirt only moments ago transformed into the efficient royal advisor she knew so well. "An hour ago."

"How is the king?"

"Devastated," she said on a sob. She fought the shivers that racked her and stared at the tapestried walls around them. Such an odd complexity, this palace. At times, the site of her greatest happiness, yet lately, the scene of too many tragedies. "Prince Milos is with His Majesty now. He sent me to fetch you."

"And Mikhail?"

Her belly flipped. Mikhail. King Jarek's and Queen Jasia's only living child. "Still sleeping." Unlike Chesna, who would not see her bed until many hours hence. "I felt it best to allow him plenty of rest before he heard the news. He'll need his strength."

Once she and her father had discussed the details of the royal funeral, she would have the misfortune to inform the five-year-old of his mother's death. Dread settled in the pit of her belly as she climbed the sweeping marble stairs behind her father.

"A wise decision," he said, "since I fear our trials are just beginning." The ice in his tone portended more misery.

Prickles erupted on her flesh, and she ran her hands down her bare arms. What else could go wrong on this horrible night?

After the strenuous birth of Prince Mikhail five years ago, Queen Jasia had suffered five subsequent miscarriages. The palace midwife then advised the royal couple to be satisfied with their one healthy son, but the queen insisted the king must have more heirs. Now her stubbornness had brought about her death.

Papa ushered her into his study and closed the door behind them. Gaze glued to the Turkish carpet beneath her slippered feet, Chesna waited with breath held.

"The queen's demise doesn't come at the best of times. I've received word from my sources in the west. Napoleon Bonaparte's armies have returned to Poland."

She absorbed this news as she would a biting salve. "He is going to Russia this time, isn't he?"

"I believe so." Papa's lips thinned into a frown.

"Then he'll invade Amatia."

"Yes," he confirmed in a hoarse monotone. "I informed King Jarek when I first received the missive, but he was too overwhelmed with Jasia's condition to heed the consequences for our country. Amatia is not Poland. We don't have well-trained soldiers ready to take up Napoleon's cause. We're a peaceful province, but our position near the borders of Russia makes us a target."

She shook her head. "Bonaparte doesn't come here for soldiers. He comes to conquer us. We're more than a stepping-stone toward Moscow. We're another piece of the pie that makes up the Corsican's grandiose ambitions to rule Europe."

"Quite true, my clever one." He moved toward the mullioned windows to look out upon the moonlit meadows below them. "And that is our dilemma, you see. If the French succeed in their conquest, an ambitious man such as Napoleon Bonaparte won't allow King Jarek to remain as the ruler of Amatia. He will offer His Majesty a choice of death or exile. I've tried to convince the king that a short time in exile would be far more agreeable to the citizens of Amatia than his death, but you know His Majesty."

Chesna nodded. "He believes in death before dishonor."

In reply, Papa gave another shrug.

"But, if he makes that choice, Napoleon will take possession of Prince Mikhail," she conjectured. "Amatia would then find itself under French rule."

"That's precisely what I fear." He turned to face her again. Moonlight cast shadows of anguish over his face. "For more than a century, the Dubrows have been the chief advisors to the royal family. We've remained loyal to our homeland and her rulers. And we must continue that tradition. I can do no more for King Jarek but provide him with my counsel and pray he heeds it. However, whether he does so or not, I'll remain by his side to the very end, even into death. It's my duty to stay with my sovereign."

"I know." Her throat tightened the words into a bare croak.

His blue-eyed gaze pierced the dark, pinpoints of wisdom in a night of sheer madness. "Do you truly understand, Chesna? When Napoleon comes, you'll be the last of the Dubrows. I won't be able to help you. You must do whatever you can to keep the Amatian throne secure."

It didn't escape her notice that he no longer considered the arrival of Bonaparte's *Grand Armée*—and his imminent death at their hands—as a possibility, but as a certainty. She was a Dubrow, however. The last of her line. And she would not disappoint her ancestors by shirking her obligations to Amatia's royal family.

"I won't fail you, Papa."

"I know you won't." He kissed the top of her head—a benediction—and opened the door again. "I have faith in you."

♥

Chesna's heart cracked as she stared at the five-year-old prince asleep in his royal bed. Amber curls set against the scarlet pillows fanned a face as pure and sweet as an angel's. He was too young to know such sorrow. How would she find the fortitude to tell him?

She sighed. Jasia would expect this one last service. And she would take charge of this moment as she had with every other incident in the young prince's life.

"Forgive me, Your Highness, but I have some very sad news for you."

The seriousness of her tone must have reached through his hazy slumber. Mikhail sat up, pushed the silken sheets away from his shoulders, and rubbed the sleep from his eyes with closed fists. "What is it, Chesna?"

She took a deep breath, prayed to the carved cherubs in his gilt ceiling for fortitude, and plowed through. "While you slept, the angels came for your mama and your baby sister. They have gone to Heaven this day."

Mikhail's gray eyes filled with tears, but he sniffed them back. "Will they return to us?"

"No, Your Highness. Our Lord Jesus decided He needed your mama and sister with Him."

A heavy silence filled the ornate room. She understood

7

the prince's struggles to rein in his emotions. From the cradle, the boy had learned that Amatian royalty did not cry. But surely, those rules did not apply to someone so young facing so much heartache.

At last, on a shuddering breath, the prince looked up into her face, his doe eyes wide and wet. "Will you be my mama now?"

Chesna brushed a lock of golden hair from his forehead. "No, Your Highness." She opened her arms, and he collapsed against her chest. "I'm still your governess, and I'll continue to care for you as I have since the day you were born. But your mama will always be your mama. No one can take her place."

"Mama will be too busy in Heaven with my sister to remember me."

She pulled away and chucked him under the chin. A smile creased her lips. "Your mama will always remember you. And you must always remember her. You must try to keep her memory alive inside your heart." She tapped his chest.

The boy looked down at her finger pressing against his ribcage. "Do you keep your mama's memory alive in *your* heart?"

"Indeed I do. And it's very difficult for me because she died shortly after I was born. I never knew her. But my papa tells me the most wonderful stories about her."

He brushed a stubby finger across the gold glinting at her ears. "You have her jewelry, too."

"Yes, that's true." She allowed herself a moment to indulge the memory. Her birthday. The ear bobs her papa had given her to show how grown up she'd become. Ear bobs that had once decorated her departed mother's lobes. With a deep sigh, she allowed the visions of that long-ago happiness to fade away. "If you need help in keeping your mama's memory alive, you may ask me anything you wish. I knew her from the day she came to Amatia. I'd be happy to tell you tales about her."

"You won't die, will you, Chesna?"

The dread lacing his words struck her like a poisoned dart. "I-I don't intend to die soon," she stammered. "But it is not my decision. It is the Lord's choice."

"But what if the angels decide to come for you next?" he pressed. "Who will take care of me if you're gone?"

"Why, Your Highness, whether I'm here or gone, your father will always care for you."

"Papa is King of Amatia," Mikhail reminded her. "He has many duties to attend to. He doesn't have time to care for me."

"Don't speak foolish thoughts." Forcing a lighthearted air, she tousled his head. "You are the most important person in your papa's life. Never forget that. And if something should happen to me, there are many people in this palace who would care for you in my stead. You have your papa, your Uncle Milos, my papa, and your servant, Karol."

Mikhail folded his arms over his chest and glared at her. "They're all men, Chesna. I need a mama."

"What of Urszula? She loves you very much."

Mikhail made a face of disgust. "Urszula is a cook. She doesn't know how to care for a royal prince."

"Irina was your mama's governess in Lithuania," she suggested. "She'd love a chance to be your governess."

Mikhail shook his head. "I can't understand Irina when she speaks. Her Amatian is atrocious."

Over the next several minutes, Mikhail found fault with every woman Chesna named. He deemed one too old, another too young. He dismissed one as not pretty enough for the position and another as too fat. One laughed like a goose, another thought like one. One shouted too much, another never smiled.

"You're the only person who loves me the way Mama loved me," he declared. "I desire no one else to care for me."

"Well then, I must remain with you until you change your mind," she teased him. "I suppose I might live until you don't need me anymore."

Mikhail threw his arms around her waist, buried his head in her ribcage, and squeezed. "I'll always need you, Chesna. Promise me you'll never leave me."

She tried to pull him away, but he clung to her with the tenacity of an ivy plant.

"Promise me," he repeated firmly. "Promise you'll always stay with me."

9

Her heart split open and wept. Such an impossible promise!

But Mikhail needed to hear her make the vow. He needed someone to believe in, someone to rely upon now that his life had changed so dramatically. He was only five years old. He needed comfort, he needed peace and, most of all, he needed to know he wouldn't be alone.

"I swear I'll stay with you as long as you wish, Your Highness," she vowed. "I won't leave you."

2

Two days later, a mournful procession crept through the streets of Simion. The city's residents wept openly as the casket that carried Queen Jasia and her stillborn daughter rode past in a cart drawn by six black geldings. Throngs of men and women lined the streets, waving black handkerchiefs and beating their breasts in grief. Children sobbed and threw flowers upon the top of the casket, blanketing the black box in colorful blossoms.

As tradition dictated, the king's Royal Palace Guards flanked the cart. King Jarek, astride another black gelding, rode behind the funeral cart with his son seated before him. His brother, Prince Milos, followed on a matching horse. The remaining royal retinue, including Chesna and her father, Bela, walked in their wake from the wrought iron gates of Opal Palace to the Church of St. Ambrose in the city's square.

When the procession turned the final curve in the road, the white spires of the church pierced the steel gray sky.

"It's hard to believe she's gone," Bela whispered to Chesna.

She nodded, too choked up with emotion to speak. Only seven short years ago, the residents of the city had blanketed another carriage with blossoms, the carriage that had transported the newlywed king and queen to the palace after their marriage ceremony at the Church of St. Ambrose.

The line of mourners slowed to a halt outside the church. Chesna scanned the expressions of the people around her. King Jarek seemed to have aged decades overnight with his drawn face and stooped posture. Prince Milos, normally gregarious and cheerful, wiped tears from his ashen cheeks with the back of his hand. Prince Mikhail, pale and shaken, did not speak. In fact, he hadn't spoken a word since their conversation on the morning of his mother's death.

Sympathy melted Chesna's grief-encased heart, and she inched forward as the king lowered the child to the ground. She knelt beside him. On a stifled cry, Mikhail wrapped his arms about her neck and buried his face in the crook of her shoulder.

Crack!

The sound of gunfire rent the air a moment before something whizzed past Chesna's head. A soldier in the Royal Guard emitted a sharp yelp, and then fell to his knees, his chest flowered with wet blood. A scream sounded, and the crowds erupted into chaos.

Chesna's heart shattered in her chest. Napoleon's soldiers had arrived.

She glanced up at the Royal Guard, who carried no arms or munitions but their decorative silver sabers. Defenseless to oppose the foe and protect their sovereign, they quickly broke ranks and disappeared into the fleeing crowd.

As the soldiers of the French army fired their weapons again and again, the air filled with oppressive smoke and disoriented the terrified people. Amatians ran in every possible direction, heedless of their own safety or that of their fellow citizens. In their haste to escape death, they pushed and shoved at one another, trampling the unfortunates who stumbled in their headlong flight.

Beside her, Prince Milos climbed upon the black and gold marble base of the city's monumental fountain. Waving his arms, he shouted above the screams and reports of the guns. "Peace, I beg of you! Please don't give in to panic!"

A screeching sound pierced the air, and Chesna's gaze turned skyward. A flaming rocket exploded, directly in front of Prince Milos. He fell on the ground, dead. His head, severed by the fiery blow, plunged into the water with a bright red splash.

Oh, God. Bile rose in Chesna's throat, hot and acrid. As his blood coursed over the cobblestones near their feet, Mikhail whimpered in horror. She swallowed hard against the need to retch. Shielding the child's eyes from his uncle's headless torso, she held him against her bosom and offered what little comfort her own fears would allow. But his soft cries turned to shrieks of terror, and his slender frame shuddered as the guns continued to crack and boom. Smoke dried her mouth, preventing any sounds of horror to pass through her lips.

"Take the prince inside the church, Chesna," an urgent voice spoke low in her ear. "Request sanctuary from Father Grigory." She looked up from the little boy's bowed head and into the harried eyes of her father. "Hurry! Remember your vow to me. Get inside the church and stay there."

Despite Bela's prodding, she hesitated. If she fled to the church with Mikhail, she knew she'd never see her father alive again. Glancing between them, her mind wavered between fear for the little boy and fear for the man. How could she possibly choose?

A large red-haired man appeared out of the screaming throngs and grasped Chesna's hand. Mikhail's personal servant, Karol, wore the same terror in his eyes Chesna bore in her heart. "We must go now. There's much to do and precious little time." Without waiting for any argument she might attempt, Karol pulled Mikhail from her arms and scooped him against his chest.

She turned again toward her father, but the smoke-filled air and sea of people had swallowed him.

"Remember how much I loved you, Chesna," her father called out from somewhere beyond her foggy line of vision. "May God be with you."

Karol's forceful nudge in her right shoulder pushed her toward the granite steps that led to the church's entrance. She'd only reached the arched mahogany doors when a sudden clatter arose behind them. With her fingers clutching the cold brass handle, she whirled.

In their panicked flight, the townspeople had upset the funeral cart, which stood unguarded. The cart fell onto its side and the casket slid out, spilling the linen-wrapped bodies to the ground. Men, women, and children trampled the deceased royals beneath their frantic feet.

"No!" King Jarek raced forward to protect his dead wife and child from being crushed by the crowds.

As the king broke out into the open, one of Napoleon's sharpshooters fired. A blossom of red appeared on King Jarek's shirtfront, and he pitched forward, his arms thrust outward in a final attempt to shield his beloved wife from harm. He landed directly atop the two bodies, still.

"Papa!" Mikhail's shriek of terror caught Chesna's attention.

She turned away from the spectacle, wrenched the door open, and raced inside the church with Karol, still cradling Mikhail, on her heels. They scrambled up the aisle, passing the empty rows of benches in a blur of gleaming brown. At the altar, Father Grigory lit the tall, pillared candles on either side of the church apse. The two adults fell to their knees on the scarred wooden floor with a loud thump.

"Sanctuary, Father," Chesna managed to gasp with her last breaths, her hands thrust toward the priest in supplication. "I beg of you. Please grant us sanctuary."

♥

As the heart-wrenching din of battle raged outside the church's stone walls, Chesna and Karol sheltered Mikhail inside. Father Grigory hovered nearby, waving incense over their bowed heads. The sickly sweet smoke only distressed Chesna's senses more. Her eyes teared. Her nostrils stung. A gray cloud of pain clamored in her head, and her stomach tumbled in freefall.

While Father Grigory prayed for divine intervention, Chesna refused to place her faith solely in God. Instead, she murmured plans to Karol, who nodded and whispered his own ideas in reply.

The report of the guns echoed through the cavernous church. Dust fell from the rafters with each dull boom. Unholy screams pierced the holy quiet.

Mikhail remained silent, but his wide eyes reflected the terror of his experiences on this dismal day. Hours passed, and the guns at last fell silent before the child surrendered to his tiny body's need for sleep. Soft snores bubbled against Chesna's chest.

Despite her own fatigue, she remained alert with Karol beside her. The priest paced to and fro. The black beads of his rosary dripped from his gnarled fingers.

Each minute that ticked by without word of the goings-on outside ramped up her dread until her mouth tasted bitter ashes and her stomach churned. King Jarek was dead. As was Prince Milos. Leaving Prince Mikhail the heir to the throne.

The king is dead. Long live the king.

But where was her father? Surely, he was also dead. If he'd survived the carnage, he would have come to the church to protect his new sovereign. Her childhood heart wept for her father's loss. Bela Dubrow had been a wise, loving parent to both her and their countrymen. Although his first priority was always the royal family, he'd never allowed Chesna to feel neglected. Somehow he must have known this day might come because the brilliant tactician had shared all his knowledge with his daughter.

If not for the child asleep on her lap, she'd crumble into emotional pieces. But her father had taught her well. Her first priority must always remain with the king. She was no longer royal governess. By the right of ascension, she was now the last of the Dubrows, the royal advisor. And Mikhail was now her sovereign. Both of their roles had changed dramatically today.

Regardless of the numbness settling over her bones, she would not awaken His Royal Highness. On a deep breath, she forced her tense muscles to relax.

As if he'd sensed her discomfort, Father Grigory leaned to whisper in her ear. "Follow me, Miss Dubrow. Let's give the prince a place to sleep."

Gingerly, she rose with her precious burden cradled in her arms. On hesitant steps, legs shaky from exhaustion and shock, she followed the priest behind the curtains that draped the altar. They descended a series of stone stairs and entered a tiny windowless chamber which contained a small wooden cot with a threadbare blanket. Mildew pierced the stagnant air.

"It isn't much," the priest said softly. "But it is the best I might offer His Highness."

Throat desert-dry, Chesna croaked out a husky thank you.

He turned away. "I must return to my prayers for the day's victims."

The victims. She stifled a sob and placed Mikhail on the cot. He never moved at her motion, too drained to sense the jostle from her soft body to the hard wooden bed. Once she had the prince—no, the *king*—settled, she sat beside him on the cot's edge and brushed a curl of hair from his forehead.

"We must work quickly, Chess," Karol said from the doorway. "Time is short."

"I know," she whispered. Despite her shaky hands, she quickly stripped the boy of his clothing. When he wore nothing but his silken undergarments, she wrapped the thin blanket about his shoulders to ward off a chill. "Is it safe for you to leave now?"

On a shrug, Karol stepped inside. "It's a chance we must take. Will the boy understand this subterfuge?"

Sympathy overwhelmed her, and she bent to kiss Mikhail's temple. "It's a chance we must take."

Karol sighed. "We're placing our lives in the hands of a five-year-old boy."

Chesna's ire blazed. "His Majesty, King Mikhail of Amatia, is placing his life in our hands. Never forget that." She rose from the cot with the royal vestments tossed over her arm and his shoes in her hand. Eyes squeezed shut, she thrust the items at Karol before she might second-guess her decision. "May God forgive us for what we are about to do."

"God understands," he replied. "Better to pray King Mikhail forgives us."

She stared at him in consternation. "King Mikhail is alive. Which is more than I can say for the rest of his family."

"Or your own." Karol must have realized his blunder because his cheeks flamed redder than his hair and he stuttered, "F-forgive me, Chess."

His bitter reminder of her father's fate roiled the acid in her stomach, but she waved away his apology. Her pain dimmed when compared to Mikhail's. Nothing mattered but

His Majesty. "Go," she told Karol. "By dawn, we must return to the palace, our plan in motion."

"When will you explain to him what we've done?"

She cast a glance at the sleeping boy. "If he doesn't awaken beforehand, I'll rouse him when you return. We'll explain our plan then. Once we've abandoned this sanctuary, we may trust no one but ourselves."

Karol nodded, his lips set in a grim line. "May God watch over you both, Chesna."

"And you also, Karol."

Without another word, he left on his errand. Alone again, Chesna knelt beside the cot. The harsh, cold stones and bits of gravel punished her knees, but still she prayed. She prayed Karol would be successful in his quest and would return to the church soon. She prayed Mikhail would understand what she'd done and that he'd keep their secret. She prayed for wisdom, for strength, for the saints to watch over the souls of all those who'd perished today. She prayed for those who'd survived. She prayed God would listen to her prayers.

At last, Karol returned.

"Done," he announced simply. He carried a bundle of filthy clothing in his arms and a pair of worn old boots in his hand.

Hands perched on the cot's edge, Chesna struggled to rise from her penitent pose. Her legs, however, had given their last and she sank onto the cot, missing Mikhail's feet by the whisper of an inch.

"Chess?" Karol asked.

She waved away his concern and focused her attention on the sleeping child. "Your Highness?" With one gentle hand, she nudged his shoulder.

He stirred, rolled onto his side, and pulled the thin blanket up over his head.

"Please, Your Majesty, you must listen to me."

The boy flipped down the blanket and opened one eye to stare at her. Obviously, her use of his new title had struck through his sleep-fogged brain. His brow furrowed, and a lone tear slipped down his cheek. "Papa?" The squeaky tremor in his voice confirmed her suspicion that he sensed the truth regarding his father's fate. "He's gone, isn't he?"

She bowed her head. "Yes, sire. Forgive our haste, but we must speak quickly."

The cot creaked as Mikhail sat up. With a shiver at the cold air, he folded his arms over his chest, and looked around in confusion. "Where are my garments?"

Chesna exchanged a quick glance with Karol, who came forward with the bundle of dirty clothes. "Here, Your Majesty."

Mikhail's expression mirrored his disgust. "Those are filthy. Where did you get them?"

Cheeks flushed, Karol backed away from the boy's indignance. "From a dead boy in the street, sire."

"How dare you!" he shouted. "I do not wear dirty garments."

"You do now," Chesna said flatly. She halted the argument he might attempt with an index finger pressed to the child's lips. "Please, Your Majesty. Listen to me. I'll explain."

Although his eyes narrowed in displeasure, Mikhail nodded.

She removed her finger and gestured for Karol to bring the clothes forward. "Do you recall what you asked of me when I told you of your mama's death?"

"Yes," he replied warily. "I asked if you'd be my mama now. But you said you could never take her place."

She shook out the threadbare shirt to remove any stray dust or insects, then slid the rough garment around his satiny shoulders. "Well, sire, I've changed my mind."

The boy looked up, one eyebrow quirked. "How so?"

"Do you understand why the French have attacked Amatia today?"

"Papa said Napoleon Bonaparte wants to seize Russia, and in order to do so, he must take control of Amatia."

"Yes, Your Majesty." She said a silent prayer of thanks that the child understood the political ramifications. "To rule Amatia, Napoleon would destroy the royal family, including you. But the French only plan to remain here for a short time before pressing on toward Moscow. They must cross the mountains before the cold weather sets in. And if they're defeated in Moscow, a fate my father claimed was all but certain, your throne reverts back to you based on your alliance with Tsar Alexander. Until then, we must keep these foreigners from discovering your true identity so they cannot harm you or take you prisoner."

One eyebrow quirked up, an expression so like his father's, Chesna sucked in a sharp breath. "And how will we accomplish this?"

She refocused on the new king. "While you slept, Karol took your garments and went out into the streets. He found a dead boy of about your age, removed his clothing, dressed him in your royal attire and left his body beneath that of your father's. By tomorrow morning, Napoleon's army will be under the assumption they succeeded in killing the entire royal family."

"So you're going to pretend to be my mama to fool our enemies," he surmised. At Chesna's nod, he clapped. "How clever of you!"

She placed her hands over his to stop the applause. "This isn't a game, sire. From the moment we leave these walls, you'll refer to me as Mama and I'll refer to you as my child. Karol will no longer be your personal valet. In fact, all the servants will treat you in the same manner they treat any other servant's child. You will have no royal privileges. Are you certain you understand what this means?"

"Of course I do. And you must not call me 'sire' anymore. Or Your Majesty." He wagged a finger of chastisement in her direction. "And I cannot be known as Mikhail lest our enemies become suspicious. What will you call your son?"

"I shall call you Zarek."

His regal brow furrowed. "Isn't that too similar to my father's name? Zarek and Jarek?"

"Yes it is, which is precisely why I've chosen it. I don't wish for you to forget your father, even for a short time. He was a great man, a magnificent king, and someone you should strive to emulate." She held up an index finger. "And I'm giving you this name for one other reason."

"What other reason?"

"Zarek is Polish for 'God protect the king.'"

The boy grinned for the first time in days. "I like it. What do we do now?"

19

"Now, we'll return to the palace, Zarek."

"Yes, Mama," he replied, the epitome of obedience as he clasped her hand.

3

Dear Chess,

Your tears and pleas haunt me. I know you doubt my promises.

—April 8, 1805

By the time Chesna slipped into Opal Palace through the servants' entrance, the French army had already taken over the residence. The royal servants huddled like sheep in the kitchens. Heartsick, Chesna took in the damage to this normally warm and organized place. Splinters of crockery crackled under her feet. The smell of spilled wine soured the air.

The marauders had apparently rifled through the pantry. Flour caked the tile floor, eggs lay cracked on the counters, rinds from fruits and vegetables littered every flat surface. Chesna tiptoed inside, anger rising with each new atrocity.

"Where are they?" she whispered to the nearest chambermaid.

"Inspecting the rest of the palace from turret to dungeon," the older woman whispered in reply.

Good. Quickly she ushered Karol and the newly-named Zarek into the fold.

When Zarek rushed to her side, Urszula, the chief cook, gasped and lifted her arms toward the ceiling. "Saints be praised. Our prince is safe."

"No, Urszula," the boy replied in hushed tones. "I'm no longer your prince."

She colored. "Of course not, Your Majesty."

"Not Your Majesty, either." He flashed a cocky grin at Chesna. "I am to be known as Zarek, son of Chesna Dubrow, until our enemies are defeated in Russia."

A simplistic explanation, but judging by the nods of approval from the household staff, sufficient.

To be certain everyone understood, Chesna stepped forward and placed a protective hand on the boy's shoulder. "Can you all remember that?"

Before anyone might answer, a French soldier appeared in the doorway. Several servants retreated at his sudden entry into their midst. But Chesna and Zarek remained rooted to the flour-coated floor.

She glared at the interloper, radiating hatred through her eyes. His face, streaked with dirt and sweat, reflected back the same disdain. Dried blood smeared his chest and sleeves. No small stain. Whose blood had spilled so recklessly yesterday? The king's? Her father's? Bile rose in her throat, and she swallowed the burning acid before it might spew from her lips. *Monster.*

He was so young, still wet behind the ears. Why, she was at least a decade older than this man-boy. But she had never taken a life. Of course, should anyone threaten Mikhail/Zarek, her soul would quickly bear that same dark stain.

The soldier broke their staring battle first. "General Jacques de Valmiere demands the servants gather in the grand hall immediately."

The servants looked at one another in confusion. The soldier spoke in French, a language unfamiliar to most of them.

Apparently impatient with their ignorance, he thrust a finger toward the doorway. "*Ouste!*"

Expressions blank, the servants herded out of the kitchens while the soldier shouted and cursed at them in French.

Although the rest of the staff couldn't comprehend the monster's invectives, Chesna understood every vile word. Beside her, Zarek stiffened, but she squeezed his hand to remind him that he must do nothing to arouse suspicion. They dared not let this foreigner discover they spoke his language as well as he did.

In the grand hall, an older man with black eyes blazing above a hooknose sat upon King Jarek's golden throne. Dozens of armed soldiers surrounded the man, each wearing the same expression of smug disgust.

"*Je m'appelle General Jacques de Valmiere,*" he announced. The servants stared at him in confusion, and he turned to the soldiers clustered around him. "Where is the officer who speaks Amatian?"

A tall, broad-shouldered man with jet-black hair and silver eyes broke ranks and stepped forward. "Here, sir!"

An audible gasp came from someone in the crowd of servants, but a quick glare from General de Valmiere silenced them all.

"You will translate," the general ordered.

On a nod, the officer turned to face the Amatians. When the general began speaking again, the officer translated the words into their native tongue.

"King Jarek and all his male relations are dead. I hereby claim the province of Amatia by right of conquest in the glorious name of the Emperor of France, Napoleon Bonaparte."

With each word the man spoke, Chesna's blood chilled another degree. By the time the speech concluded, ice had frozen in her veins.

Not so, Zarek, who broke from her hold and shouted, "You may tell your cowardly emperor he'll never rule Amatia!"

"Zarek," she hissed. "Silence."

The general looked about the cluster of servants, then faced his officer, beetle brows knitted together into one angry caterpillar. "What did that boy say?"

Chesna breathed a sigh of relief. Thank God the general hadn't understood Zarek's outburst. She prayed the translating officer would not betray the child.

But Zarek pushed through his wall of bodyguards and stood alone in the center of the hall. He confronted the furious general, a mouse daring to confront a lion, his face flush with hostility. "I said you may tell your cowardly emperor he'll never rule Amatia," he repeated in flawless French.

"Insolent brat!" The general shot up from the throne, one hand outstretched to strike.

With a sharp cry, Chesna raced forward to block the coming blow. The general's hand slapped harmlessly against the mutton sleeve of her gown.

"How dare you?" The general's soulless gaze burned through her like the fires of hell. "Who are you? And who is this boy?"

Despite her shaky legs, Chesna straightened and placed a protective arm around Zarek's shoulders. "I am his mother," she announced in French.

No sense in feigning ignorance of their language since Zarek had already given away that particular secret. Now, her objective would be to prevent these vile ruffians from learning any other truths. To that end, she shoved Zarek's little face into her skirts.

May His Majesty forgive me my transgressions...

The translating officer stared at her, wide-eyed, but she ignored him and trained her gaze on the general glowering down at her.

"Where is the boy's father?" he demanded.

"Dead," she stated flatly. "He was killed in yesterday's attack."

The general resumed his perch on the throne. *Usurper.* "For a servant, you and your son speak French well. Why is that?"

Chesna's brain sought some easy answer, but exhaustion had long ago claimed her wits. Before she could conjure a reasonable excuse, an older woman stepped from the circle of servants.

"Because Zarek isn't a mere servant's son. He is the son of King Jarek."

Rage melted the ice in Chesna's veins to molten lava. She turned to face the late queen's former governess, fists tight, and posture stiff. "Irina!"

Shocked murmurs ran through both sides of the hall's occupants, but Chesna burned white hot. The betrayals around her accumulated like autumn leaves. Tears gathered in the corners of her eyelids, but she wouldn't show these traitors any weakness. "Don't say any more, Irina."

General de Valmiere held up a hand for silence. When the grumbles died, he turned his snake eyes on Chesna. "Is this true?"

"Of course not," she said quickly.

With a sharp cry, Zarek huddled deeper inside the folds of her gown as if to avoid notice. She placed a hand on his shoulder and prayed he didn't sense her nervous tremors.

"Do not believe her," Irina retorted. "She'll do whatever she must to protect that child. Chesna's always been an ambitious viper. And now that King Jarek is gone, she'll stop at nothing to place her son on the throne in his father's place."

Cradling Zarek even closer, Chesna turned her rage on Irina. "Why?" Shock stole the volume from her voice and her question came out a scratchy whisper. "Why would you do this?"

Irina tossed her head. "I came to Amatia with Queen Jasia. The queen was a good and loving lady." She thrust an angry finger in Chesna's direction. "But this evil woman hated Jasia. She wanted King Jarek for her own. Queen Jasia was heartbroken when she discovered that Chesna would present the king with a child a few months after Prince Mikhail's birth. And when the child arrived, King Jarek insisted Zarek be given the same privileges as the true prince. They even shared the royal nursery."

When intimidation didn't still Irina's tongue, Chesna resorted to begging. "Irina, please. Don't do this."

"You wicked woman!" Irina spat at Chesna's feet. "I'd rather see Amatia ruled by a foreigner than by your bastard get."

"Irina," Karol shouted, but whatever else he intended to say couldn't compete with all the shouts from the other servants.

The uproar inside the grand hall swelled. Why? Why had Irina turned against them? How could she betray their king so horribly?

"Enough!" the general bellowed, snapping Chesna from her reverie.

At once, all noise and motion stopped. Even Zarek

froze.

General de Valmiere turned his beet-red face to the soldier who'd originally herded the servants into the hall. "Captain Dumont, take the staff back to the kitchens at once."

On a crisp salute, the soldier turned to the crowd of stunned onlookers. "*Ouste.*"

Chesna pulled Zarek from her gown and grasped his hand, prepared to follow, until the general's next order stopped her dead. "Captain Gabris. Take this Chesna and her bastard son to the dungeon. Lock them there and then, return here."

"Yes, sir."

"Majors Roucher and Montfort," the general continued, "will remain. The rest of you men, see to setting up camp."

Chesna, with Zarek nearly attached to her side, backed away from the crowd of dirty, sullen soldiers.

Captain Gabris reached for her hand, but she whirled away, covering Zarek from his view. "I don't need your assistance."

"I should imagine you don't," he said, his smirk evident in the humor that laced each word.

One arm around Zarek's shoulder, she strode from the hall toward the vestibule that would lead to the bowels of the palace. Only after she knew they were alone did she face the captain.

"Welcome home, Pietor," she said with all the hatred stored inside her heart.

"Thank you, Chesna," he replied blandly.

4

While they'd been in the grand hall, she'd never shown a hint of recognition toward him, but she'd known him immediately. How could she not? His face had haunted her dreams for seven years. Still, she couldn't help but study this stranger who walked beside her in the vestibule.

He was older, as was she. At one time, they'd seen eye-to-eye, but now they were quite far apart, and not merely because of the difference in their heights. He was a stranger to her now. Oh, he still had the same gray eyes, eyes that used to light up at the mere sound of her voice. But now they looked at her in disgust. The same thick black hair curled around his oval face, but now the length ended at the top of his nape, the *French* fashion, as opposed to the shoulder-length tresses she'd tugged to gain his attention in their youth. He still had the same aquiline nose, but now he held it so highly in the air, she wondered how he didn't walk face-first into walls.

The broad shoulders that used to hoist her in the highest branches of the orchard trees to find the ripest fruit were now encased in an enemy uniform. And his lips, the same lips that once would kiss her into fits of giggles, compressed into a deep frown of revulsion.

He was Pietor, and yet he was not *her* Pietor. The young man to whom she'd pledged her undying love in a spring meadow had become a man she couldn't bear to be near. Pietor *Gabris* had forsaken his name and his country, as well as her heart.

"I suppose this is why you haven't bothered to write me in the last six years," she remarked in a tone as emotional as a tree stump.

She grabbed a lit torch from a nearby wall sconce and proceeded forward. But with the torch held aloft in her left hand and Zarek's tenacious grasp on her right, she had to wait for Pietor to pull open the door to the staircase that led to the cells. He brushed past her, and his profile called up visions she'd rather forget.

...I will rush home to you...

...I swear upon the soul of my late mother, I will return to you...

...I will not forget you. I will not forget my promise to you...

Liar.

The moment he yanked on the handle, the musty air of centuries of misery assailed her nostrils. No matter. No prison could compete with her bitter memories of Pietor.

"I would have wagered the lure of the whores of St. Petersburg made you forget me," she said.

"Had I known you'd join their sisterhood so soon after my departure, I might not have forgotten you so quickly."

The barb struck tender flesh, but with right on her side, she shook off the sting. "You were far too busy becoming one of Napoleon Bonaparte's lackeys to remember the lonely girl waiting for you in Simion."

"Obviously you found a way to occupy yourself in your solitude."

"I didn't wish to wither on the vine," she replied with an impudent toss of her head.

"Wither? You barely waited until you were ripe before you allowed yourself to be plucked." He gave a curt nod in Zarek's direction. "Is he really King Jarek's son?"

Did she hear a touch of jealousy in his tone? Oh, she hoped so. She squeezed Zarek's arm, a silent reminder he must do nothing to reveal the truth to this traitor. "Yes, he is. Look closely at him. He has the stamp of his father all over his face."

As they stood at the bottom of the stairs, Pietor, two steps above, scrutinized the boy. Chesna waited, fully aware of the conclusion he'd eventually draw. Even without the regal demeanor, this child was King Jarek in miniature. He had his father's golden hair, warm gray eyes, and clefted chin. Pietor's lips compressed again, and Chesna hid a smile.

Her heart chastised her for finding pleasure in his anger. But after years of bitter loneliness, the revenge of the moment tasted too sweet not to savor for a while. "The resemblance is startling," she said. "Isn't it?"

"Yes," he replied softly. "There is much of his father in him."

"I was speaking of the resemblance to you." She strode ahead on the muddy floor. "You had a very similar look as a child, though with your mother's dark hair. Papa always said a family's traits repeat themselves in their descendants. And after all, you and Zarek are cousins."

His hand clutched her sleeve, slowing her to a stop. "Be quiet, Chesna," he whispered. "From now on, you must be careful what you say and to whom."

"Why?" She whirled to face him. "Is it possible your compatriots don't know who you are?"

"My compatriots know I was born and raised in Simion and that I became disenchanted with the Amatian way of life when I left for St. Petersburg," he replied tersely.

A smile of victory twitched her lips. "I'll wager that means the general is unaware your father was an Amatian prince."

Beside her, Zarek inhaled sharply, but she squeezed his arm again. Another reminder.

"No one knows Prince Milos is my father, and I'd prefer that information remain a secret," he admitted.

"Well, then, you'd best pray for your general's swift command to move on to Russia," she replied airily. "The longer you remain here, the better the chance someone will reveal the secret of the *other* royal bastard."

Now Pietor sucked in a breath. "*Touché*, Chess. But again, I warn you, if you want to live to protect *your* bastard, you will take care to keep your secrets close."

Did he think to threaten her? He should know better. She'd never back down from him. Had he forgotten her so completely? Forgotten the games she'd played with Master Arno? How she'd always advised him to stand up to Prince

Milos once and for all?

Then again, if he'd stood up to his father the last time she'd suggested it, he never would have abandoned her for St. Petersburg and Napoleon Bonaparte. *Traitor.*

"How much blood is on your hands already, Pietor? How many former friends, compatriots, and family members did you slay today? Perhaps it was a blessing your father died when he did. It may have been God's way of preventing him from discovering his beloved son grew up to become a traitor to his homeland."

He tightened his grip on her sleeve. "Would you put aside your childish animosity long enough to tell me what happened to my father? How did he die?"

"A French rocket blew his head from his shoulders during yesterday's invasion. I was standing right beside him at the time. My sleeve is coated with his blood and brains."

"By God!" He pulled his hand off her arm to stare at his fingers with horror.

Satisfaction rippled through her nerves. One small recompense for the way he'd hurt her so many years ago. And how he'd hurt her again now.

Swallowing her bitterness, she continued toward the row of cells with Zarek by her side. Thankfully, the boy remained silent.

"You've changed, Chess." Pietor shook his head in disappointment. "You've become harder."

Her tone darkened to match the air around her. "I grew up, Pietor. I'm no longer the naïve young girl who believes in a faithless man's promises. I've learned to be more careful with my heart."

He stopped her outside one of the dismal cells, but this time he grasped her hand instead of her blood-stained sleeve. "Perhaps you should have guarded your virtue as closely as you guarded your heart. Tell me, how long did you wait for me before you sold yourself to the highest bidder?"

She pulled from his grip and glared at him. "I may have sold myself to a king, but I never sold my soul to the devil. Which of us, do you think, is more of a disappointment to our fathers?"

"My father might not approve of what I've done but he'd

understand why I did it."

"I doubt that." She turned to place her torch in one of the empty sconces lining the dank gray walls around her and suppressed a shiver of revulsion.

She hated the dungeon. She hated the blackness and the heavy wet air that smelled faintly of mold, despair, and death. She hated the cold walls made of gray stone and the rusted iron bars that imprisoned hearts and souls as well as beings. Most of all, she hated the rats that shared the quarters with those unfortunates imprisoned in these cells. She'd hated rats since she was a child. And now, she couldn't help but think of Pietor as the King of the Rats.

"Did your father approve of your relationship with my uncle?" The edge in his tone could shave a full month's beard.

"My father might not approve of what I've done but he'd understand why I did it."

"I doubt that."

More than underground places, she hated the way he turned her words back on her when she turned his words back on him.

"Believe what you will." She waved him off. "Your opinion means nothing to me."

"There was a time when my opinion was the only one that mattered to you." He grasped her wrist again and pulled her close against him, his hard body pounding awareness into her soft flesh.

She'd loved him so desperately once. But not again. Never again. Her heart couldn't survive another broken promise. Chesna yanked her wrist out of his hand and took a step backward. "I told you, Pietor. I've grown up since then."

His gaze caressed her from head to toe, blazing with light as he studied the length of her. "I can see that."

Fire erupted beneath her belly. She placed a hand flat against the bodice of her gown. The heat that emanated from inside the muslin nearly scorched her skin. Quickly drawing her hand back down to her side, she stood a bit taller, almost on tiptoe, so she might look him in the eye. "Why have you come back?"

He ignored her question while the intensity of his gaze

continued to send ripples of heat over her skin. "You were always such a pretty child, Chess, but now you're exquisite. Why, your eyes are the very same shade of blue as the wildflowers in the meadow outside the palace. And that thick honey hair." He reached out a finger to touch the long tress draped over her shoulder, brushing the back of his hand across her breast.

The intimate contact forced the breath out of her lungs in one sharp gasp.

If Pietor heard the sound, he ignored it as he ran his thumb across the silken curl held between his fingertips. "I wager a man might wrap himself in this and feel as if he were enveloped in a soft cocoon of spun gold. It's little wonder you bewitched my poor uncle. You could tempt a saint to sin."

Chesna backed up against the wall near the row of cells. Moisture seeped into her back, and murky water soaked the hem of her gown. She remained too awed to do more than stare at Pietor. He still held her hair between his fingers, yet she felt powerless to fight. He stood so very close to her, close enough to touch. If she reached out a hand, the heat of his flesh would sear her fingertips. But her arms remained by her sides as she fought within herself to remember what he'd brought home with him.

Pietor, on the other hand, leaned forward, placing his palms flat against the wet stone wall to block her escape. "I've waited a long time for this," he whispered as his mouth came toward hers.

Sensing his objective, she punched a fist into the inside of his elbow. His hand flew off the wall, and she sidestepped him before he could do little more than taste cold wet granite instead of the lips he'd anticipated.

"How dare you touch me!"

He whirled, mouth twisted in a grimace and eyes more frigid than the snowy Carpathian Mountains. "What, Chess? You're a discriminatory whore?"

"Yes, I am," she retorted. "I choose my own lovers."

"Well if my uncle could satisfy you, you'll have no complaints with me. My bloodlines may not be as pure as the king's and I may not wear a crown upon my head, but you won't find me lacking in any other way. And your papa always said a family's traits repeat themselves in their descendants."

Dragging Zarek with her into one of the squalid cells, she slammed the door shut with a loud thud. She didn't need to say a word.

Zarek did it for her. "Stay away from my mama, French pig!"

5

Most of my compatriots speak of little more than Napoleon Bonaparte and revolution.

—*June 23, 1805*

Pietor climbed the dank stairs back toward sunshine and warmth. Chesna Dubrow. Her name alone roused his senses. She'd always been lovely. But now? Now, she rivaled the summer sun in brilliance. And God, how he still desired her! As he climbed the staircase back to the main level, his body hardened at the memory of her silken hair, soft skin, the flush in her cheeks...

Once, a long time ago, he'd dreamed of a future with her. Of marriage and children and a lifetime of love. But that was before he learned the truth.

On a growl, he pushed thoughts of Chesna from his mind before his insides burned. He had to focus on his duties, not on the woman he'd lost. Besides, she'd made a new life for herself. A life that didn't include him. He had no reason to feel guilty about leaving her behind.

By the time he reached the grand hall, he had his emotions and desires well in check.

General de Valmiere still sat upon King Jarek's former throne, leaning back against the red velvet and stretching out his poultry legs, his feet perched on the golden footstool. The image jolted Pietor. How often as a child had he sat on the thick crimson carpet runner, Chesna beside him, as Bela and the king discussed the latest news from Russia or Poland?

Bela Dubrow. Another black mark on Pietor's soul. Obviously, Chesna's father had also perished in yesterday's skirmish. Nothing else would have kept him from protecting the palace and its residents from French occupation.

And here was the proof of France's total occupation, he thought as he refocused on de Valmiere's present location. A foreigner on Amatia's throne. His stomach flipped, and he quickly scanned the rest of the massive room. From the wall of portraits, his ancestors stared at him with condemnation. The last in the line, his uncle, demanded answers. Answers Pietor could not provide.

To the right of the throne where de Valmiere now reigned, Major Hugo Montfort paced. His booted heels click-clacked over the marble floor tiles in a staccato rhythm. "The child is King Jarek's bastard. He is a threat to the emperor and must be disposed of. Say the word, General, and I'll have him executed."

"I disagree, General," Major Francois Roucher, on the general's left, added. "Surely we can counteract the boy's threat to French rule without resorting to murder."

Pietor's heart stuttered in its beats. They planned to kill Zarek? His cousin? Once again, he dared a glance at King Jarek's portrait. This time, his uncle seemed to beg for mercy on his son's behalf. Perhaps guilt made the man appear so, but dear God, how much blood would Pietor have on his hands when all was done? Before long, like Lady Macbeth, he'd never remove the stains. His brain scrambled to come up with a reasonable alternative to Montfort's murderous scheme.

At last, he seized upon one desperate thought. The very idea crushed any dreams he still harbored, but he'd long ago learned that the greatest benefits for mankind often required devastating sacrifices from individuals.

Besides, time was quickly draining from his side of the hourglass.

"You'll forgive my interruption," he said as he strode into the middle of the debate. "But the child is only a threat if we allow him to be one."

Montfort stopped pacing long enough to stare at his underling in surprise. "Oh?"

General de Valmiere sat up higher. "What exactly are

you thinking, Gabris?"

"The ascension laws of this country are quite clear, sir," he said with false conviction. "The king's bloodlines must be purely noble. No bastard is permitted to inherit the throne."

Roucher let out a relieved sigh. "So, Zarek is no threat to the emperor. Therefore, we might leave the boy alone."

But Montfort shook his head. "What of the boy's mother? You heard what the old woman said. This Chesna wishes to place her child on the throne at all costs. *Zarek* may be no threat to the emperor, but his mother is another tale."

"Then perhaps we should grant her wish," the general said. "Zarek and his ambitious mother could be a boon to the French cause, rather than a hindrance."

Montfort folded his arms over his chest. "How so?"

"The child is still young, too young to have formed any loyalties that must be dissuaded."

"If he's dead, he won't have any loyalties," Montfort grumbled.

"But if he lives, he could be raised as a loyal French citizen."

"Forgive me, General," Roucher said, "but what good would that do?"

de Valmiere shook a finger. "Remember Tsar Alexander's solution for Lithuania, gentlemen. The same rules might apply to Amatia. Zarek may not be eligible to be king, but he could be named grand duke. We might surround him with advisors who are loyal to Napoleon Bonaparte and to France."

The dawn of understanding lit up Roucher's face. "With a fellow Amatian on the throne, the residents of this province would be more cooperative toward us."

"And if we marry the boy's mother to an officer who is devoted to the emperor," Montfort interjected, "we'd be assured the child was raised with the proper beliefs and allegiances."

"An excellent idea, Montfort," de Valmiere exclaimed. "But first, we must find the perfect officer to raise the boy. Any suggestions?"

Roucher strode forward, a wolfish smile on his face. "I'll marry the wench."

Pietor's fists clenched. He'd pound the smarmy major into a bloody mess before he'd allow him to touch Chesna.

But the general shook his head. "I appreciate the sacrifice you're willing to make, Major Roucher, but I fear you won't do."

"Why not?"

"You're already married." Montfort poked Roucher in the ribs. He then turned his sharp gaze to Pietor. "What about Captain Gabris?"

Pietor flinched. "Me?"

Marry Chesna? Good God, no. Marrying her would be disastrous. For both of them.

"Are you married, Captain?"

"Well...no, but—"

"Then you're the perfect choice," Montfort replied. "You were born and raised in this country. You know the language and the customs. Surely the Amatians wouldn't find fault with one of their own countrymen raising the boy. And we might feel secure knowing the child is being brought up by a man who has proven his loyalty to the emperor time and time again."

The general's gaze swerved to Pietor, his scrutiny more intense than the heat of a roaring fire. "You might be correct, Montfort. How long have you been with us now, Captain Gabris?"

Pietor swallowed the lump that rose in his throat. "Over four years."

"Details," de Valmiere demanded. "Where'd you come from? How'd you land under Major Montfort's command? Come, come, man. Now's not the time for modesty."

But Pietor said nothing more. His heart tossed questions that buzzed more loudly in his brain than anything his superior officers might ask. Did they really consider him a fitting husband for Chesna? Could he come full circle with his arrival home? And did he still want to marry her?

He hadn't lied when he'd told her she'd grown harder. The gentle dove he'd ignored over the last several years had grown into a strong-willed woman. A woman who'd do whatever she must to protect Zarek. And the husband chosen for her would have to contend with keeping them both safe from a host of enemies.

No. As much as he still desired her, he could not marry Chesna now. Too many obstacles stood between them. And Zarek's existence only complicated an already unpleasant state of affairs.

"Gabris came through the student initiative at St. Petersburg." Montfort's voice broke through Pietor's musings. "Before joining our ranks, he served in the Young Guard under Major Paul Campignon for three years. Do you recall hearing of the incident at Mt. Santruscen when Campignon lay wounded under heavy enemy fire?" At the general's nod, Montfort added, "It was Gabris here who saved the major's life. Campignon promoted Gabris to first lieutenant, then a year later to captain. Since then, Gabris has made a name for himself as a loyal follower of the emperor's cause. I say he's the perfect bridegroom for the late king's mistress."

A heavy silence filled the room while the general and two majors studied Pietor as if he were a traitor and they were his firing squad. Pietor itched to move, to break their stares, to free himself from the net closing in around him.

"I respectfully decline the honor, General," he said at last.

"It is indeed an honor, Gabris." de Valmiere smiled. "But it's also an order. Return to the dungeon and fetch your bride. Montfort, you go to that church in town and bring us back a priest. We have a wedding to plan."

♥

Inside the dungeon cell, Chesna sat on a stone bench, Zarek cradled in her lap. Although his head remained buried in her bodice, his telltale sniffles suggested he fought against tears.

She understood his struggles. In the last few days, the world had shifted. As if, on a whim, God had rolled the earth upside-down.

Queen Jasia, King Jarek, Prince Milos, and most of all, her father. Gone. Dust. Cut down when Amatia needed them most. When *she* needed them.

Never again would Papa call her his clever girl. She'd

never again advise Queen Jasia from behind the curtains during the Women's Council. Prince Milos's laugh, booming and full of mirth, would never again echo in the grand hall.

And the one person she'd thought gone forever from Amatia had returned. The prodigal son. The prodigal *lover*. Pietor. In an enemy's uniform. With blood on his hands. Curse him!

Her heart had never recovered when he'd suddenly stopped writing to her six years ago. Six years, three months, and twenty-two days ago. At first, she'd assumed he'd found another woman to love. Furious, she'd written at least a dozen letters to him, demanding he tell her the truth. If he were truly happy with someone else, despite the ache his loss caused, she would release him from their childhood vows of marriage and a life together. He'd never replied. When another year elapsed and even his father received no word from him, they had all assumed he'd died. And Chesna had died a little, too.

That was when her father had found her a place in Queen Jasia's household, a diversion from her pain. And after Prince Mikhail's birth, she transferred all the love she'd once showered on Pietor to this clever, brave, royal child. A devotion she'd never once regretted. Not even now, when she and he faced certain death, thanks to Irina's betrayal.

What on earth had possessed Irina to make up such a tale? Her fingers curled into fists at her sides. She hoped Karol had taken the Lithuanian to task for her interference. Of course, her words had already stirred up a hornets' nest. Exactly how deadly the sting had yet to be determined.

"Mama?"

At Zarek's call, Chesna's heart lurched. She should have been a real mother by now, not a temporary parent by proxy. But she tossed aside her bitter memories and righteous anger. Only the prince mattered.

Perhaps Pietor's betrayal had been a blessing after all. Childless, she suffered no torn allegiances. Her loyalty would always remain with the royal family. She was a Dubrow. She could do no less than her ancestors. No less than her father, may God grant him peace.

Tears sprang to her eyes and to regain control, she took

a moment to kiss the top of Zarek's head. "Yes?"

"What will happen to us now?"

"For starters," a voice drawled from outside the cell, "your mother and I are to be married."

Chesna shot up, nearly spilling Zarek to the filthy floor. She quickly righted the boy on the bench and flung herself at the tiny barred window in the cell door. Pietor's grinning face appeared on the other side.

Her stomach twisted. Married? Madness. He couldn't possibly expect them to simply continue on as if nothing had occurred over the last seven years—not to mention the last twenty-four hours.

On a deep inhale, she forced a calm far from the storm brewing inside her. "That was a long time ago, Pietor. I have no intention of marrying you now."

The shadows from his torch distorted his expression so that he looked as if she'd offered him a dead rat for dinner. "Your intentions are of no consequence, my dove. Whether you wish it or nay, you will be my wife before nightfall."

"I am not your dove, nor will I be your wife. I'd rather spend my life in this cell than marry you."

A clank of steel on rust, and the cell door squealed open.

Pietor stepped aside and swept her a low bow. "Then by all means, Chesna, do share your sentiments with General de Valmiere. He is the one ordering our immediate nuptials."

No. Ridiculous. Why on earth would a French general give a whit about some old, long-forgotten romance between her and Pietor?

With a swish of soggy skirts, she slipped past him. "I don't know what you told the general to insist upon something so outrageous, but I'll disavow him of your nonsense straight away." She turned, extending a hand. "Come along, *son*."

Zarek immediately popped off the bench. "Coming, Mama."

With Zarek's hand clasped in hers, she strode up the slimy staircase. Beneath the folds of her gown, her legs shook with exhaustion and shock, but she maintained a perfect grace so that the odious traitor wouldn't notice.

She'd let him see no chink in her armor.

Head high, she swept up the grand staircase to the main vestibule. The replicas of swords and shields from years gone by welcomed her, gave her strength. She squeezed Zarek's hand as they trod the scarlet carpet from the vestibule to the arched doorway leading to the grand hall. On either side of them, magnificent statues of the ancient Amatian deities guarded the entrance. Perion, the supreme god, held a bolt of lightning in his upraised fist. Velos, god of the underworld, sat astride a fire-breathing dragon. She paused for a brief moment at the statue of Svarila, goddess of war, who stood dressed in a man's toga, one breast bared, shield held over her head to ward off the blow of an invisible enemy. Wind-swept hair formed a cloud around her fierce but exquisite face.

If you gods ever existed, please lend me your great gifts to fight for the good of the people. Grant me the power of Perion, the ferocity of Velos, and the strength of Svarila.

Chesna squeezed her eyes shut as she passed the last statue in the line. Overlooking the hand-carved arch that separated the vestibule from the grand hall, Zora, goddess of beauty silently mocked her. Zora. The bride of the heavens. How perfectly ironic.

The arch they walked under depicted a placid sea at dawn, an homage to Zora's reputation as the purest maiden, brighter than the sun, the most honorable of all the gods and goddesses.

"Ah, here comes the bride now," de Valmiere announced.

Chesna glared at Zora's image, and then bent to Zarek. "Wait here."

Leaving the child under the watchful eyes of the ancient gods, she strode forward to the throne where the usurper still sat. Rage blossomed anew, but she allowed thoughts of Svarila to squelch her violent emotions.

"General, forgive me," she said, head bowed in obedient penitence. "But I must speak."

He offered her an imperious wave. "Speak then."

On a deep inhale, she chose her words carefully. "Your officer told me of your plans for us, and I would beg you to reconsider. I have no wish to wed at this time."

The general's eyes narrowed. "Understand this, madam. I am not a patient man. Your former lover may have indulged you due to your position in his bed. And as much as I envy the old man his good fortune, for the sake of your son, I'd prefer you wedded before you're bedded by another. And since, as I've said, I am not a patient man, that wedding will take place now."

Pietor stole up behind her, wrapping an arm about her waist. As if she were already his possession.

Chesna's temper soared, drowning out Svarila's calmer guidance, and she broke from his embrace on a shout of frustration. "I'd rather die than marry this pig!"

"If that is your wish, *mademoiselle*." The general shrugged and turned to Major Roucher. "Take her back to the dungeon."

"No!" Zarek rushed forward and threw himself at Chesna's feet. "You mustn't die. You promised me you'd never leave me. Don't leave me, Mama! Please!"

"Zarek, be silent," she chastised.

He quieted immediately, but remained on his knees, teary eyes pleading his case.

"Well, *mademoiselle*?" the general barked. "What is it to be, death or marriage?"

Chesna stole a glance at Pietor, who stood expressionless, then cast her eyes on Zarek draped across her feet. Kneeling, she helped him rise and leaned close to his ear. "Never show such weakness to outsiders, Zarek."

He shook his head, lips clamped in a grim line.

"Zarek, come now. Stand up."

His reply came as quietly as her request, but with a lot more steel. "Not until you remember your promise to me, *Mama*."

She offered him a sad smile. "You needn't have bothered to go to such lengths. I can't make good on my threat. You and I both know that."

Without her, Zarek might forget his parents and his duties to Amatia. If she chose death, Zarek would become Napoleon Bonaparte's lackey, much like his cousin Pietor had. Zarek needed her. Amatia needed her. But, still...

Marriage to Pietor? If she chose marriage, she'd be legally bound to Pietor Gabris for the rest of her life. Several years ago, she would have rejoiced at the idea. But that had been before Pietor became the man she didn't know, the one who stood before her now, loyal to a foreign usurper and intent upon destroying the country she loved.

What if she agreed to marry anyone but Pietor? Would she be executed for making demands? Or would this General de Valmiere choose someone else for her to wed? What if he ordered her to marry that paunchy old man by his side, Major Roucher? The way he leered at her, his fat tongue running over his thin lips, kinked her stomach into knots.

Her papa always said the enemy you knew was easier to manage than the stranger you didn't know. At least Pietor had been born and raised as a loyal Amatian. His father had been a royal prince. He'd loved his homeland once, had listened to her counsel and heeded her advice. Perhaps, he could do so again. If she married him, she might persuade him to forget about Napoleon and France, especially once de Valmiere and his cohorts left for Russia.

The grand hall remained as silent as a church as Chesna considered the choice set before her. Death or marriage? Death or marriage?

"I'll marry him," she finally announced in defeat.

"I knew you'd see reason," the general remarked then turned his eyes to Pietor. "Well, Captain Gabris, will you wed the wench?"

Pietor flashed a brief inscrutable look at Chesna before replying. "If you command me to do so, General, I'll marry her."

The general clapped his hands with childish delight. "Splendid!"

6

The moment Pietor agreed to the marriage, one of the general's cronies appeared in the grand hall, dragging Father Grigory behind him. The general ordered the priest to waive the banns and hear the bridal couple take their vows.

If de Valmiere's orders surprised the elderly priest, he never showed any reaction. He simply nodded and draped his stole around his bony shoulders. "I will need to hear their confessions first. Is there a private chamber I might use?"

"No private chambers," de Valmiere growled and pointed to the farthest corner of the room and the row of Doric columns wrapped in gold. "Set up two chairs over there."

The majors scrambled behind the throne for the two gilt and scarlet chairs normally reserved for guests of His Highness. Chesna watched the two men attempt to lift the heavy furniture with no success and hid a tired smile. But her lips quickly took the downward turn into a wince when they pushed the chairs across the floor on ear-splitting squeals. At last, the chairs sat in their designated place.

"Set them side to side, facing opposite directions, rather than facing one another," Father Grigory instructed, "to protect the privacy of the penitents."

After the men had rearranged the chairs to the priest's recommendations, he wrapped an arm across Chesna's shoulders. "Come, my child. I'll hear your sins first." His eyes narrowed in Pietor's direction. "I should imagine your list will be shorter than his."

He led her to the dark corner and sat her in the chair that faced away from the throne. "And now my dear," he said as he took the other chair. "You may begin."

Within the semi-privacy of their makeshift confessional, she apprised Father Grigory of all that had transpired in the last several hours. She summed up with, "I even sought strength from the ancient gods in the vestibule." The moment the blasphemy left her mouth, she wished she could take the words back. Had she just imperiled her immortal soul? As terror flooded her heart, she dared to ask, "Is that a sin, Father?"

"It is never a sin to seek guidance from the familiar. Your papa would often review the legends and myths of our ancestors to find answers to problems within the realm. He sometimes spent hours in the Hall of Heroes, studying the armor or seeking guidance from the ancients."

She'd forgotten that fact. Or, perhaps, she'd buried the memory deep inside her heart. Why else would she have imitated Papa's actions in the vestibule?

"Are you certain you wish to wed this man, my child?" Father Grigory asked. "You're placing yourself in grave danger."

"I don't have a choice, Father," she replied. "I've vowed to protect the prince, and I must do so, even if it means my life."

Father Grigory sighed. "May our Lord watch over you and keep you safe," he intoned before assigning her a light penance for her sins.

When she rose, her lips already moving in the familiar prayers, Pietor strode across the room to take her place. She averted her gaze from his and quickly returned to Zarek who sat cross-legged on the blood-red carpet runner near the throne.

She sat beside him and wrapped an arm around his waist.

"I'm sorry, Mama," he murmured.

Her hand traced slow circles of comfort over his back. "Hush, Zarek. You've done nothing wrong."

"If not for me, you wouldn't have to get married."

"If not for you, I'd have no reason to smile every day of

my life," she replied.

No other words passed between them as they waited what seemed an eternity for Pietor to complete his confession. So, Father Grigory had been correct. Pietor had a great deal to unburden from his soul. Discomfort tickled down her spine. All too soon, she'd be married to this monster.

At last, the priest made the sign of the cross and Pietor did the same. Dread chilled Chesna's skin to gooseflesh. In ten more steps he'd be beside her. Nine...eight...seven...

"Shall we tie the knot, my dove?"

She'd miscalculated. Badly.

♥

No one offered Chesna a moment's respite to change her gown or even wash her face. Thus, at her wedding, she wore the same black dress she'd worn to Queen Jasia's funeral, the garment stained with the blood and brains of poor Prince Milos. She'd lost her shoes somewhere and never found them. Smoke and grease coated her hair. Dirt and dried tears stained her cheeks. Still she put up no argument.

Until the general bowed low before her. "I'd be happy to act in the place of your father and escort you to your husband."

Then, Chesna put her bare foot down. "My son will have that honor." She reached a hand out to Zarek.

Chesna Dubrow married Pietor Gabris inside the grand hall of Opal Palace. Soldiers of Napoleon Bonaparte's army served as their only honored guests. No family members rejoiced. No friends offered congratulations. No feast, no music, and no revelries brightened the dismal pall hanging over the bride and groom.

When Father Grigory instructed Pietor to place a ring on the bride's finger, he looked at the priest, askance. Obviously in their hastily made plans, no one had considered a wedding ring.

Zarek withdrew a gold band from a chain around his neck and handed it to Pietor. "You may use this, sir."

"Thank you, lad." Pietor took the ring from the boy and

gave it to Father Grigory to have it blessed. "I promise it shall be returned to you as soon as possible."

"That won't be necessary," Zarek replied in his most imperious manner. "As it was a gift from my father, it is now my gift to my mama. She may keep it until she no longer has any use for it."

His barbed words hit their target right between the eyes. Pietor blinked.

Zarek looked up at Chesna, a grin spreading from ear to ear. For the briefest moment, she saw Pietor as a child in Zarek's smiling face. Memories tumbled in her brain. Memories of swimming in the clear waters of Lake Matya, of climbing trees in the orchards and foot races in the meadows. Memories of days stuck inside the classroom under the watchful eye of their tutor, Master Arno. They'd shared many happy days. How could Pietor have forgotten all those wonderful times? How could he have forgotten her?

She squeezed her eyes shut. Tired. She was so very tired. And terrified.

Svarila, abide with me a while longer.

Pietor's grip on her wrist shook her back to the horrors of the present. As he slipped the heavy golden band on her finger, she glanced down. The inlaid crown set with tiny rubies winked back. Oh, God! She hastily folded her fingers into a fist to hide the ring from view.

Zarek had given her his royal signet ring, a ring that showed his link to the throne.

Perhaps Svarila had heard her plea because Pietor never noticed. Despite his years away, had he given the ring more than a cursory glance, he certainly would have recognized the significance of that particular piece of jewelry.

"I now pronounce you man and wife," Father Grigory announced suddenly.

Chesna blinked. It was done. She was married.

Her brain barely managed to accept this new fact when Pietor grasped her about the waist and pulled her up against his chest.

The priest's next words made her head spin.

"You may kiss your bride."

Pietor's lips came down on hers. Resentment drained like water from a leaky barrel. With one hand pressed against the back of her neck, he tilted her head ever so slightly, slanting his own head to engulf her mouth.

His breath mingled with hers, warming her insides. Shivers rippled across her skin. His lips sealed hers, blocking out everything but him. When he opened his mouth into a wide o, her mouth was forced to do the same. She no longer had any control. Her lips belonged to him and moved in direct rhythm to his.

Nothing mattered but Pietor. Every cell, every pore awakened as he breathed life into her. She lost her will beneath his hot breath and...oh!

Was that his tongue sweeping across the inside of her mouth? She'd forgotten the bliss of his special kisses. But memory returned quickly now. Ripples of icy heat trickled from her nape to her toes. His tongue slid over the insides of her teeth. Her heartbeat sang in her ears, a rhythmic thumping similar to drums of war.

When he drew her warm breath into his mouth, her knees buckled. At last, he broke away, and she slumped against his chest, breathless, debilitated, and only dimly aware of her surroundings.

"Until tonight, my dove," he murmured against her ear.

He placed her hand inside Zarek's and turned away.

With a crisp salute to the general and majors, he left the grand hall.

7

During the brief wedding ceremony, Pietor had ignored the portraits of his ancestors. He kept his gaze focused straight ahead, never glancing to the right for fear he might see disapproval in the faces of his father or uncle. Nor did he glance to the left to see whatever disgusted expression covered Chesna's face. All too soon, the priest had pronounced them married.

And before he considered the consequences, he pulled his wife against him and kissed her. Fool! He'd never forgotten the taste of her lips, how just holding her made him complete. Ten years had elapsed, yet she still managed to transform him into a boy unable to control his basest desires.

If not for the men surrounding them, he would have bared her to his hot gaze. Only years of army discipline stifled him from tasting her sweetness.

Instead, when his burgeoning need grew impossible to ignore, he broke away from his wife. After a terse goodbye and salute to his superior officers, he stalked from the grand hall, refusing to halt for anyone or anything. If he stopped moving, he might start thinking about their upcoming wedding night. A dangerous pastime.

Even when he reached the heavy wooden doors that led to the flower-filled meadow outside the palace, he never slowed his pace. He trod across the stone path, boots crunching bits of rock beneath his heels. The path gave way to high grass, but Pietor barely noticed. All his thoughts remained firmly on moving first his left foot, then his right. Over and over again.

When he finally stopped, he found himself in the middle of the meadow. The wildflowers he'd earlier compared to the shade of Chesna's eyes danced beneath the sun's rays on the warm summer breeze. Past the azure blooms sat the two flat boulders that faced the eastern horizon. As children, he and Chesna had spent hours seated on those boulders.

A silvery fish leaps into the air before splashing back into the crystalline waters of Lake Matya.

"Tell me again, Pietor," Chesna's sixteen-year-old voice asks. "Tell me all the places we'll go." She sits upon her boulder, entwining daisies in her hair.

They look ridiculous. And yet, so perfectly Chesna.

Pietor smiles. "Name a place, my dove, and we'll travel there."

Her pretty blue eyes widen. "I want to live in America."

"America? So far? Why?"

"Because America isn't like England or France or Russia. It's new and different. I want to live in a land where I can be a part of something special. Where my children can forge new paths, new lives. Create their own traditions so they won't be subject to silly rules and expectations."

Smile flips to frown. He understands her message. The heated arguments between Pietor and his royal father always upset her. He picks up a flat stone and skims it over the lake's surface. "Even America has rules, Chess."

She leans back on her arms, face tilted toward the sun. "Yes, but in America, a person is not defined by his parentage. I don't mind rules. Provided those rules are fair to everyone..."

Lake Matya had been their paradise, a Garden of Eden where they fished, swam, sailed, and told each other secrets. They'd challenged one another to foot races down to the meadow. Sometimes, he'd let her win those foot races just to see the brilliance of her smile. All those years ago, he would have given her the moon just to see her smile.

The forest beyond, with its deep glades and rolling hills, provided hours of adventure for two teenagers attempting to avoid adult scrutiny. Beneath the shelter of the pine boughs, he and Chesna had experimented with the first fumbles of passion. Although they'd vowed to wait for their wedding night to fully consummate their love, they'd indulged curiosity with innocent kisses and tentative explorations of each other's bodies in the privacy of the forest. Even now, Pietor couldn't look at the tree line without picturing his beautiful Chesna, bodice unlaced, lips swollen from his kisses, and her hair a mussed golden cloud around her sparkling eyes.

Damn her. For the last seven years, he'd tried to avoid anything that reminded him of Chess. But everywhere he turned held her presence. He'd found the women in St. Petersburg exactly as she had described them on the day he left Simion: painted, pampered, and predatory. In his classes, he'd missed her teasing, her clever mind, the way she outwitted their tutor, time and again. During the autumn months, he walked along the Neva and suddenly wished she was beside him to see the majestic colors of the city. Winter evoked images of their snow fights, gliding along the frozen surface of Lake Matya, and the pink in her cheeks from wind and cold. Spring brought cornflowers and their magnificent blue color, the exact shade of her eyes. Each summer he longed to return home, to see her, touch her, beg her to be patient with him. But he could not.

He'd asked Bela for Chesna's hand before leaving for St. Petersburg. Bela had insisted Pietor agree to his father's demand to complete his education first.

"Go to St. Petersburg. See a bit of the world and learn about life. And when you return home, if you and Chesna are both still of the same mind, your father and I will agree to your marriage."

So he did as Bela and his father wished. He went to St. Petersburg. And there, he learned a great deal about life. He heard about revolutions occurring throughout Europe and the New World. He discovered that while he lived a life of privilege and excess in Simion, others less fortunate starved in the streets.

He read the works of Jefferson, Rousseau, and Voltaire.

He agreed with their ideas, particularly Rousseau's opinions that the multitudes wallowed in poverty and obscurity so that a few nobles could live with honor and wealth. He learned of the success of the Revolution in America and how the citizens of the United States now governed themselves. He studied their Constitution, their Declaration of Independence, and their patriots.

But none of what he learned about events in foreign lands affected him as badly as what he'd discovered occurring inside the hallowed walls of the Opal Palace in Amatia. On one fateful day, he made up his mind to take a stand. He left the university and joined many of his fellow students in championing Napoleon Bonaparte's cause. Once in the Young Guard, he worked hard to learn the art of warfare and quickly rose through the ranks to become captain.

He only regretted that in his quest for answers, he'd left Chesna behind. Her letters had nearly broken him. The misery in her written words bled all over the pages. But he'd turned his back on her. Something he'd sworn he'd never do.

Still, he'd done as his father and her father had advised. He'd seen more of the world than he'd ever wished. He'd learned far too much about life. And he'd come home to wed Chesna Dubrow. Just as Bela had predicted. Just as he'd always intended.

A raucous twang overhead drew his gaze to the flock of geese that soared in their usual v pattern across the clear, blue sky. He bent and picked up a stone to hurl at the noisy birds. His missile fell far too short of the target—intentional, of course. He had no reason to hurt the creatures. He merely envied them their freedom.

How much simpler life would be if he and Chesna could sprout wings and fly away. Carefree. They could leave all their troubles here, explore those exotic destinations they had dreamed of. Go to America. Perhaps there, they might find peace.

But, no.

Chesna would never leave Zarek. And he, God help him, could never live in the same household with the king's son. Even for her...

Frustration itched under his skin. Chesna, always a spitfire, now had a child to protect. These days, she resembled the magnificent goddess of war who guarded the vestibule. He could almost see her in Svarila's garb, one sweet breast bared for his touch.

Every fiber in his body turned to steel at the picture in his mind.

By all that was holy, he needed a distraction. And quickly.

He looked out toward the west of the meadow. Units of soldiers loitered near row upon row of tents. How his uncle would despise seeing his once beautiful lands so badly abused.

With fresh determination, he stalked to the grounds where Montfort's regiment had set up camp. A burly sergeant strode past, and Pietor called to him. "Deveaux?"

Sergeant Deveaux halted and offered a perfect salute. "Sir?"

"Fetch my saber," Pietor growled. "And a dozen men looking for some exercise."

"Yes, sir."

Thoughts of Chesna would have to wait. His excess energy needed to be expended on the dueling field. Later, he'd find a way to deal with his new wife and stepson.

♥

Chesna and Zarek returned to the kitchens where a crowd of people besieged them with questions and comments.

"What happened?"

"Chess, are you all right?"

"What did the general and his men do?"

"Did you see Pietor? Imagine. Prince Milos's son, a traitor to his homeland."

Finally, Karol stepped into the fray of curious faces and rapid-fire interrogation. "Shoo! Back to work. You will find out everything later. For now, there is still too much work to do to repair the damage in here."

Chesna tossed him a grateful smile and then bent to kiss Zarek on both cheeks. "You're a brave lad. But I must speak to Irina and Karol now. Go with Urszula, and she'll give you something to eat."

Urszula, bless her, never hesitated before taking the boy's hand in her plump one. "What would you like today, hmm? Perhaps your favorite wheat cakes with honey?"

"Yes," he exclaimed and quickly scampered to the servants' table, his hunger clearly overriding all sense of royal propriety.

Once certain he was out of earshot, Chesna turned her rage on Irina. "Why?" She twisted the gold band that encircled her finger with ferocity. "Why did you tell them the king was Zarek's father?"

Irina's expression reflected no regret. "He's a child, Chesna. Much too young to be involved in the intrigue you planned. Sooner or later, he'd have tripped up and given away his true identity. He very nearly ruined everything when he confronted the general. That's what made me think to tell the lie. I only sought to protect him."

Despite the logic in Irina's argument, Chesna refused to be appeased. "But to tell them he's a royal bastard, Irina?"

"Think, Chess. If he's a royal bastard, it explains why he's so well educated. He can still wear most of his own wardrobe, which is too fine to be that of a servant. He'll be able to sleep abovestairs and not in the servants' quarters. The boy will retain the life he's lived for the last five years, yet he remains safe from French ambition because they know he can't ever inherit the throne."

Chesna thrust out her left hand to show the gold band on her finger. "By taking matters into your own hands you made our circumstances a thousand times worse. You threw me to the wolves. I'm married to an officer in the French army now."

Irina gasped, and Karol's complexion paled.

"Oh, Chess, I'm so sorry," Irina exclaimed. "It never occurred to me—"

"No, I imagine you didn't think your solution through fully," she whispered. "Your recklessness has placed all of us in grave danger. Especially Zarek."

"For heaven's sake." Irina clucked her tongue. "You should have married years ago. I don't understand why your father allowed you to turn away all those suitors in the first place. You might not be happy about their choice of bridegroom, but your marriage doesn't endanger Zarek or anyone else in this palace in any way."

Her hands tightened into fists at her side. How could this woman be so foolish? "Are you mad?"

Before she might throttle Irina, however, Karol stepped between them, his expression grim. "When Chesna's husband claims his marriage rights from her this evening, he'll discover she was never the king's mistress," he announced flatly. "Nor could she be Zarek's real mother. That means Zarek's true identity is still in jeopardy."

"Oh." Irina's complexion paled to the color of clouds, and her tone plummeted to regret at last. "What will you do now?"

Fear crawled into Chesna's throat, and she swallowed hard. "I'll have to be certain my bridegroom doesn't find out the truth about me."

"But how?" Irina persisted.

She forced a casual air. "I won't allow him the opportunity to claim his husbandly rights. I'll insist we must not sleep in the same bed until we know each other better."

Karol laughed bitterly, and Chesna sent him a baleful glance.

"Forgive me, Chess, but do you have any idea what drives a man? No mortal male in good health will resist the lure of bedding you. A man in his death throes would crawl to the marriage bed if you were the prize waiting for him. By God, I'm surprised he didn't carry you upstairs already." He stroked his bearded chin. "The general must have a great deal of control over his men."

"Or perhaps Pietor isn't a mortal male in good health." After all, he'd had the opportunity to wed and bed her years ago. But he'd only married her under orders from his commanding officer.

"Pietor?" Karol's voice echoed through the kitchen, halting all other conversations among the servants. "They married you off to that traitor?"

Crash! Someone in the crowd dropped a tray of dishes. Chesna's nerves, already brittle, snapped, and a scream of shock escaped her lips.

Karol pulled her into his arms and held her against his wall-like chest. After so many hours of feigning strength, she allowed herself a full minute to surrender to her terror. Shudders racked her from head to toe, and tears welled in her eyes.

"We'll come up with a plan, Chess," Karol crooned while he rubbed circles in her lower back.

On an enormous exhale, she straightened and broke away from her protector. "I already have," she said. "I plan to tell him that I'm in mourning. Don't forget, I lost both my father and my lover, the magnificent Jarek, yesterday."

"Chesna!" Irina waved a finger near her nose. "How tactless of you. You would use yesterday's tragedy for your own benefit?"

Chesna dropped her hands to her hips and faced Irina squarely. "When you are the lamb headed to slaughter, Irina, you may lecture me about tact. In the meantime, I'll use any means available to keep Zarek safe. If my grief can hold my husband at bay until de Valmiere and his men leave here for Russia, I will take advantage of the tragedy to prevent a far greater one. I will do whatever it takes to protect Zarek. I would die for him. I would kill for him. I will allow nothing to harm that child."

Karol took her shaky hand in his. "Chess, you and I should take a walk."

"Why?"

"Trust me." He pulled her toward the doorway that led out of the kitchens and into the courtyard. "You need to know what to expect tonight."

8

On the floor in the royal nursery, Chesna rolled over onto her side and squeezed her eyes shut. In the bed above her, Zarek slept deeply. Little wonder. Poor child. He'd survived so much since yesterday. Thank God, he'd fallen asleep so easily. She would have expected all the strange and violent events to devastate him, but he seemed to suffer no ill effects from the series of tragedies.

Not so Chesna. She'd finally found the time to wash and change out of the horrid black mourning gown. Rather than leaving the gown for the laundress, she'd ordered one of the chambermaids to have it burned. She'd never wear it again and it held no sentimental value, despite the fact it had become her wedding gown. Her wedding had been a farce. And now, she faced her wedding night with dread.

After Karol dragged her into the courtyard, in his own halting manner, he explained what she might expect from Pietor this evening if she couldn't persuade him to leave her alone. His descriptions of the act of lovemaking made her giggle. She'd, of course, known a few of the details from stolen interludes with Pietor so many years ago. But Karol's formal, stilted conversation, combined with his odd choice of terms for body parts had transformed something she recalled as beautiful and wondrous into the ridiculous.

Still...

She and Pietor were no longer the young lovers who'd pledged their troth beneath a cathedral of pine trees. And while she hadn't traveled any farther down the path of love after his departure, she assumed Pietor's time in St.

Petersburg had broadened his education in all ways. Would he really expect her to yield to him tonight? Would he force her? And if he did, could she fool him into believing she wasn't a virgin?

Sleep would elude her until she knew the answers. Surrendering to her worries, she rose and strode to the window that looked out over the west end of the meadows. Dismay infused her soul.

Overnight, the views from this window had changed from peaceful, natural beauty to filth, noise, and ugliness. The wildflowers, which had covered the grounds so proudly yesterday, lay crushed and broken under the boots and hooves of Napoleon Bonaparte's army.

In the grasslands behind the meadow, hundreds of tents now stood in long gray rows. As far as the eye could see soldiers, still clad in their sooty and blood-stained uniforms, wandered about the fields. Others sat in large circles, gambling or drinking. Still another group had given into their fatigue and slept off the excesses of battle.

Already, rotting garbage and human waste littered the lawns that surrounded the encampment. Fat black flies buzzed everywhere. Birds of prey hovered in the bleak sky, an omen of what might yet occur in Simion.

Even if these vile men departed tomorrow, the lands around the Opal Palace would never be the same again. Nor would the inhabitants.

She supposed she should be grateful that only the odious General de Valmiere and his most trusted officers would reside inside the palace. But the thought of devils lying in beds meant for King Jarek and Queen Jasia, Prince Milos, and her father curdled in her belly. Their loss sliced bone deep. To have others usurp their places so quickly proved almost unbearable.

On a deep sigh of remorse, she pressed her forehead against the glass windowpane. A sudden glint of light passed the corner of her eye. Curious, she opened the window and gripped the sill to lean out.

Pietor. She nearly tumbled when she spotted him. He stood almost directly below her window, fencing with another soldier, an older man with arms the size of tree trunks. The clang of steel on steel rang through the air.

She'd seen him duel many times in the past. Master Arno had insisted Pietor learn the gentlemanly art of fencing. But fencing with rapiers bore little resemblance to the harsher battle waging below. In those long ago days, she'd relished watching him lunge forward with his weapon, loved the sensual motion of parry and thrust.

For today's match, he'd removed his jacket and shirt.

Pietor, the boy, had disappeared. In his place stood a hardened man of muscle and sinew. Lithe and agile as always, he now possessed a strength to his movements that he'd lacked years before. The tight muscles of his chest and forearms bulged and relaxed with each lunge and feint. Perspiration dotted his rippled flesh, glistening beneath the afternoon sun as he stepped forward and back, into and out of direct light again and again.

Her belly quivered. Her mind hurled her back in time to stolen moments in the forest when she and he were barely old enough to understand love. Pietor's hands, hot and seeking, played her body like a fine instrument. He knew exactly where to touch her to evoke the sweetest music.

She squeezed her eyes shut against the traitorous memories. To no avail. Her weakened mind strolled the path, despite the dangers.

How would his hot, sweat-slicked skin feel pressed against her own? Would he feel as hard as he looked? Or would he feel more tensile, like warm clay? And how would he taste? A flicker of heat fluttered in her bosom and ignited flames throughout her blood. She placed her hand flat at the bottom of her stomach. The same blaze she'd felt through the muslin earlier seared her palm.

A tremor weakened her knees, and she gripped the windowsill to keep from falling. Her palms pressed into the ledge as her fingers tensed and relaxed in a rhythm similar to that of Pietor's muscles below. Her breathing followed the same tempo, long, deep inhalations followed by shorter, shallower exhalations.

She forced her eyes open to find Pietor's gaze fixed upon her. He winked as if he sensed her thoughts. Without changing his focus from her, he swept his arm in one swift motion and quickly disarmed his opponent. The larger man's saber fell to the ground.

"Mama, are you listening to me?" Zarek's demand snapped her out of her haze.

She whirled from the window to find the boy sitting up, alert and sharp-eyed. "Forgive me, Zarek. I didn't hear you."

"Your cheeks are all red." He pointed to her face. "You should move away from the strong sun."

Her cheeks flamed anew at his remark, but she offered him a carefree smile and quickly pulled the sash. "I agree, my darling. It's far too dangerous for me to stand at the window right now."

♥

Disappointment stung as Pietor watched the sash cover the window above. He hadn't realized he'd chosen a practice site in such close proximity to Chesna's bedchamber. And yet, he should have remembered. The location of the royal nursery hadn't changed in over a century.

Despite his faulty memory, he'd sensed the exact moment Chess leaned out the window. A tingle stirred the air like electricity before lightning strikes. And suddenly, he became twenty again, deliberately flaunting his skill to taunt her, to tease her into a state of arousal so that she'd practically fly with him into the forest where they might be alone.

Damn her. He had to regain his focus. But she enchanted him. Still and after all these years, Chesna was a fever in his blood, the one woman he could never forget or ignore.

Another challenger. That was what he needed right now. More battle, fewer memories. He signaled to the next opponent, but Major Montfort stepped between them before the competition could begin.

With hands upraised, he barked, "Captain Gabris, the general wishes to speak with you at once."

After a hasty glance at the closed window overhead, Pietor handed his saber to Sergeant Deveaux. He retrieved his shirt and coat from the branch of a nearby tree. While stuffing his arms into his sleeves, he followed Major Montfort into the palace. Montfort didn't speak as they passed the pair of soldiers who stood guard at the doors.

His silence left Pietor with jumbled thoughts to trouble him.

What now? Did the general already second-guess his plan to marry off Chesna rather than kill her and the child? Pietor's gaze strayed to the armory where the ancient weapons of war displayed the courage of his ancestors. God knew he'd do everything in his power to save them both, but he was only one man, and his battles had only seemed to increase since his return to Simion.

General de Valmiere still sat on the golden throne in the grand hall, now smoking a hand-carved ivory pipe filled with sweet-scented tobacco. Pietor had to bite back the thought that the general certainly enjoyed the fruits of his soldiers' labors. Rather than speak treason, he saluted and waited for his next orders.

"Ah, Gabris. Excellent." de Valmiere waved a hand. "Leave us, Montfort."

The major saluted. "Yes, sir." He turned away, and his boots clacked across the tiles.

Only after the door had closed behind him did the general speak again. "Gabris, do you realize why I insisted you marry that young woman today?"

"Yes, sir." Pietor nodded. "Her child might prove an asset to the emperor."

The general blew a long curl of smoke into the air and smiled knowingly. "Yes, Captain, that is true. But in order for the child to be of any use to us, his mother must be restrained. Are you aware who your wife is, Gabris? She is Chesna Dubrow, the daughter of Bela Dubrow. You recognize that name, of course."

Pietor opened his eyes wide with feigned astonishment. "Of course, sir. Everyone in Amatia knows Bela Dubrow. Members of the Dubrow family have been the advisors to the kings of Amatia for over a century."

"Well, no more." The general took another long draw on the pipe. "Bela Dubrow is dead."

A lump of guilt rose in his throat, and he swallowed hard. "Are you certain, sir?"

"Dubrow's body was discovered this afternoon in the square. He must have put up a terrible fight. Montfort informed me he counted no less than a dozen bayonet wounds in the man's chest."

As if Pietor himself lay beneath a bayonet, pity pierced his heart a thousand times over. Poor Chesna! Did she know? She'd adored Bela, always seeing him as more god than man. Now she would have to accept the fact he was mortal after all.

"Did the major happen to say where they disposed of Dubrow's body?"

He needed to know, for his own sake as well as Chesna's. Eventually he'd want to pay his respects to the man's remains—if possible.

"Dubrow and all the members of the royal family were interred in the graveyard at the Church of St. Ambrose." The general sighed, took a thoughtful puff on his pipe. "That old priest wouldn't agree to waive the banns and perform your marriage until we allowed him to bury the bodies with the care and honor due to peers of the realm."

Pietor frowned and stifled the tickle in the back of his throat. "Forgive my impertinence, sir, but with the loss of Dubrow as well as the entire royal family, France's position as conqueror was secure. Which made my marriage to Bela's daughter unnecessary." And an even deeper thorn in his side.

The general removed the pipe from his mouth and leaned forward, elbows on knees. "Make no mistake, Captain. While Bela Dubrow's demise was a stroke of good fortune, the daughter still concerns me. Chesna seems to have her father's gift for strategy coupled with a thirst for power, a dangerous combination. I'm not surprised she bore a royal bastard. But now, I believe she'll use her child to gain her own objectives. The Dubrows have always relished their political position. Chesna Dubrow will stop at nothing to retain her family's power over the people."

If the general believed that, he clearly did not understand Bela *or* Chesna. But Pietor remained mute on the subject.

"It will be your duty to see your wife respects her new station in the palace," the general continued. "She is the child's mother, but her contact with Zarek must be closely guarded and very limited. Under no circumstances is she to be alone with the boy. She might poison his mind against us. You will be responsible for seeing that Zarek becomes loyal to France and the emperor."

"I'll do my best, sir."

"Your best may not be enough, Gabris. This is Bela Dubrow's daughter. The servants and residents of this city will naturally look to her for guidance. If she defies our rule, they will follow suit. But if she accepts her defeat gracefully, we will have a peaceful transition of power here. I don't care how you gain the wench's cooperation. Beat her, threaten her, do whatever you must. But I want her humbled. Immediately. I'd advise you to take control from the start. In the marriage bed."

Pietor forced a lewd grin. "I admit, I'm looking forward to bedding her. I've never had a royal mistress. I wager she must know a great many tricks to keep a king's interest."

"And she'll no doubt use those tricks in an attempt to keep you out of her bed." He wagged a finger. "Brook no games from her. Show her who is master in your household from the very beginning."

"Believe me, General. She may have wiles." He shook a fist. "But I can be very persuasive when it comes to besting a woman in an argument."

9

Rousseau, Franklin, and Voltaire—your heroes, yes? What a wicked girl you are, to bandy those names about, all the while knowing their ideals threaten the king's rule by giving power to the citizens.

—*July 30, 1805*

Chesna remained in the royal nursery for the rest of the day. Even when Karol arrived to escort them to the kitchens for dinner, she declined.

"I can't eat," she told him. "I simply can't."

No lie. Her throat closed up every time she thought about the general and his men dining on Urszula's culinary specialties. She could not—would not—pretend those vile men were welcome in Opal Palace.

Karol nodded sympathetically. "I'll bring Zarek back after the meal. Get some rest, Chess. You'll need your strength."

He didn't add *for tonight,* but the words hung in the humid air between them. Still, she thanked him while he scooped Zarek onto his shoulders. The two males left moments later, the boy's laughter lingering behind.

Alone for the first time in days, Chesna kicked off her shoes and settled into a chair with one of her father's favorite books. The moment she opened to the first page, his image popped into her mind, familiar and comforting. With no one to see her, she allowed herself to fall apart. Tears flooded her eyes and streamed down her cheeks. When the pain in her heart sliced her in half, she set the book on the floor, curled her legs up to her chest, and rocked. A lullaby from somewhere in her past echoed through her head.

The soft song and her sheer exhaustion worked in harmony to finally lull her into fitful sleep. Nightmares haunted her. Visions of smoke, dead bodies, soldiers with blood dripping from their fingertips filled her mind. Suddenly, Pietor's image appeared. From his hand dangled her father's head, his body sliced clean away.

"You're our only hope, my clever girl," Papa's head said.

She awoke with a start. Zarek's chatter in the hallway reached her ears. Quickly, she sat up and swiped her fists across her cheeks. Before Karol brought Zarek inside, she pasted a smile on her features.

Her smile flipped when Zarek entered, not with Karol, but with Pietor.

His steely gaze took in her appearance from head to bare toes. "You didn't come down for dinner," he said with a frown.

"I wasn't hungry." She rose from the chair to reclaim her status as his equal. "I found the company distasteful." To brook any argument he might plan, she turned to Zarek, her false smile nearly cracking her cheeks in half. "As for you, my darling, it's time for your bath and then we shall ready you for bed."

"I hate my bath," the boy grumbled.

She chucked him under the chin. "I know that. But I will not allow a dirty boy to sleep in a clean bed."

To her shock and dismay, Zarek turned pleading eyes to Pietor. "Please?"

"Don't expect me to argue with your mama on your behalf," Pietor said. "Go take your bath."

Zarek sighed. "Yes, sir."

The boy scampered off toward the bathing chamber where, judging by the sudden echo of chatter, the servants were already filling his tub.

The moment Zarek disappeared, Pietor stepped closer. "Chess? Are you ill?"

The concern in his tone roiled her stomach. She'd die before she confessed her dreams to him. As grateful as she was that he hadn't gainsaid her about the bath, such a simple gesture didn't allow him the privilege of her trust. He'd lost that gift many years ago.

"Thank you for bringing Zarek to me. But I hate to keep you from your duties. You may leave now."

When he shook his head, shivers raced up her spine.

"My only duties concern you and Zarek. I'll be staying here."

She fought to remain calm and keep the smile pasted on her face. "Very well. Make yourself comfortable while I see to my son."

On stiff legs with an even stiffer spine, she strode into the bathing chamber.

No matter what he tried, she would not fall prey to him. Not again. Never again.

♥

Pietor had expected her to scream or throw something when he made his intentions known. But she surprised him with her mild acceptance. After she left the room, he settled in the chair near the window and picked up the book on the floor.

Antigone. In Greek. Oh, yes. Chesna could always surprise him.

With a sigh derived from part exhaustion and part frustration, he placed the book on the table beside the chair. He had never had the patience to learn Greek. He had never had much patience for any of his lessons. Thinking about it now, Pietor leaned his head against the back of the chair and stared at the gilt ceiling. He had a sudden recollection of their old tutor, Master Arno, chastising him for his laziness.

"You are allowing a female to best you in your studies," the tutor says in disbelief. Then he turns to Chesna and exclaims, "No man will ever wish to marry a woman who is smarter than he is."

But Chesna never backs down from an argument. And she refuses to feel inferior simply because she's a female. "Any man who loves me already has the wisdom of Solomon," she retorts with a wink in Pietor's direction. "If he chooses to marry me, it will only prove that his intelligence is beyond measure. I shall be his counsel, his steadfast ally, and his willing bedpartner."

After which, Master Arno throws his hands in the air and storms out of the study, leaving the two giggling children to scamper off and play...

Pietor shook off the memory. Poor Master Arno. He had never known how to deal with Bela Dubrow's exasperatingly intelligent daughter.

Regardless of the circumstance, Chesna always refused to allow her temper the upper hand. He should have remembered that. She loved to fence words and she hated to lose an argument, but she never let anyone see her angry. It was somehow beneath her to show such a weakness to an outsider. Master Arno never learned that, but Pietor had. He had simply forgotten.

Through the large windows, darkness fell. Night's lullaby of crickets and wolves enveloped the room. Giving into his exhaustion, he closed his eyes. When he opened them again, he started. The room lay still and quiet. He must have fallen asleep. Chesna hadn't returned from Zarek's bath, but Pietor sensed hours had elapsed since the two left him in this room. Rising, he stretched and took a moment to gain his bearings.

He and Chesna had spent many hours in this room as children. Little had changed in the ensuing years. To the right of the playroom would be the bedchamber of the royal governess, to the left, the bedchamber of the royal children. In which room would Chesna hide?

Hands outstretched, he felt his way in the darkness toward the doorway on his right. Slowly, he turned the knob and poked his head around the jamb to the unlit quarters of the governess. Nothing stirred. No one slept inside. He lit the lamp, emblazoning the room in mellow gold. Despite her absence, Chesna's presence permeated the walls. The furnishings, light and feminine, reflected the occupant. Honeysuckle tinged the air. He paused only long enough to smile at the large four-poster bed with cloth of gold draperies, which monopolized the center of the room, and then he backed away, leaving the door ajar.

Chesna wouldn't willingly lie in that bed with him. But if he had to carry her kicking and screaming from her hiding place, he'd have her there tonight. He would not give her an opportunity to escape.

Staying close to the wall, he crept silently to the second door. He placed his hand on the knob and turned. Locked, of course. He laughed softly. By God, he had married a scheming wench. Still, he refused to be outwitted.

He returned to the playroom, to the windows overlooking the meadow and opened them wide. Placing his knees upon the sill, he crawled to the ledge that ran alongside the exterior of the palace. The ledge was quite narrow, narrower than he remembered, but he inched his way to the windows of the children's bedchamber.

Simion in July could be unbearably hot, so hot that the bedchamber windows needed to remain open at night in order to allow whatever breeze stirred to enter the room. But the breeze would not be the only thing to enter the royal nursery on this humid evening. Pietor swung his legs inside and landed on the carpeted floor with a soft thud.

These quarters were just as dark as the other two, but his eyes had become accustomed to the lack of light. Here, the furnishings were twice the size of the other room's, and crimson cloth replaced the gold. Like the windows, the draperies were left open, the obvious preference for air over privacy. Pietor's sharp gaze quickly scanned the tiny form sleeping beneath the bedclothes. Zarek. So where had Chesna hidden herself?

He stepped inside the room and very nearly fell over her. She slept on the floor at the foot of the child's massive four-post bed, the gold carpet as her mattress, her bent elbow for a pillow.

He knelt and scooped her into his arms. Exhaustion must have taken hold because she never stirred as he rose and walked to the door. Traversing the ledge again, dangerous enough for one, would prove fatal for the two of them. Thus, he took the safer and faster route, the corridor.

Cradling his sleeping wife, he fumbled with the doorknob until he heard it click open. Once safely inside the playroom again, he pulled the door closed behind them. He anticipated a great deal of shouting in these rooms in a short time and he did not wish to awaken Zarek with the violence of the coming argument.

He made his way to the governess's bedchamber and kicked the door closed with his foot. Gently, he placed Chesna in the center of the bed, returned to the door to lock it and did the same with the windows. Assured she had no means of escape, he sat beside her on the edge of the bed and brushed the curtain of golden hair from her face.

"Wake up, my dove," he cooed in her ear.

"Mmmm," she mumbled and rolled over onto her side.

"It's our wedding night, Chess," he reminded her.

10

Chesna sat bolt upright. "No." She shook her head and scooted to the farthest corner of the bed. "You can't expect me to... I'm in mourning... It's only been a day since I lost..."

As she stammered through her explanations, she tried to rise, but Pietor grabbed her wrist to keep her on the bed.

"Zarek," she said. "I must stay with my son. He might need me. He's only a little boy and he's been through so much."

"Zarek is sleeping soundly," he replied smoothly. "If he should wake, you'll hear him call you. But right now, *I* need you."

Her eyes widened in alarm. "Do you think to force yourself on me? You would resort to rape?"

Despite the ugliness of her words, he laughed. "I have no intention of raping you, Chess. In fact, I don't intend to touch you."

"You don't?" Now she sounded disappointed. "Why not?"

"Frankly, the idea repulses me. I'm not the least bit interested in tasting my uncle's leavings." He snorted in disgust. "I choose my own whores, thank you."

She gasped as if he'd slapped her. "I am not a whore!"

"Nor are you the pure innocent I left behind when I traveled to St. Petersburg." He jerked his head in the direction of the other bedroom. "The boy sleeping next door is proof of that."

She dipped her head, but not before he spotted the rosy flush creep into her cheeks. "What do you want then?"

"My commander ordered me to marry you and I've done so. He also ordered me to bed you, but there are some things I can't bring myself to do, even in the name of duty."

"So why not allow me to sleep in my son's chamber?"

"Because I don't wish it gossiped about the palace that I defied orders. My men might believe I can't control my wife and lose respect for me. From now on, you and I must appear as a true married couple. We will sleep in this bed side by side every night. During the day, you will play the role of meek and obedient wife, bending to my will in all instances."

She lifted her gaze from her knees. Her eyes burned rage hot enough to broil him. No doubt, on a spit. "What if I don't agree to your demands?"

"If you don't agree to my *requests*," he corrected, "or if you are thinking of agreeing with me now but defying me tomorrow, I remind you that you are my wife now. I have the right to bed you or beat you at any time in any place. And you do not have the right to deny me."

Her lips tightened into a grimace, and her eyes narrowed with undisguised hatred. The ugly words he'd uttered hung between them, bitter and angry—not how he'd ever envisioned their wedding night. But the sooner Chesna accepted her new position in the household the better.

He inched closer to whisper in her ear. "Are we in agreement, *wife*?"

"We are," she said at last, her voice whisper soft.

At her agreement, he leaned against the silk-draped headboard and stared at the golden canopy above them. "Good girl." He praised her as he would a prized pet— dangerous, but necessary to test her.

Chesna stiffened and shot him a look that suggested he might have won this battle, but the war had only begun. Perfect. The last thing he wanted to do was break her spirit.

"What happens now, *husband*?" she asked, arms folded over her chest.

"Would you like to talk for a bit?"

She raised a suspicious eyebrow. "Talk?"

Pity stabbed his heart. She never used to be so on guard around him. He understood the reason for her caution, but he certainly didn't relish how awkward they'd become together. "We haven't seen each other in seven years. Wouldn't you like to know what I've been doing in that time?"

"I know what you've been doing," she retorted. "You've been following a madman in his quest for power."

"And I know what you've been doing," he snapped. "And with whom."

"It's far better to bed down with a king than to bed down with vipers."

He offered a mock salute. "Is that another of your father's maxims?"

"No, I thought of that one on my own. I don't need to hear the fiery words of a stranger to stir me into doing what's right."

"You may not believe so, but I'm fighting for a good cause. I'm fighting for the future of our country."

"Are you mad?" She slammed a fist into the bedcovers. "You're selling our country's future. To a despot. And the price we'll pay is much too high. Just yesterday Amatia lost its current king, its future king, and both of our fathers."

He blinked. She knew? How? When?

"You know about your father?" he said huskily.

"Know what?" Her face drained of color, and her eyes widened. "What have you heard about my father?" Her fingers curled into his collar. "Have you seen him? Is he alive? Where is he?"

Ah, so she didn't know. And now, he'd have to tell her. Pietor took her hand, patted it consolingly. "I'm sorry, Chess. He's gone."

"He's gone?" She yanked her hand away as if he'd tried to set her fingers on fire. "What a genteel way to say my father was murdered."

"He wasn't murdered. He died valiantly, fighting for his country. A hero's death."

"Oh, I feel ever so much happier about his loss now." Every word from her lips dripped sarcasm. "It might have been much more painful to have him here with me. Better he died valiantly than have him live through yesterday's onslaught." She steadied her gaze on his. "How do you know he's gone? Did you kill him?"

"No." A slow stream of tears slid down her cheek, and

he used his thumb to catch one on his fingertip. "I'm sorry, Chess. I loved your father dearly."

She slapped his hand away from her face. "Your so-called love didn't prevent his murder. Or the murder of your own father, for that matter."

"Perhaps not, but I didn't kill anyone."

"Don't think yourself innocent because their blood doesn't stain your hands. Your inaction killed them both. You might have stopped this tragedy from happening at all, but you were too much of a coward."

His breath erupted in a disbelieving snort. "I should have stopped Napoleon's forces from invading Amatia? How? I'm only a man, not a god. For one brief moment, forget the fact you and I are on opposite sides and think fairly. The battle lines were drawn a long time ago. General de Valmiere planned to come here whether I accompanied him or not. Surely your father's spies made him aware Napoleon had set his sights on Moscow. The emperor's invasion of Poland should have been a clear warning Amatia would be next."

Silence reigned for several minutes, while he guessed she weighed his words against her emotional pain.

Finally, she sighed. "What happened to my father?"

How much to tell her? As little as possible. Certainly he'd have to avoid the ugly details. "He was buried along with the royal family on the grounds of St. Ambrose," he replied evasively.

"I want to see his grave."

Rather than pursue this conversation, he turned off the lamp. "Go to sleep."

"I want to see his grave, Pietor. I need to say my goodbyes to Papa."

"Go to sleep, Chess."

"I'm too upset to sleep. I can't help but think about Papa and what he must have suffered before he died."

The general's earlier comments echoed in his head like a death knell. *Montfort informed me he counted no less than a dozen bayonet wounds in the man's chest.*

He couldn't ever tell her the truth. "You might fall asleep if you were a bit more comfortable," he noted.

"If you wish to make me comfortable, leave my bed. I

cannot relax with you here."

"I've already told you, your lack of virtue is safe with me."

"Nothing of mine is safe with you," she shot back. "Not my father, and certainly not my son."

He shook his head. "I see you still love to fence words."

"And you still love to fence, although now you use a saber."

He kept his lips together lest his smile light up the darkness. "I saw you watching me this afternoon."

"Yes, how fortunate you were able to put your dueling skills to such good use, killing the innocent."

"Enough battle for one night. Go to sleep," he repeated more firmly.

Thankfully, she yawned once or twice but let their conversation drift away. Within minutes, she surrendered to sleep.

Meanwhile, Pietor sat upright, staring at the ceiling. His mind wavered between regret and pride at what he had accomplished so far. He still had a long way to go before he could count his actions as a victory.

While Chesna might have slept deeply, hers was a restless sleep. She tossed and turned for hours, kicking her legs and arms in wild recklessness. The parts of her husband not bruised by her flailing limbs suffered enticement by her more seductive movements. Sometime after midnight, she finally found a comfortable position. Unfortunately for Pietor, this position involved her arm wrapped about his neck and her leg thrown over his side. Her thigh rubbed against his as she sighed in his ear.

Pietor swallowed his rapidly beating heart each time it rose into his throat. How in the devil's name could he keep his desire in check until morning? Come the dawn, he vowed to himself, he'd leave this bed and spend the day vigorously battling against other soldiers in the hope that, by tomorrow evening, he'd be too exhausted to feel the temptation he experienced now.

♥

Morning arrived far too slowly for Pietor. He spent the night still dressed in his uniform, which was meager protection from his wife's roaming arms and legs. When the sun finally rose, the sensual environment became even harder to ignore. Sunlight streamed through the windows and onto the bedcovers, surrounding the occupants in an aura of heated gold. The songs of chirping lovebirds danced on the apple-scented morning air. After withstanding the torture until his muscles tingled from lack of motion, Pietor slipped from the bed. Despite his sudden action, Chesna remained in a deep sleep.

He quickly washed, changed into a clean uniform, peeked on Zarek, who also still slept, and then returned to the bedchamber where his exhausted wife lay.

Married. He and Chesna were married. Despite the years, the misunderstandings, and their opposing wills, they'd fulfilled the vow made so long ago.

Her beauty, golden hair fanned across the lacy pillow, face relaxed in the peaceful realm of dreams, and perfect lips parted only enough to let air into and out of her lungs, stirred him. If only he'd had the opportunity to share his secrets with her, to tell her what he'd discovered in St. Petersburg and to confide his plans to her. Perhaps this current impasse would not exist between them. But would they have married before now? Or would a wedding between them have become an even less likely possibility?

He stole a quick glance heavenward. No doubt, Bela Dubrow had refused to allow something as inconsequential as death to prevent him from interfering in their lives one last time. So did he owe the old man gratitude or grief for this final matchmaking attempt?

When he could tarry no longer, he awakened his wife with a gentle shake on her shoulder and a soft coo in her ear. "Chess, it's morning."

She came awake with a jolt. "I'm awake." She struggled to sit upright and peer at the brightness outside the windows. "Goodness, it's late. I should look in on Zarek."

He waved a hand toward her. "The boy's sleeping soundly. I looked in on him earlier."

The sheet slid away to reveal a creamy shoulder where her gown's laces had come undone. He quickly turned to stare out the window. Beneath their chamber, the military units already drilled.

"How long have you been awake?" she asked.

"All night," he admitted, his gaze fixed on the routine of march, salute, present arms, and the rest of the commands as automatic to a soldier as breathing. At last, he turned to face her again. Thank God she'd used his inattention to rise and straighten her dishabille. He offered her a disingenuous smile. "It's been a long time since I've slept in a soft bed, much less in a place as grand as the Opal Palace. I had trouble getting comfortable. And of course, I overindulged at dinner. I'd forgotten what a wonderful cook Urszula is. Just the memory of last night's meal has my mouth watering to break my fast today. You missed a grand feast yesterday, Chess. Amatian duck with honey glaze, sweet peas in cream, root vegetable puree dotted with bacon, and her flaky oat bread with maple butter. Delicious."

Now Chesna turned away. "I'm not hungry."

"Oh, no. Not again." With a deep frown he strode in front of her. "You will not hide yourself away in this room another day. You are my wife now. You'll make our guests feel welcome in this palace even if the emperor himself appears on our doorstep."

Spots of color appeared in her cheeks. "Napoleon Bonaparte wouldn't dare show his face here. He sends his barbarians to conquer us in his name, but he remains safely hidden in France."

"I'm not certain where you gleaned your information, my dove, but the emperor is in Austria these days."

Her lips twisted into a disapproving moue. "Semantics. As for your General de Valmiere and his band of ruffians, they are not guests and they are not welcome here. Lastly, this is not *our* doorstep. This is the Opal Palace, home to the royal family of Amatia for more than two centuries."

"No longer," he reminded her. "The royal family is dead."

"All but my son," she reminded him.

"Which is why we were coerced into this marriage," he summed up. "It will be our duty to raise Zarek together."

She tossed a long tress over one shoulder. "Hear me now, Pietor. I will not allow you to fill my son's head with your twisted loyalties and insurrectionist thoughts. Zarek is my child and I will raise him as I see fit. Without your treasonous influence."

"We can discuss the details of the boy's upbringing later," he replied blandly. "But now, you should wash up and dress while I tend to Zarek."

Her hands settled on her hips. "You're not listening to me. Zarek is my child, and I'll tend to him myself. I've cared for that boy without your help for more than five years. I'll continue to care for him without your help."

The morning sunlight streamed through the glass behind her, illuminating the sheer fabric of her sleeping gown and shadowing her legs to perfection. Pietor couldn't help but stare at the curvaceous hips and tapered limbs peeking from beneath the filmy gown.

Impatient with his growing reaction to the temptations she offered, he tore his gaze away from the inspiring view and growled, "You'll do as I say, my meek and obedient wife. I'll tend to Zarek while you prepare yourself to go downstairs and dine with us."

Thankfully, she moved out of the sun's path, toward her dressing closet. But she gave him a smile as cold as Lake Matya in January. "And you may go to hell, my hateful and arrogant husband. You think I've changed since we last saw one another? What about you? My appearance might seem different, but at least my values have remained the same."

He quirked a brow. "Have they, Chess? When I last saw you, you were still an innocent maiden. You can't claim that title anymore."

"And when I last saw you, you swore on the soul of your sainted mother you wouldn't forget me. What happened to the honorable young man who left Simion seven years ago, Pietor? How could you follow a monster like Napoleon Bonaparte? What could he possibly offer you that your father couldn't? Power? Glory?"

"By God, you're such a little fool," he chided. "You know nothing about me. You have your own view of what I should be and where my loyalties should lie. And because I don't measure up to your expectations, you assume I've changed."

"You're absolutely right." Although she'd softened her tone, the impact only strengthened the power of her words. "I don't know you. The man I knew would never betray his country in so violent a manner. Tell me. Were the deaths of so many innocents worth your noble cause? Did you gain enough satisfaction from the rivers of blood that ran in the streets upon your homecoming? Does it please you to know how honorably *your* father died while defending his country? Was all that savagery enough to sate you? Or will you need more innocent blood shed in the name of your glorious emperor? Who will be your next victim? My boy? Tell me now so I might kill him myself before you and your army of brutes get your bloodied hands on him. I'll show him mercy with a swift death. But you'll destroy him slowly and then crush him like an unwanted insect."

He winced. By God, the woman had a tongue sharper than a rapier. And worse, he couldn't deny her accusations without divulging secrets he'd sworn to protect.

"Get dressed," he ordered as he strode away from her vicious words. "I'll rouse Zarek. When the boy is dressed and ready, we'll return to escort you to the dining hall. Do not challenge me again, madam."

11

The minute Pietor closed the door behind him, Chesna sank to the floor, her hands covering her face. She'd married a monster.

But she gathered her tumbling emotions and refused to surrender to tears or feminine vapors. She was still a Dubrow, and her ancestors would never forgive her if she allowed self-pity to destroy the royal family.

Zarek. The heir to the throne. He needed her now more than ever. She would give no quarter. She'd die for him. She'd kill for him. She could do no less than her father, her grandfather, and all the Dubrows who'd come before her.

On unsteady legs, she rose and saw to her toilette. A short time later, she paced the bedroom in a soft gray muslin gown, perfect for her mood, her hair held in place with a black velvet ribbon. Her melancholy dissipated, however, when Zarek's smiling face appeared in her doorway.

"Good morning, Mama," he exclaimed as he dropped Pietor's hand and raced to embrace her.

She caught him against her waist. Recalling her earlier angry words about killing Zarek before Pietor and his brutes might, she squeezed as if she'd never let him go. "Good morning, my darling boy."

Please, God, keep him safe. Help me protect him.

"You're crushing me," he whined.

Despite her pain, she laughed. "Forgive me." She

loosened her hold only slightly, but enough for him to break away.

He stayed close, however, and picked up a fold in her dove gray skirt. "You look very pretty this morning."

"Why, thank you." She swept him a low curtsey, then tousled his hair. "And you look as handsome as your father."

"Ahem!" Pietor, still standing in the doorway, glowered. "Shall we join the others in the dining hall?"

Fear slammed Chesna like a hammer between the eyes, but she blinked, inhaled, and nodded. A Dubrow would never show weakness to those hateful soldiers downstairs. Ignoring his outstretched arm, she took Zarek by the hand and slipped into the hall to descend the grand staircase.

She stumbled only once, but Zarek, with the wisdom of his forefathers, announced quickly, "Sorry, Mama. I didn't mean to trip you."

Inside the dining hall, the general and his minions gathered about the long mahogany table, which was set with the palace's finest china and glittering silver. The matching sidebar, banked against the stone wall, nearly buckled under the weight of savory breads, sizzling sausages, boiled eggs, fresh ripe summer fruits, and wheat cakes, all held in sterling serving dishes kept hot by lit candle nubs. The aromas tantalized Chesna's tastebuds, reminding her she hadn't eaten a bite in two full days.

But her appetite disappeared when she spotted de Valmiere seated at the head of the table, King Jarek's place of honor. While he talked to his underlings, he shoveled forkfuls of egg and sausage into his arrogant mouth. What a beast, to usurp the place of a man so dearly loved by everyone who knew him.

While this horrid man and his cronies sat comfortably in the dining hall, eating, drinking, and laughing, the royal family's bodies grew cold in their graves. By God, she hated to see these men here. And with good reason.

"Who invited the whore?" a voice chimed from the far end of the table.

Guffaws of ribald laughter followed the remark.

"Chesna's my wife, Dumont," Pietor announced through clenched teeth. "And I expect you to apologize to her at once."

Chesna looked over the throng of soldiers staring at her, mouths agape, and lifted her chin high. No apology could atone for the multitude of insults they'd dealt her over the last several days. Swallowing her pride, she touched a hand to her husband's forearm. "No, my lord. It's obvious Zarek and I no longer have a place in this room. We'll join the other servants in the kitchens. With your permission, sir."

His expression softened to one of sympathy, but she shot him a look full of hatred.

On his nod, she curtsied nearly to the floor, head bowed to hide the fire in her eyes. Then, taking Zarek's hand again, she turned and left the dining hall.

"She's your wife now, eh?" The vile Dumont's question stopped her from moving past the foyer. "That explains the dark circles under your eyes. While the rest of us fought the heat and mosquitoes last evening, you rode the royal whore."

To her shame, the hall reverberated with lewd laughter. Releasing her hold on Zarek, she bent to whisper, "Go see Urszula and make sure she fills you a plate twice your size. I'll be along in a moment or two."

"Yes, Mama." Zarek seemed unaffected by the men's crude comments, a fact which gave Chesna pause to thank God for the innocence of youth.

"Receiving royal treatment, Gabris?" another officer shouted. "You always were a lucky devil."

"Is there a sweet honeypot beneath her gown, Pietor?" Dumont's voice rang out again. "Or did you find some vinegar between those legs?"

Chesna, ears burning with humiliation, prayed her husband might say something—anything—to defend her. The little girl inside her hoped that, perhaps, a piece of the Pietor she'd once loved still hid inside the hateful man she'd married. But he remained stone silent while the insults to her character flowed like a spilled cask of wine.

"Did you make her kneel before you and swear her loyalty to France before you plowed her field?"

"*Merde.* What a sight that would be to behold, eh? Her saucy little bottom rising in the air while her golden head lay at your feet."

"I'd want her golden head placed slightly higher than my feet, fellows."

General de Valmiere's chortles rose above the braying din. "I wager Captain Gabris had to beat that saucy little bottom before he plowed her field. By God, I made the right choice, giving her to you to control. Very well done, Gabris. It only took you one night to tame the bitch and bring her to heel. Very well done, indeed."

Still, Pietor said nothing. And Chesna, alone in the foyer, castigated her foolish heart for caring. She pulled her hair from its ribbon and wrapped a tress around her finger. Blast him!

She should have realized by now that the boy who'd vowed to love her forever had left Simion on that long ago day and disappeared. The man she'd married yesterday might as well be a stranger who bore the same name and a keen resemblance to her childhood sweetheart. And she would be far better served if she thought of him in such a way.

The pain of betrayal sliced so deeply, her chest hurt too much to breathe. She wanted to flee, to leave the Opal Palace, toss off the heavy mantle of responsibility that weighed down her shoulders and buried her in muck. But she could not, would not, abandon Zarek.

With a sigh of defeat, she turned from the ugliness in the dining room and headed for the kitchens, crushing the strip of black velvet beneath her heel.

The hum of conversation halted the moment she stepped inside. She scanned the dozens of people seated at their benches in the crowded servants' dining area. Only the sound of her heartbeat thundered in her ears. A vast array of expressions, from anticipation to deep concern to sheer dread, met her gaze. Yet, no one spoke. Apparently, no one knew exactly what to say or how to ask the question uppermost in all their minds.

"Well?" Irina burst out at last. She rose from her place across from Urszula at the first table and stared impatiently at Chesna, hands on her hips.

Chesna dropped her attention to the floor and wished for a trap door she might fall into.

"Chesna," Irina's strident demand stirred the air. "What happened last night?"

After a quick glance toward the far end of the table where Zarek sat in avid conversation with several other children, she murmured, "He never noticed I wasn't..." Bile rose in her throat, and she swallowed, then grimaced at the harsh taste. "...what he thought me to be."

"Well, thank God for that," Irina exclaimed as she resettled herself before her plate of ham, eggs, and pastry.

Around her, the other servants all returned to their meals.

All but Karol, who stole up behind her and placed a protective arm around her shoulder. "Are you feeling all right this morning, Chess?"

The concern in his tone became her undoing. A block of tears filled her head, seeking release. Rather than allow them to escape, she simply shielded her face behind a veil of hair and nodded.

But her response must have lacked conviction because Karol cupped her chin, tilting her face to meet his gaze. "Did he hurt you?" he demanded angrily.

"More than you'll ever know," she confessed on a sob.

Before she began to weep in front of the entire household staff, she broke away and raced out of the kitchens.

Nearly blinded by torrential tears, she stumbled up the staircase. The old battle implements silently mocked her clumsy ascent.

Forgive me, Papa. I've shamed you today.

She wanted to show strength, wanted to pretend the enemies' barbs bounced off her as if she hefted one of the ancient shields for protection. But every minute she'd stood outside the dining hall, listening to their insults and slurs while her husband said nothing, sapped another ounce of fight from her bones. Now, all she wanted was to curl into her bed and cry until her eyes drowned.

Outside her bedchamber, she halted.

Strange voices came from inside. Someone was in her room! Who?

Pietor?

No. Aside from the fact she'd left him downstairs

preening for the barbarians, she'd recognize the silken timbre of his deep, dark tongue. These men were harsher, more guttural in their speech.

Her tears evaporated beneath the heat of her outrage. Inside the nursery, she found an assortment of debris. Zarek's favorite toys lay strewn across the floor, many in pieces that could never be reassembled. Pages, torn from his books, scattered like fallen leaves in late autumn. Anger lit the fuse of her temper, but she tamped down any emotional outburst with fists clenched tightly at her sides.

Once she'd sidestepped the carnage in the nursery, she entered her bedchamber and stopped short. Two soldiers stood amidst the disgrace that had been her neat and orderly quarters only an hour earlier. Gowns, shifts, and pantalettes sat in a rainbow of color and fabrics in one corner. Her scented powders dusted the tabletops with cloying perfume. A rare breeze blew papers across the floor near her bed.

But she stifled a cry when she spotted her mother's earrings, a memento of the woman she'd never known, crushed into glittering pieces in the nap of the carpet.

Her gaze honed in on a fat soldier with a mouse for a moustache standing before her armoire. One meaty arm rifled through the drawer that held her undergarments.

"What are you doing up here?" She kept her tone even, almost conversational, despite the fury riding high inside her heart.

A second soldier, this one thinner and clean-shaven, stepped back from her bookcase. His face bore an expression of resentment, as if she'd overstepped herself by questioning his appearance in her room. "General de Valmiere ordered us to inspect these rooms and remove any items we considered traitorous to the Empire."

The first soldier held a lacy chemise between his extended fingertips.

The thin hair of Chesna's patience snapped. She lunged across the room and yanked her underwear from his filthy hands. "My clothing is not your concern."

"Well, now," the second soldier drawled, "that might be, but these books look rather suspicious."

With her chemise clutched to her chest, she whirled to

find the thin man waving her father's copy of *Antigone*. She strode toward him, hand outstretched to grab the book before he could damage the pages. "There's nothing suspicious about my books."

He pulled the book up over his head, out of her reach. "Oh, I'm not so sure about that. There's some very strange-looking writing inside this one. Since I can't read it, I can't say it isn't dangerous now, can I?"

"The writing is Greek," she retorted. "It's a tragedy by Sophocles, a famous Greek philosopher." On tiptoes, she extended her hand toward the link to her father. They'd already destroyed her memento of Mama. Now her father's memory seemed doomed to the same fate. "Would you please give that back to me?"

One hand still holding the book away from her desperate fingers, he snaked an arm around her waist and pulled her up against his chest. "Give us a kiss first."

She squirmed in his hold, craning her neck to avoid his lips while still stretching toward the book. "Please return that to me."

"I said, give us a kiss first." He tightened his hold and to her horror, she smelled his foul breath, like putrid eggs, near her cheek.

"Release me, please." To her dismay, her voice trembled, which only made both men chortle.

The one holding her leaned so close she had to bend backwards to avoid his smacking lips. "Come on now. We know who you are. You were a royal mistress. Now that we've conquered your king, we get his spoils. That means you have to serve us. Me and my friend over there."

She dared a glance at the fat one, whose eyes narrowed and his smile widened.

"You will release her immediately."

The voice, soft yet lethal, carried enough threat to make the soldier drop his hands to his sides.

Freed from his grasp, Chesna skittered backward out of reach before she turned to where Pietor stood in the doorway, a wide-eyed Zarek by his side. But Pietor's focus remained locked on the thin soldier still holding her father's book.

"Return the book to the lady, Sergeant Lorelle," he

remarked in the same soft, level tone.

Cheeks flaming, the soldier named Lorelle thrust the leather-bound book into her hands.

On a relieved sigh, she took the book and wrapped it protectively in her undergarments, then clutched the bundle to her chest.

"What kind of havoc are you and Beaulieu involved in up here?" Pietor's glare could freeze a bonfire.

"We were only doing what General de Valmiere told us to do," the soldier murmured.

"Oh?" Pietor raised an eyebrow. "The general ordered you to accost my wife?"

"N-no, s-sir," Lorelle stammered. "The general ordered us to bring your belongings up here and told us to be certain no insurrectionary items remained behind."

"I'm still waiting to hear where the general's orders included putting your hands on my wife."

"We didn't know she was your wife, sir," the fat one, Beaulieu, replied.

"It doesn't matter what you knew, Private Beaulieu. The ladies of this household are not here for your enjoyment. General de Valmiere has ordered that there will be no raping or pillaging while we are in Simion. Now get out of this room, both of you!"

"Yes, sir." They nearly fell over themselves to leave the room.

But Chesna's attention centered elsewhere. On shaky legs, she staggered to the center of the room. She knelt in front of the shattered jewelry and stared at the crushed pieces of gold. Hopeless. The finest goldsmith couldn't repair the damage wrought by the ignorance and greed of Napoleon Bonaparte's minions. Setting aside her garments and book, she gathered the bits of gold and precious stones into her cupped hand.

"Chess?" Pietor's question, more tender now, came from behind her. "Are you all right? What happened? Did they hurt you?"

She closed her fingers around the earring bits before he might see them. He held enough power over her. She wouldn't allow him to gloat about this latest victory against her will. She looked up at him, brow furrowed. "How did you know I was here?"

"Zarek came to fetch me from the dining hall. He said you were crying when you left the kitchens."

With the earrings safely tucked in her fist, she rose to face him. "Zarek was mistaken." She threw her shoulders back, allowing no weakness. "I do not cry."

Expressionless, he brushed a thumb across her tear-stained cheek. "I thought as much."

Before he might contradict her statement, she quickly changed the subject. "Why did you interfere with those men?"

His jaw practically hit his chest. "You need to ask me such a thing?"

With an air of nonchalance far from the turmoil simmering in her belly, she shrugged. "You didn't defend me against the general and his aides in the dining hall."

He blinked, confusion evident in his silver eyes. "No one touched you in the dining hall."

"No, but the insults they hurled were just as hurtful."

"I ordered Captain Dumont to apologize to you," he reminded her. "You deemed it unnecessary."

"Because at the time, he didn't know I was your wife. I'm talking about afterwards."

"Afterwards?" His brow pleated in deep lines. "You left for the kitchens afterwards."

"I didn't leave right away." The heat of shame warmed her face. But then, she remembered, his sin was far greater than her eavesdropping. "I lingered long enough to hear them talk about me. About my saucy little bottom in the air and my head at your feet. Or a few inches higher if de Valmiere had his way. And whether I had a honey pot or vinegar under my skirts." The words tumbled from her lips in a torrent of anger and pain. "You said nothing, Pietor. You didn't even attempt to defend me against their insults."

"What's this, Chess?" He snorted. "You take offense to the truth?"

She gasped her outrage and stamped a foot.

"It's a bit late for distress now, don't you think?" he continued. "You should have shown more concern for your reputation before you lay beneath King Jarek while he sweated above you."

Ready to slap the smarmy smile from his face, she uncurled her fists, dropping her mother's broken earrings to the floor. But first, she stole a quick glance at Zarek, whose face clouded with concern. Two deep inhales and exhales quelled the violence.

Pietor, on the other hand, apparently remained unaware of the boy's interest in their conversation. "If you had taken a care then, your resentment might be justified now."

She wanted to argue, to tell him he should have done something—said something—to inform them that he wouldn't tolerate their slurs against her. But ever mindful of the child listening intently, she opted to let the matter drop.

Not so Pietor. "Men are men, Chess. They do not mince words for polite company. They believe in calling a whore a whore."

Her too-fragile emotions could take no more. "And I believe in calling a pig a pig." She turned her back on him and strode toward Zarek, one hand outstretched. "Come, my darling. Let's clean up this mess and then we'll begin your lessons for today."

But Pietor stepped between them, a solid wall of animosity. "No, Chess. You'll no longer spend as much time with Zarek as you used to."

She already knew the answer, but she took a deep calming breath and asked the question anyway. "Why not?"

"You may unfairly influence the boy against the emperor," he explained. "I will now be responsible for Zarek's care and education."

Her rage became some physical monster, eating her alive from the inside out. She wanted to scream the roof down around him. She wanted to pick up the nearest heavy object and beat him with it. She wanted to kill him for destroying her life.

But calling on her last ounce of dignity, she fought those inclinations. With a nod of graceful defeat, she strode past him to leave the chaotic room. "Very well. I trust you'll clean this mess. After all, your friends caused the destruction."

Just as she reached the doorway, she turned back to

him and, in a voice whisper-soft, told him, "I hate you, Pietor Gabris. God cursed me the day He sent you back to Amatia. May He forgive you for what you have done here because I never will."

A red mist floated before her eyes as she whirled from the room and ran back down the staircase to the grand hall.

What had she ever done in her life to deserve this torment? And to have her once so very dear Pietor be the instrument of her misery seemed more than she could bear. He had ruined her life. He had brought his horrid soldiers and his vile emperor here to destroy everyone and everything she had ever loved. For all she knew, her husband might have been the man who killed her father. And she had vowed before God to love and obey him until death parted them!

Her feet landed on the tiled floor in the grand hall with an angry stomp. The absurdity of her situation struck her the moment she heard the sound. Where in this godforsaken palace would she go now?

Six armed soldiers stood before the large mahogany doors that led to the courtyard and beyond. She couldn't simply stroll outside. The enemy's tents and garrisons of soldiers covered the pastureland. And she certainly didn't wish to come face-to-face with any more members of Napoleon's trained ruffians. If she spotted another arrogant face above another bright blue uniform, she might be forced to kill someone.

She didn't dare go back to the kitchens. Karol, Urszula, Irina, and all the others would wish to know every detail of her wedding night and why she left the kitchens so abruptly earlier. Besides, she couldn't bear to see their sympathetic faces. Pity would only break her.

She refused to return to the nursery to listen to her husband fill her child's head with poison. If she had to hear Pietor spouting his nonsense about the Great Emperor Napoleon Bonaparte and his grand plans to rule Europe in the peoples' name, she might throw herself out the window to escape.

Any of the other rooms inside the palace which might have been a haven in the past would now be off limits to her, including her father's bedchamber and his study.

She couldn't think of a single place to go for succor. She'd never felt so strange, like a prisoner without a prison cell.

So she turned and headed for the one place where she belonged. To the one place where she might find solitude, but not peace. She would never find peace again.

12

"I hate you, Pietor Gabris. God cursed me the day He sent you back to Amatia. May He forgive you for what you have done here because I never will."

Pietor stood stock still while Chesna's words reverberated in his brain and in his heart. She couldn't possibly hate him more than he hated himself. The fact that his animosity kept her and Zarek alive couldn't soothe his conscience.

A tug on his shirt caused him to look down into the boy's tempestuous eyes, eyes like his father's. And his uncle's. And like Pietor's. A trait repeated in all the royal family's descendants.

"Why don't you like my mama?" Zarek demanded.

Non-plussed, he offered the boy the truth. "I like your mama very much."

"No, you don't. You make her angry. And you make her cry." That steady royal gaze pinned him as securely as the chains on a condemned prisoner.

"I don't mean to do either of those things, Zarek," he replied.

"Then why do you?"

After a decade of dealing with grown men, he'd forgotten how tenacious children could be when a topic mattered to them. Especially any child raised by Chesna, who refused to lose a debate, mainly on principle.

"Did your mama happen to tell you I've known her since she was your age?"

The boy's eyes grew round with wonder. "No."

"Well, I have."

Why he chose to reveal that secret to a mere slip of a boy, he couldn't fathom. But if Zarek allowed such information to get into the wrong hands or *into the wrong ears*, all three of them could be executed.

"You mustn't tell anyone," he added in a conspiratorial whisper.

"I won't. I promise." On a nod, Zarek bent to scoop up some shiny metal on the carpet. "Did you know her mother?"

"Chesna's mother?" The question threw him for a moment. But he shook off his confusion. "No. Why?"

The boy held out his hand. "These were her mama's."

A sigh escaped Pietor's lips. He recognized those familiar pieces now irretrievably crushed to near dust. While he took the shattered jewelry from Zarek's hand, memories flooded his brain.

Chesna's thirteenth birthday. The sparkle of gold when she tucks her hair behind her ears and the blinding smile on her face.

"They were my mother's. Papa says as long as I have these earrings, I have a piece of her with me. Do you think I might look like her when I wear them?"

Poor Chess. By God, how much more indignity could she withstand? He had to find her, somehow ease her pain without giving away his own motives. But he couldn't leave Zarek. And they should clean up the destruction de Valmiere's men had caused.

Then again, he thought as he took in the bits of lace and silk scattered around the room, perhaps he should have one of the chambermaids gather Chesna's things. The work was too intimate, too *personal*, for him.

He paused. But not too personal for a husband, which, he reminded himself, he was.

Her husband.

He shoved the shattered earrings into his pocket and gestured to the destruction around them. "Why don't you pick up your toys while I see to the rest of this mess?"

Afterward, he'd leave Zarek with Karol while he went after Chesna. Right now, she needed a friend. But in the hornets' nest that was Opal Palace, not even the closest friends were trustworthy. Unfortunately, he was the best she could hope for.

♥

Pietor searched for hours. With each minute that ticked by, his panic rose. Where could she have gone? Or had someone else accosted her—this time, with more success than Beaulieu and Lorelle had?

He finally found her in the late afternoon. She sat, imprisoned in the dungeon, in the very same cell she had occupied before their marriage ceremony.

"Go away," she muttered when he stopped outside her cell. "I don't wish to see you right now."

"I don't care if you wish to see me or not. Do you have any idea how long I've been searching for you?" He pressed his face against the barred window so she might see his impatience. "I've been tearing this palace apart for three hours. I've searched every nook and cranny, every crawlspace, every cupboard. I looked from the rooftop to the root cellar with no luck. I was just about to wade through Lake Matya in search of your drowned body when it suddenly occurred to me where you might be." He dropped his hands to his sides. "And by God, here you are."

She never flinched at his tone, never gave any reaction at all. In fact, she didn't look up from the cold stone slab, but finally, she did wave a hand at him in dismissal. "Don't fret, Pietor. I promise I'll be in our bed tonight. Until then, go away and leave me alone."

Her animosity stung. Not that he didn't deserve her barbs. Especially after the insults he'd hurled at her in their chamber. Yet, she had to understand that despite their opposing positions, he still cared about her welfare. "Is that why you think I'm looking for you? To be certain you're in our bed six hours from now?"

She rose from the bench and approached the door of the cell, only speaking when they were inches apart, but separated by even rows of cold wet iron. "That's our agreement."

He scowled. "And until tonight you intend to stay down here?"

"I have nowhere else to go." She gestured at the dank gray walls with a broad sweep of her arm. "This is the only place where I might be alone."

"You can't stay down here. Do you want to make yourself ill?"

She shrugged, but said nothing in reply.

"Dammit, Chess! Come out of this cell immediately!"

He knew he'd made a mistake the moment the words left his mouth—a moment too late.

Chesna would never be intimidated by anyone who shouted at her. Her stubborn nature reacted in exactly the opposite fashion when confronted with someone's anger. She remained mute, the hint of a casual smile playing on her lips while he stood on uneasy feet, regretting his outburst with every silent moment that slipped by.

"No," she said at last, in a voice as serene as an untouched forest. "I believe I'll stay here a while longer."

"I could have your things moved down here permanently," he threatened.

Her smile broadened. "What a wonderful idea. Would you include my father's copy of *Antigone* with my things? And an oil lamp or a few candles might be in order. It's a bit too dark for reading. And if you wouldn't mind, perhaps you could ask Karol to bring me some bread and cheese? I haven't eaten in quite a while."

Pietor's temper flared, but he maintained an even, moderate tone. "If you'd like something to eat, you'll join us in the dining hall for the dinner hour."

Her lips twisted in a moue of distaste. "I sincerely doubt the 'royal whore' is welcome in the dining hall. I might spoil the meal for the delicate bellies of such hardened soldiers."

"Then you will go to the kitchens with the rest of the servants. It's time you realized you're no longer the darling of the household, Chess."

"Believe me, Pietor, the events of the last few hours have crystallized that idea in my mind." Her voice cracked, and her brittle tone raised the hackles on his nape.

He brushed his fingertips over the shattered earrings in

his pocket. Yes, he'd imagine she understood her new place with or without his reminder. But she couldn't give up. Not yet.

He clucked his tongue. "No doubt your father would be very disappointed to see you hiding down here."

"I'm not hiding," she retorted with an impudent head toss. "I'm a prisoner. I can't leave this cell."

"No one's keeping you here. You may come and go as you please." He wagged a finger. "Don't forget. You promised to be in our bed every night. You may stay in this cell all day every day, if that's your wish. But at night, you will be in our bedchamber. Beside me."

She folded her arms over her chest. "Yes. Of course. You wouldn't want your fellow blackguards to lose respect for you. You don't care if your wife despises you, as long as those rats in uniform believe you've managed to beat her saucy little bottom before you plowed her field." On the last outraged word, she turned from the cell door. Returning to her stone bed, she sat on the edge and stared up at the ceiling. In a softer voice, she added, "Fetch me in time for the dinner hour, please. One loses all sense of time here in the dark."

She'd scored her victory.

Properly chastened, he could do little more than nod. "Of course."

"Don't forget *Antigone* and the candles."

Sympathy flipped to ire. But he tamped down his emotions with fisted hands. He knew her well enough to understand she was trying to bait him. Apparently, she hoped he would browbeat her and demand she leave the cell with him now. She probably hoped to appear as the voice of reason while he shouted and reacted like a madman.

And while part of him burned to drag her out of this dank cell by her hair, another part of him longed for the opportunity to rub salt in her wounded pride when she finally gave up this inanity and admitted defeat on her own.

"I won't forget," he promised.

He turned from the cell and walked up the staircase, back to the warmth and sunlight above, while his wife smoldered in the musty darkness.

♥

Chesna didn't remain alone in the dark for long. Karol came down to the dungeon with a tray prepared by Urszula containing bread, cheese, and watered wine.

Unlike when Pietor found her, Chesna greeted Karol with a warm smile and ushered him into her cell as if she played hostess of a magnificent soiree. Flashing a wide grin, he reciprocated her nonsense with a click of his heels and a low bow.

"Madam," he intoned with the formality befitting a royal servant, "I've brought you a light repast."

On a giggle, she sat on her stone bench, and he placed the tray on her lap before sitting beside her.

"So?" the gruff man asked. "Now that there is no one to hear us, tell me the truth. What happened between you and Pietor last night?"

"Nothing." She took a nibble from the golden bread slathered with soft white cheese, chewed, swallowed. Delicious. The tang of cheese, mixed with the sweetness of honey baked into the bread, woke up her tastebuds and made her stomach dance in anticipation of a hearty feast.

Meanwhile, Karol frowned. "I can't help if you don't confide in me."

With the bread a breath from her teeth, she paused. "I *am* confiding in you. Nothing happened. My husband didn't touch me last night."

"Why not?"

She arched a brow. "You sound surprised."

"I am surprised." His cheeks flamed brighter than his hair. "You forget, I was a fixture in this palace before you were born. I've watched you grow up. Half the men in this city have admired you from afar since the first changes from child to woman appeared in your face. Trust me when I tell you, you've been the subject of many a young man's nighttime visions."

Now Chesna's cheeks flamed. "You're being fanciful."

"No, I'm not. And out of all those young men, no one was more devoted to you than Pietor. He was the man who used to write sonnets comparing the sparkle in your eyes to everything from the dew on wildflowers to the stars in the winter sky."

Despite the agony of her current circumstances, she smiled at the memory of those pretty poems.

"What happened to him in St. Petersburg?" Karol demanded. "What's wrong with him?"

"Nothing's wrong with him. At least, I don't believe so."

"Of course something's wrong. Why else would he leave you alone? After all the years he's pined after you, how could he not bed you once you were married?"

Her belly tumbled in freefall, humiliation complete. She lowered her head to stare at her feet. "He said he didn't wish to taste his uncle's leavings," she murmured. "He believes the lies Irina spewed, that I was King Jarek's mistress. So now, the thought of bedding me disgusts him."

"A traitor with a sense of moral outrage? What a surprise." He clasped her fingertips, squeezed gently. "At least his hesitancy works to our advantage. Now you and Zarek will remain safe from the French ambition."

She returned her attention to her meal, but her appetite had faltered yet again. She pushed the tray onto the empty seat on her left. "We're safe *now*. But what if he suddenly changes his mind and decides to pursue me after all? Regardless of our detailed discussion yesterday, I honestly don't think I could fool him if he were to suddenly press the matter."

Karol nodded solemnly. "Then you must use this current respite to your advantage."

"How?"

His steady gaze honed in on her, and she squirmed on the bench. "You might want to try charming him. Rather than fighting and insulting him and his choices, try to talk to him. Understand him."

"Understand him? I don't want to understand him. He murdered my father, his own father, the king—"

"The French army is responsible for their deaths, Chess. Not Pietor."

Resentment shot her from her seat. "He's a member of the French army."

"He's also a member of the Amatian royal family. Which is why I asked you what happened to him in St. Petersburg.

Aren't you the least bit curious?"

"No," she rasped through a throat thick with unshed emotions. To release some of her anxiety, she paced the filthy floor.

"No?" He leaned back, gaze still sharp on her. "The man left here pledging his undying love to you. He asked your father for your hand before he left Simion."

She stopped. "He did?"

"Bela didn't tell you?"

Speech abandoned her, and she shook her head. Tears skimmed her eyelids.

"He made Bela promise you'd wait for him to come home."

"You're lying," she whispered harshly.

"No, I'm not. Pietor never wanted to go to St. Petersburg. You know that. Something powerful must have happened in Russia to make him turn his back on you."

"I know what happened. Napoleon Bonaparte led him astray. He forgot all about me, all about Amatia, and all about any promises made."

Slapping both hands on his thighs, Karol rose. "Then you'll have to find a more powerful argument to win him back."

"I don't want him back. I want him gone." She wanted the *old* Pietor, the one who loved Amatia, loved *her*.

"Regardless of what you want, your first responsibility is to the prince. Mikhail is Amatia's only hope."

"Mikhail is dead," she reminded him sharply.

"*Zarek* is our only hope," Karol amended. "And *you* are Zarek's only hope. You must protect him at all costs."

Pressure pounded her skull. So much rode on her feeble shoulders. How could she possibly accomplish everything to everyone's satisfaction? Her legs resumed their pacing, if only to give her brain something banal to focus on. "Papa always wished I'd been born a son. I had hoped by protecting Zarek from Bonaparte's men, I might prove my gender wasn't a detriment to my involvement in government policy. But I was wrong."

"Never doubt yourself, Chess. You've done very well in this game so far."

"I've done very well for a *woman*," she corrected bitterly.

"But a man wouldn't have been forced into marriage to protect the prince."

"That's true," he agreed. "But any men ordered to protect the prince are either already dead, or in hiding. Like me. You're all we have left. Don't disappoint us. You must protect Zarek."

She shivered. "How? I'll do whatever I can, but Karol, I'm so afraid."

He pulled her into his embrace. "I'd be more concerned if you weren't afraid, Chess. But don't let fear override your common sense. I'll protect you as best I can." He ran a large hand over her hair, soothing her nervous tremors. "And never believe you're less than capable because you're a woman. Bela would be very proud of the strength you've shown in the last few days."

"Excuse me," a voice drawled from behind her.

Chesna whirled. Pietor stood against the wall, arms folded over his chest, the cell door open beside him.

She ripped away from Karol. "Where's Zarek?"

"With Urszula. I thought perhaps you might wish to wash up before dinner," Pietor continued in a tight voice. "I didn't realize you were receiving men down here."

Before she could do more than gasp, Karol's beefy arm shot out to grab him by the throat. "I wouldn't sound so haughty if I were you, Pietor *Gabris*." Between each syllable, Karol shook him like a wet cat. "You may be grown now, but to me, you're still the same child who cried on my shoulder when your father punished you for breaking Urszula's best cooking pot." He released his grip on Pietor and returned his attention to Chesna, hand outstretched. "Come, Chess. Dinner's waiting."

With Karol's hand to lend her strength, she passed her husband who sputtered like a fish suddenly pulled out of Lake Matya.

13

Long after the meal concluded, Chesna remained in the kitchens, dreading the moment she must return to her bedchamber. She didn't have the courage to face Pietor tonight. After she and Karol had left the dungeon, she'd returned to her rooms to change her gown. All evidence of the soldiers' damage from earlier had disappeared. Including her mother's shattered earrings. She regretted their loss, wished she hadn't allowed her anger to lose the last link she had with the woman she'd never known.

Pietor had taken Zarek into the dining hall with his cronies so she didn't even have the child to distract her from her jumbled thoughts while she listened to the servants' chatter during the meal. Now, she threw herself into helping the kitchen servants with table clearing, dishwashing, and floor sweeping.

Finally, Urszula would allow her no more opportunity to avoid her fate. "Shoo! Out of my domain. You have other more important duties to attend to."

She blanched.

"If it helps," Karol whispered, "remember what I told Pietor earlier about crying on my shoulder. He was a child once, too. You knew him then, knew exactly how to handle him. I'll wager you still have that special touch."

He winked, and she offered a wan smile in return.

With the enthusiasm of a condemned prisoner, she climbed the stairs. Every step made her feet feel heavier until by the time she reached the top landing, she would've sworn her legs were made of lead.

She managed to drag herself into the nursery where

Zarek played on the floor with a pile of wooden blocks. Pietor sat at her desk, writing in a leather-covered book. No doubt to combat the stifling heat, he'd removed his uniform jacket, loosened the ties of his shirt from around his throat, and rolled up his sleeves past his elbows. Bent over the desktop, he looked more like the Pietor of old than the soldier she'd come to despise.

Except for his hair. She missed the way the ebony length used to brush his shoulders. Now, the close-cropped curls reminded her how far from her he'd truly gone.

"Mama!" Zarek shot up from his pile of blocks and wrapped his arms around her waist. His tight hug rejuvenated her, reaffirmed the drive to protect him at all costs. If she'd sacrifice her life for him, she could certainly swallow her pride and find a way to make peace with Pietor.

He looked up then and offered her a nod. "Chess." The single syllable nearly bit her flesh.

She attempted a bright smile. "Pietor."

His posture stiffened in the chair, as if he prepared to fight off a series of physical blows. From her? A flush of heat steamed her neck and cheeks. How could she possibly break through this impasse? She might as well try to talk her way through a brick wall.

"I trust you enjoyed your day today."

He relaxed slightly, leaning back and extending his legs. "I spent most of the afternoon with Zarek. You've done well, Chess. He's an intelligent boy."

"Look, Mama." Zarek held out a slate. "Pietor and I worked hard today."

She took the board from him, studied the precise words drawn by the adult and the crude but legible copies Zarek had created. After Zarek had written each word, Pietor had written a sentence using the new word to increase the boy's vocabulary. A flicker of hope danced when she noticed everything had been written in Amatian, not French.

"We worked on numbers, too," Zarek said. "And then Pietor took me swimming in Lake Matya."

She whirled to face Pietor's indulgent smile. "You did?"

"Too much studying numbs the mind," he said smoothly. "Especially in this heat. I may have forgotten a few things when I left Simion, but I've always remembered how refreshing the waters in the lake felt on a hot, sticky day when my brain buzzed with numbers and letters." His voice lowered to a whisper that brushed her spine like a lover's fingertip. "Do you remember, Chess?"

His words, a kiss on her bare nape, evoked memories long buried. Memories of his mouth on her mouth, on her neck. A tingle erupted beneath her flesh, traveled slower than tears through her blood.

She shook off the sensual haze, but couldn't hide the tremor in her voice. "I remember." On a long exhale, she returned her attention to Zarek. "What shall we read before bed tonight, my darling?"

But Zarek shook his head. "I don't want you to read to me tonight, Mama."

One hand outstretched to escort him to his bedchamber, she pulled up short. "Why not?"

"I want Pietor to read to me."

"Oh." Betrayal stung deep. From the moment she'd been given the responsibility of caring for him, she'd never had to share his attentions with anyone else. Not even the queen. Now, after only one day in Pietor's company, one swim and a few hours of lessons, the boy's loyalties had shifted.

She'd failed. Failed her father, failed the royal family, failed Amatia. Most of all, she'd failed Zarek. But, no. She wouldn't give up so easily. Zarek was five and Pietor was a new toy for him. Eventually, he would disappoint the child, just as he had with her so many years ago. And she would be there to pick up the shattered pieces when Pietor broke another tender heart.

Pietor had finished whatever he'd been writing and swerved to watch the power struggle between them. Because she sensed he'd enjoy an emotional scene, Chesna capitulated with grace.

"Pietor?" She flashed a serene smile in his direction. "I believe your services have been requested."

His eyebrows shot up in surprise. "Why don't we both read to him tonight?"

"No." Zarek folded his arms over his chest and used his most imperious tone. "Mama reads to me every night. I want you tonight. Let Mama rest for a while. I don't like the circles under her eyes."

So that explained his demand. The boy still cared about her. Hiding a relieved smile, she forced a wide yawn. "I *am* rather tired."

"Very well." Pietor rose. "I'll read while you rest. What shall we read tonight, Zarek?"

"*Antigone*," the boy replied. "Mama wants me to learn Greek."

He jerked his head in Chesna's direction. "You planned this."

But humor overtook her, and she could barely vocalize her denial. Giggles rippled through her belly, rose into her throat, and passed over her lips.

"Imps," he growled. "Both of you."

How Zarek knew about Pietor's weakness for languages, she couldn't fathom. But somehow, the boy had turned the tables on the man. And oh, she enjoyed watching Pietor squirm for a change.

Finally, he sighed. "*Antigone* in Greek. But I warn you now, you mischievous young pup, your lessons tomorrow will not be as easy as they were today. I'll make you pay for your nonsense." He turned narrowed eyes in her direction. "As for you, madam, you seem to take great delight in my situation."

Her giggles subsided at the edge in his tone.

"Enjoy your mirth now, Chess. I'll make you pay for your disrespect when I return to this room."

Oh, God. What had she done? She was supposed to charm him. Instead, she'd raised his ire. She immediately sobered as he scooped Zarek onto his shoulders and strode away.

Pietor sat at Zarek's bedside struggling through the jumbled Greek contained in Sophocles's tragedy. Occasionally, the boy would laugh before correcting his pronunciation. Once or twice, he actually covered his ears and winced.

But at last, Zarek apparently took pity on Pietor's fractured tongue. He yawned twice, stretched his arms out wide, and snuggled beneath the thin bedsheet. "You will read again to me tomorrow," he announced with a wave of his hand. "Please send in Mama now to kiss me goodnight. She'll wish to hear me say my nighttime prayers before I sleep."

Pietor bit back a retort. The boy certainly had his father's demeanor, didn't he?

"Of course," he replied with a deep bow. "Your wish is my command, sir."

Zarek must have missed the sarcastic edge in Pietor's tone. He simply waved again. "You are dismissed until tomorrow."

Chess had her hands full with this lad. Yet, she'd done an amazing job in educating and raising the boy. If the child lived long enough, he'd be an intelligent, just man someday. And now, Pietor had as much invested in seeing Zarek reach that potential as Chesna did.

When he reentered the playroom, he found Chesna pacing ruts into the carpet.

He cleared his throat. "Ahem!"

On a squeal, she looked up suddenly, terror written in her wide eyes and pale face.

She feared him.

The knowledge chilled him. Not Chess. Not now. She couldn't give up yet. She needed to stay strong for all that was still to come.

The Chesna he'd left behind had feared nothing. Not man, nor beast. Certainly, she'd never feared *him*. She'd always challenged him, questioned him, charmed him, loved him. But fear? No.

The Chesna he knew in the past would never crumble easily. Then again, the Chesna of old had a powerful father to sustain her. And no one to worry about except herself. Unfortunately, the Chesna he married lacked the daunting support of Bela and had the added responsibility of protecting Zarek from the vipers who lurked nearby. Including himself.

Chesna Dubrow would face any enemy bravely and damn the consequences. But Chesna Gabris folded under pressure because the consequences involved a five-year-old boy.

Well, he'd rather have her despise him than fear him. Because despite de Valmiere's orders, he'd never intended to break her spirit. He'd only hoped to gain her cooperation.

As she continued to stare at him with her worried look, he sought some way to ease her tension. "Your son has requested your presence at his bedside for his nighttime prayers," he announced with the posture of a royal majordomo.

"Of course." She skittered past him, sideways like a crab avoiding a fisherman's net.

And as she slipped around him to see to the child, that familiar sense of guilt nagged him. Perhaps, she had every right to fear him. He'd abandoned her too long ago to make amends now. Seven years. And he could never atone for neglecting her for all that time. He shoved his hands into his pockets, touched the pieces of her mother's earrings lying within the folds. No wonder she despised him—she considered him one of the monsters who'd destroyed her home.

With his thoughts still centered on the two visions of his wife, the vibrant girl of the past and the shadow he'd married, he sank into the nearest chair.

♥

When Zarek dismissed her, Chesna tiptoed into the playroom. Pietor sat on the settee, a deep frown etched into his face. Time to swallow her pride and protect her charge.

Meekly, she approached him and bowed her head. "I apologize for laughing at you, Pietor." Her voice shook, but she plowed on and knelt at his feet. "My behavior was inexcusable. I humbly await your discipline for my disobedience."

He shot up, his boot missing her temple by mere inches. "Chess, for God's sake, get up. What are you thinking?"

She blinked, but rose unsteadily. "I...I mocked you. Because you couldn't read Greek. You said you would punish me when Zarek was abed."

"Did you honestly believe I would beat you?" His thumb brushed her chin, tilted her face to meet his. Electricity crackled in her veins. "Chess, I was a poor student ten years ago. I'm still a poor student now. You always teased me about my weakness. I would expect you to remark upon it. Whether you wish to believe me or not, nothing's changed between us."

She shook her head. "Everything's changed between us," she murmured.

"Only in your imagination, my dove," he replied in a voice so soft she barely discerned the words. He patted the cushion on the settee. "Come. Sit beside me."

Tears glistened on her eyelids, and she shook her head again.

"Chess, I would never hurt you." Again he patted the cushion, this time with more energy. "Never."

He already had. First, he'd left her behind. And then he'd returned, bringing destruction with him.

When she made no move, he leaned forward, hands outstretched in supplication. "Please?"

Dread weighed her down. She acceded to his plea, remaining alert for a sudden move on his part. Even while she perched on the edge of the settee, she kept her posture stiff and her feet poised to fly should the need arise. As if he thought to ease her tension, he slid closer, diminishing the space between them, until his thigh pressed against hers. Heat radiated between them. His left arm snaked around her shoulder, and his fingers meshed in a curl of her hair. She bit her lip, but otherwise remained motionless. When she didn't attempt to stop him, he lifted the tress and rubbed the strands across his cheek.

"Still as soft as silk." He nuzzled her neck, and she gasped. He withdrew, leaning away from her, but he took her chilled hand in his warm clasp.

His index finger stroked the inside of her palm in a slow up and down motion. Zarek's gold ring flashed like a beacon in the dusky light of the room, and she hastily pulled her hand away to bury the telltale item in the folds of her gown.

"I'd like to beg a favor from you."

Suspicion slinked up her spine. "Oh?"

"Yes." He offered her a self-deprecating grin that did nothing to allay her fears. "I think I'm in dire need of a review of my Greek. Would you be kind enough to tutor me so that your son doesn't have to correct every other word I utter?"

Relief flooded her from head to toe. She smiled. "I always told Master Arno that the man who married me would appreciate my intelligence."

"And as always, you were right. So?" He held out *Antigone* toward her. "Where shall we begin?"

She opened their lesson with a simple statement, but his garbled translation brought her to a fit of giggles. Once she reined in her humor, she gently corrected him. He repeated her correction, a little clumsily, but after the third attempt, managed to wrap his tongue around the awkward sounds. Despite exhaustion sapping the strength from her brain as well as her bones, she managed to sit upright and converse in the foreign language with relative ease. But as the hour progressed, she struggled to remain awake. At last, she yawned and leaned her head back, closing her eyes.

"Go to bed, Chess," he said with a gentle nudge.

She opened one eye. "What about you?"

He held up *Antigone* and tapped the cover with his finger. "I have some more reading to do, but I'll join you shortly."

With a weary nod, she rose from the chair and stretched the kinks out of her back. Once on her feet, she headed to their shared bedchamber and closed the door behind her, but didn't lock it. What would be the point? She had agreed to sleep in the same bed with her husband and she would keep her promise regardless of how uncomfortable it made her. The consequences she faced if she broke her promise seemed more uncomfortable to contemplate.

After slipping out of her muslin gown and undergarments, she tossed them into a small wooden chest in the corner of the room. Once each week, the laundress would enter each of the bedchambers and remove the dirty garments from the chest. She'd return the laundry after the servants had washed and pressed each item to perfection.

Chesna had never had a personal maid. She never saw a need for one. She wore very simple clothing—a chemise, a petticoat, a short blouse, and a dress that laced at her bosom comprised her summer wardrobe. In the winter, she added woolen pantalettes and an extra chemise to fight the biting winds. She wore her hair loose down her back as befitted a young unmarried woman in Amatia. Of course, that had changed now. Now she would pull it back from her face with a bit of ribbon.

Reaching into the drawer of her armoire, she pulled out a plain white sleeping gown and tossed it on over her head, then tied the laces around her throat. She moved to the bed and drew back the sheets, smoothing them down with the palm of her hand. She settled herself on the soft featherbed and sighed deeply with a mixture of contentment and sheer exhaustion. She fell asleep the moment her head touched her pillow.

♥

For another hour, Pietor remained inside the playroom, reading his Greek and fighting to keep his thoughts off his wife asleep in the next room. A useless exercise. Memories of her had filled his head for seven years. Living with her constant presence only enhanced those long-ago images. Every minute spent with her reminded him of how much he'd missed her while he'd lived abroad.

So many times in the past he'd wished to see her, to share his secrets with her and to listen to her counsel. Now he could see her anytime he wished but he still didn't dare to share his secrets with her. So he kept his own counsel.

After another hour of futile attempts to concentrate on the foreign words on the pages, he surrendered to his feeble mind's need for rest. He rose from the chair and extinguished the lamp before feeling his way in the dark to their bedchamber. Once inside, he sat on the edge of the bed and pulled off his boots and hose, taking care not to awaken Chesna. He rose again and quickly stripped out of his clothing, then tossed the garments into the laundry chest.

Nude now, he slipped beneath the bedcovers. Chesna mumbled when his weight sank into the bed. He remained completely still beside her for a long moment, not even daring to breathe. In the darkness, she sighed in her sleep. He relaxed his position slightly, waited another moment or two, and then rolled over onto his side. Wrapping an arm about her waist, he pulled her up against him. The scent of honeysuckle surrounded him.

She didn't make another sound. But she wiggled her bottom against his pelvis in a delightfully seductive manner. Pietor stifled a groan at her actions and forced his thoughts onto the most unpleasant topics he could think of. He reviewed the grievous battle wounds he'd seen in his years in the army, marches through bitterly cold terrains in the dead of winter, the painful thought of his father's grisly death.

Just when he thought he had control of his emotions and the ache in his manhood had eased, Chesna rolled over suddenly and threw her leg across his waist. Immediately, the ache returned in full flourish.

Good God, she didn't make her nearness easy for him to ignore at night. During daylight hours, they managed to avoid any close proximity. The palace was a perfect place for two people to evade each other. With so many rooms and so many residents, one could easily become a faceless member of the crowd. But at night, Chesna instinctively sought out the man lying beside her. And for now, her surrender to him in sleep proved enough.

Placing his head back on the pillow, he positioned himself so the top of her head lay tucked beneath his chin. Satisfied she wouldn't move, he closed his eyes and slept.

Just after dawn, a pounding on their door awakened him. Chesna gasped and shot up.

Before he could calm her anxiety, a man burst in and shouted, "The general demands to see you both downstairs at once!"

GINA ARDITO

14

The young soldier who stood in the doorway glanced at Pietor's bare chest for a brief moment before turning his attention to the woman in the bed. His lupine gaze scanned her from head to waist, taking in her disheveled hair and her bare shoulder where her sleeping gown had fallen to her elbow. Pietor watched the corporal's eyes light up and knew exactly what the young pup thought. He stared at that flawless ivory skin and imagined how he'd like to taste her for himself.

"Have you seen enough yet, Corporal?" Pietor growled as he pulled the sheet up to cover his wife.

"Yes, Captain. I mean no, Captain. I mean—" the soldier stammered.

"Out!" Pietor bellowed, pointing a finger at the door. "Tell the general we'll be with him shortly."

"Yes, sir." The corporal saluted and backed out of the room.

When the door closed again, he turned to Chesna who stared at him agog. "W-where is your sleeping gown?"

"I don't wear one," he told her with a disarming smile and a slow wink. "Soldiers rarely do, you know."

"Oh!" Her cheeks blazed, and she turned to stare at the bedpost, no doubt fighting to hide her embarrassment. "You knew they would send someone up here this morning, didn't you? That's why you're not wearing a sleeping gown. You wanted that man to think we had..."

"Not quite true, Chess," he announced. "Oh, I knew the general would want to ascertain we're living as a true man and wife. That's why I insisted we must sleep in the same bed every evening. But I didn't know he would send someone to burst in on us this morning."

"Then why aren't you wearing anything while you're in my bed?"

"This is my bed, too. And I've already told you, I never wear a sleeping gown or a nightshirt or any other garments while I sleep. Except my uniform, when we're on patrol. But to truly sleep comfortably, I prefer nothing to hinder me." He leaned closer, and to his amusement, she sidled to the farthest edge of the featherbed. "Come, come, Chess. Don't play the shy sparrow with me. Didn't the king remove his royal robes when he climbed into your bed at night?"

Her cheeks grew redder, and her eyes widened for the briefest moment before she apparently regained control. "Of course he did. But you are not a king."

"Oh?" He arched a brow. "I don't compare favorably to my uncle then?"

"No," she replied, smugness riding high in her tone.

"How can you be certain if you don't look?"

"I did look."

But she wouldn't face him, and her obvious embarrassment had him biting back hoots of laughter.

"You're an attractive man, Pietor," she said haughtily. "But you can't hold a candle to my dear Jarek. Your uncle had much more to recommend him than a crown."

So she wanted to play, did she?

"What could he possibly have that I don't?" he pressed. "Uncle Jarek was an old man with a big belly and gray hair. How could I not compare favorably to that? Be honest. Have you ever seen a younger virile man in the nude?"

"I've no need to see any other man in the nude. Jarek wasn't as old or as big bellied as you recall. You saw him through the eyes of a child. I saw him through the eyes of a woman."

He snorted.

"And if you're concerned about his virility, let me assure you your uncle was a masterful lover. Why, he could touch me with a fingertip, and I would melt like snow in July."

She lied. He knew she lied. And yet, he couldn't help but needle her. "Really?"

"Yes, really. One look from across a room was enough

to turn my knees to jelly." Her tone grew hushed, her expression dreamy-eyed. "And when he kissed me, I lost all sense of what was occurring around me. The moment his lips touched mine, our souls intertwined."

She went overboard now, but he let her continue the lies, waited to see how far she'd traipse along this path. She closed her eyes and leaned her head back against the headboard, sighing dramatically. "Even now I can remember how he made me feel when he would lie down beside me and take me in his arms..."

Enough. The visions in his head nauseated him.

"Get up and get dressed," he fairly roared, cutting off her description of his uncle's prowess.

Her attempt to hide her smile was weak at best. She actually thought she'd won this round. But to prove his own point, Pietor rose from the bed and strutted naked before her.

Her entire body seemed to turn pink, and she squeezed her eyes shut. "Get dressed, Pietor."

"Why? Does my appearance distress you?"

She refused to answer him, but tilted her chin higher in the air.

"Shall we call this battle a draw, my dove?"

"Agreed," she mumbled, eyes still tightly closed.

When Chesna and Pietor reached the grand hall, General de Valmiere pointed an angry finger outside the arched windows. "What is the meaning of this?"

Pietor exchanged a glance with Chesna. "The meaning of what, General?"

"Not you, Captain. Ask her." He turned to thrust his finger at Chesna. "You! Look out there and tell me what's happening."

Offering her husband a confused shrug, she strolled to the wall of windows and leaned forward. Outside the main gate, throngs of women fought to push their way past the soldiers blocking the entrance to the Opal Palace.

She turned back to de Valmiere with a broad smile. "Today's the tenth of July, General. It is the day of the

Women's Council."

"What does that mean, *madame?*"

She sighed. "When Queen Jasia first came to Amatia, she asked King Jarek for four days a year to be put aside for the women of the country. On those days, the queen hears grievances and passes judgment for crimes committed against the female population. The tenth of July is one of those four days. No doubt, the women have come to have their queen's ear."

"Their queen is dead," de Valmiere reminded her.

Because she sensed he intended to hurt her with his bluntness, she ignored him. "Many of these ladies have traveled for weeks. Entire families have been known to make the trek to Simion for a few minutes of their sovereign's time. It is entirely possible they do not know what has happened here in the past few days. What they do know is they wish to be heard and they will not leave the grounds of Opal Palace until someone listens to their grievances and provides a solution for each of them."

"Captain Gabris will answer their complaints," the general ordered with a wave of his hand. He started to walk away.

Her next words stopped him in his tracks. "These women will not speak to Captain Gabris."

He whirled to glare at her through beady, snake-slit eyes. "Why not?"

"Because he is a man."

"Of course he is a man. I know that."

"So do the women outside these walls," she replied blandly. "Therefore they won't speak to him."

A slow tic appeared at the left side of the general's cheek. "You may tell these women if they don't speak to Captain Gabris, they leave here unheard."

"Forgive me, but you're being foolish, General," she said. "They've come to speak with Queen Jasia and they will not air their grievances to any man. Not even you. They trusted the queen because she was one of them. She was a woman. She understood their woes and their helplessness. They'll only speak to another woman. And if you try to remove them from the grounds of the palace without allowing them their day of reckoning, they'll run you and your men out of here on the points of swords, kitchen knives and any other sharp implements they can find."

de Valmiere threw up his hands. "God deliver me from Amatian women! You're all given far too much freedom to say what you wish and do as you please. Your King Jarek's first mistake was in listening to his wife's advice."

A slow rage simmered in Chesna's blood, but she kept her tone emotionless. "You've never taken advice from a woman?"

"When I need to know how to birth a babe or how to run a household, I'll take advice from a woman," he snapped. "Women are too ignorant to be involved in government affairs."

Chesna had heard this argument from countless other men and she always gave the same reply. "If women are ignorant, it's because men have made them so. Given the same educational opportunities as a man, a woman can think for herself. Men fear an educated woman might desire their positions of power, but don't be afraid. Women have no need to make fools of themselves in the name of glory and honor. We're too intelligent for that."

"In France, our women know their places," he grumbled. "They leave their governing to men."

"Yet despite their ignorance, hundreds of Frenchwomen lost their heads during your Reign of Terror," she retorted. "If I were sentenced to be executed by the governing men of my country, I'd insist upon having my say before I met Madame Guillotine. Perhaps if your women had governed themselves, their blood would not have flowed so rampantly through the streets of Paris."

The general's face turned near purple as he sputtered. "Do something about your wife's tongue, Gabris, or I'll be forced to do it for you."

He turned again to walk away, but this time, Pietor stopped him. "General? What do we do about the women?"

"Let your wife handle them. But you stay by her side."

"And the boy?" Pietor asked.

The general's face went blank. "What boy?"

"My son," Chesna reminded him. "Zarek. Pietor should stay with Zarek while I see to the Women's Council."

de Valmiere strode away with the corporal close behind.

"Let the servants see to the brat. Your husband stays with you, madam. To be certain you and your band of Amazons do not plot to overthrow us all."

Chesna waited until the general and his minion had left the hall before she gave her opinion of the man. "Idiot." She lowered her voice to a gruff mumble and imitated him. "'Be certain you and your band of Amazons do not plot to overthrow us all.'"

"Hush, Chess."

"Forgive me," she apologized most insincerely. "But the man is an idiot. If all of Napoleon's officers are such halfwits, we should have no trouble ousting them from Amatia before long."

Pietor shook his head. "The general is a ruthless soldier and a brilliant tactician. If half of Napoleon's officers had his abilities, France would be the supreme ruler of Europe. It would be wise of you to remember that."

"You are as much an idiot as the man you follow. France will never be the supreme ruler of Europe. Napoleon is too ambitious for his own good. If he doesn't surrender in Amatia, he will surely surrender in Russia."

"And you're an idiot for daring to say such things aloud," he warned her. "For now, I suggest we forget this fascinating discussion and deal with your Women's Council. Agreed?"

"Agreed," she announced with a sigh.

Her second surrender of the day, and it was still early morning. She'd have to make certain this capitulation didn't become habit for her. No matter how charming Pietor might find a meek and obedient wife.

Chesna ushered Pietor into the Reception Room where Queen Jasia had always heard the complaints and problems of the female population of Amatia. Out of respect for the late sovereigns, Chesna refused to sit upon the throne that had once belonged to the queen, but asked Pietor to fetch two plain wooden chairs.

When he returned with the chairs, she placed one in

the center of the floor directly before the dais. She ordered the second one set behind the throne, hidden by a cluster of velvet drapes and intricate tapestries that covered the wall from ceiling to floor.

"You sit there," she said, gesturing to the chair behind the draperies.

The hackles on his neck rose. "Why? Will your Amazons revolt if they know there's a man in the room?"

"You lived in this palace for more than ten years, Pietor," she replied. "During that time you accompanied your father on many excursions through the villages of this country. While your features may have changed somewhat since then, it's still possible one or more of these women might recognize you. Unless you wish for the general to learn you are Prince Milos's son, you should remain out of sight."

Her reminder startled him. She showed more concern about his identity than he did. When had he become such a fool? He couldn't afford any mishaps at this stage. Still, her concern couldn't possibly have anything to do with his truth.

"Why should it matter to you if I'm recognized?"

"If the general learns who you are, he'll punish you severely for lying to him. He might even have you executed." Folding her arms over her chest, she shuddered violently.

Warmth filled his heart, and he reached for her. "I have no intention of being executed, but it's nice to know you still care about me."

She shrugged, simultaneously breaking his hold on her. "Don't be ridiculous, Pietor. If de Valmiere executes you, what will happen to Zarek and me? I could be forced to marry that Major Roucher or Major Montfort next."

She could have slapped him to gain the same reaction.

"I appreciate your thoughtfulness," he bit out.

"Did you expect more? Why?" Without waiting for an answer, she waved her hand toward the curtains. "Go. I'll have the soldiers escort the first ladies inside only after you're behind the draperies."

As she'd stated, only after he'd retreated to his hiding place did she allow the women to enter.

By now, information regarding the fate of the king and

queen had apparently spread throughout the crowds, causing an outpouring of grief. The women who appeared before Chesna seemed embarrassed to bother her at such a sorrowful time. Their own problems were suddenly insignificant in light of the goings-on in Simion. But Chesna insisted Queen Jasia would wish the Women's Council to continue despite her death, as a testament to how much she had been loved and respected by her people.

Within the first few minutes, Pietor realized Chesna's mind mirrored her father's. She listened to the women's complaints, asked only the most pertinent questions, and gave sound advice to each and every female who asked for it.

A widow from the farming village of Larisa sought Chesna's counsel to deal with her wayward daughter. "Zora is lazy and refuses to help me in the fields," the woman complained.

The daughter, a girl of about seventeen years of age with golden hair and bright green eyes, stepped forward to defend herself. "Mama forgets what it's like to be young and pretty. If I spend all my days working on the farm, I'll never catch a fine husband. I'll be dirty and smell of animals. I should not be toiling from sunup to sundown with such menial chores. We need a man to help us, and I need to look my best so I might find the perfect man."

"Is there a certain man you wish would help you?" Chesna asked.

"No, madam," Zora replied. "I have not yet found a man that suits me."

"Of course. One should never settle for less than the best."

"Do you see, Mama?" Zora turned to her mother. "She understands my dilemma. Why can't you?"

"Tell me, Zora," Chesna continued. "What sort of man would suit you?"

"He must be wealthy," she answered without hesitation.

"Wealthy?" The sharp new octave indicated that requisite piqued Chesna's interest. "Why must he be wealthy?"

"Mama has worked so hard her entire lifetime," Zora said. From his position behind the curtains, Pietor dared a peek and noted the girl's lack of sincerity in her arrogant posture. "If I had a wealthy husband, we might have servants so Mama would be able to rest in her elder years."

"Perhaps, I might know someone." Chesna leaned forward and folded her elbows atop her knees.

"Really, madam?"

"Yes." Chesna said.

Even in the shadows, Pietor understood the victorious smile evident in her inflection. He almost felt sympathy for the ignorant Zora. Almost.

"I know the perfect man," she continued. "Allow me to tell you about him. His name is Heronim and he's been serving here in the palace since before I was born. He is nearly fifty years of age, but very big and very strong. Why, if he were capable of standing erect, he would be well over six feet tall. He spent his childhood on a farm in Calinot, just a few miles from Larisa so he's familiar with your village. And he knows all there is to know about crops and farm animals. Best of all, after so many years of devoted service to the royal family, he would come to you with an enormous purse."

"I'm grateful for your kindness, madam." For the first time since appearing before Chesna, Zora sounded hesitant. "But, he seems a bit old. I mean, is he healthy enough to run a farm?"

She shrugged. "Well, he is missing several teeth and most of his hair. Also, he's a bit hard of hearing. You might need to speak loudly in his presence. Then there is the matter of that running sore upon his knee from his riding accident. Hot poultices are needed nightly to keep the sore from becoming too badly infected. But I assure you, he's still very strong. And once you're married, his wealth will make it possible for you to hire workers to help with the farm."

Zora actually backed up a step. "Perhaps, this man would be more suitable to my mother. After all, they would be close to the same age."

"But your mother was already married. She isn't seeking a new husband." She turned toward the older woman. "Are you?"

"No, madam. I'm quite content to remain a widow. I

only wish for someone to help with the work to be done on our farm."

Chesna clapped her hands. "Then it's settled. I'll have Heronim summoned here immediately. How fortunate for you that Father Grigory happens to be in the palace today. We can have you married in an hour's time. You'll have everything you've ever wished for and your mother will have the help she needs so she might rest in her elder years. Isn't that wonderful?"

"But..." Zora's voice suddenly sounded small and frightened. "I had always thought to marry for love."

"Really?" Chesna replied. "How odd. You didn't mention love when I asked you a moment ago what would suit you. But never fear, Zora. I'm certain you'll grow to love Heronim in time. After all, marriage is forever."

"I-I..." Zora stammered. "I thank you for considering me worthy of him, madam, but I believe I'd rather wait for a man I might love *before* I wed."

"But what of your mama?" Chesna asked. "She needs help on the farm, but should rest in her elder years."

Zora released a deep sigh. "I'll help Mama."

"What a loving daughter you are!" Chesna's tone rang with false admiration. "But remember. If you find your work is too difficult for you, your mother may send me word and I'll have Heronim appearing at your doorstep in a thrice."

The older woman cackled. "Thank you, madam. You are indeed a wise and gracious lady. May God bless you."

Zora only said, "Come, Mama."

The two women quickly left the Reception Room. Before the next problem could be brought to her, Pietor called out from his hiding place behind the curtain. "Chess? Who is Heronim? I don't recall anyone in the palace with that name."

"There is no Heronim in the palace," she called back.

He had to hold both hands over his mouth to keep his laughter from being heard by the next woman who entered...

15

Chesna spent a full day and half the night inside the Reception Room ruling over the Women's Council while her husband remained in the shadows. Most of the women came forward with minor complaints, neighbors feuding over land boundaries, fathers who refused to pay their daughters' dowries, sons who spent too much time in gambling halls, and petty arguments between family members. Other problems required more finesse and tact to find a solution. Aside from the widow and her lazy daughter, a distraught young woman sought justice from Chesna because her betrothed had deflowered her, disgraced her, and then refused to marry her.

"Oleg betrayed me," she wept. "He swore he loved me and he played me false. My parents have disowned me with nothing but the clothes on my back. They tossed me out into the streets. They claim I've disgraced them with my wanton behavior." She fell to her knees, her hands held out in supplication. "You must believe me, madam. I would never have allowed Oleg to take liberties with me if he hadn't sworn to marry me."

"When were you to be married?" Chesna asked her gently.

She bowed her head. "In a week's time. He told me I would feel less nervous about our upcoming wedding if we celebrated our bridal night earlier. If I gave myself to him, I would know there was nothing for me to fear after our marriage. I believed him. Why wouldn't I? Now I am ruined!"

Sympathy welled inside Chesna's heart. "Do you love him?"

"I don't know, madam. I thought I did, but how can I love a man whom I can't trust? If he would betray me in such a manner before our wedding, what will my life be like once I'm tied to him in marriage? How can I love someone who would treat me so shabbily? Do I dare to hope he regrets what he did to me? Or is he boasting about his conquest to his friends and neighbors? How can I know what is truly in his heart?"

The young woman's questions struck a deep nerve with Chesna. She had the very same questions since her marriage to Pietor. How could she trust the man who'd betrayed her time and again? At times, she thought she glimpsed the young man she'd loved inside the stranger she'd married. But which was the true Pietor?

And if she had no ready answers for herself, she certainly didn't have an easy solution for this woman. Perhaps this young lady's arrival was an omen. Perhaps in finding a solution for Oleg's jilted betrothed, Chesna might find answers to her concerns regarding Pietor.

"Marriage is a serious consideration," she finally told the woman who still stared at the floor. "You must not wed in haste and you must not wed a scoundrel simply because he dared to take advantage of you. But if your parents have disowned you, you must find a place to live. Look at me." She waited until the young woman had raised her head so she could see the understanding in her eyes. "Would you be willing to work here at the palace until you have made a decision regarding Oleg?"

For the first time since her arrival, hope flourished on the woman's face. "Oh yes, madam! I would do anything you wished. I'm an excellent cook and my mother is a seamstress. I learned a great deal about sewing from her. I could work in your kitchens or in your laundry or in your stables. I would be a scullery maid if that were your wish. I would scrub your floors until they glistened. I would do anything at all."

Chesna bit back a chuckle. The girl's eagerness spoke volumes. "Very well. Let's see if Urszula can use some more help in the kitchens. But first, what is your name?"

"Monika Lokash," the woman told her.

"Welcome to the Opal Palace, Monika. Once you're settled, we'll send for this Oleg."

Monika's face paled, and she gasped. "Oh, no, madam. I could never face him again. I would be too ashamed."

"You must face him, Monika. Only after you've seen him again will you be certain of your feelings for him." Chesna allowed her voice to rise, to carry to the man hidden behind the tapestry. The man who'd betrayed *her*. "You have nothing to be ashamed of. It's Oleg who should regret his scurrilous actions. But we'll allow you some time to think about your predicament before he arrives. And if you decide not to marry Oleg, you'll still have a place here at the palace."

Monika crawled forward to kiss the hem of Chesna's gown. "Oh, thank you, madam! Thank you."

Chesna pulled her skirts away. "Stop that, Monika. I'm not royalty. I am a servant here, just as you are. And to that end, you must call me Chesna." She rose from the chair and assisted Monika to her feet. "Come with me. We'll get you settled here at once."

♥

Leaving Pietor in his hiding place, Chesna escorted Monika to the kitchens. She introduced the newcomer to Urszula, who, as Chesna expected, took the young lady under her wing like a mama bird with a chick. When she returned to the Reception Room a short time later, she carried a tray Urszula had prepared. The fragrance of roasted lamb tickled her nostrils and enticed her stomach to growling.

"Pietor?"

He stepped out from behind the draperies, grinning like an idiot. "We're done? All the women have had their day of reckoning?"

She nodded and sat on the floor, tucking her legs beneath her gown. "Until October when it begins again. We missed dinner, but Urszula prepared a small feast for us." She placed the tray on the dais.

He turned his eyes to the ceiling and folded his hands

as if in prayer. "God bless Urszula. I'm famished." He sat beside her and reached for a joint of lamb. "I thought we'd never finish with this women's nonsense."

Her temper spiked. Not another male who belittled the problems of women because they didn't deal with such weighty subjects as war and conquest.

"It isn't nonsense," she retorted. "Those women needed guidance, and I gave it to them. That's nothing to scorn."

"You did well, Chess," he remarked as he bit into the aromatic meat with gusto. "Your father would be proud of you."

His mention of Bela sliced into her heart and cut her to the quick. Why did he continue to remind her of her father's loss? Did he think he'd eventually wear her down if she suddenly realized she no longer had Bela's wisdom and strength to support her? So many women were trapped in lives mired in unhappiness for no other reason than the helplessness of their gender. And now she had joined their ranks, forced to marry one man because another man ordered her to do so.

If her father were alive, this never would have happened. And her father wasn't alive because of the man who dared to mention him to her now.

"Papa was always proud of me," she announced. "Why wouldn't he be? I never betrayed his trust."

"You mean he approved of you writhing with pleasure beneath the king?"

Rage smoldered, but she bit her lip and said nothing.

"What, Chess?" he pressed. "No clever witticisms? No snappy retorts? No excuses or apologies for your wanton behavior?"

Before answering, she took a healthy bite from her favorite bread and cheese, swallowed the morsel, but not her anger. "I don't owe you an apology. Everything I've ever done, I've done for the good of Amatia. I'm a Dubrow. It's my duty to place my country above my own wants."

"You're a Gabris now," he corrected her.

"I was born a Dubrow, and I'll die a Dubrow. You and your general may have forced me to marry you, but that doesn't change who I am."

"I didn't force you to marry me. I was just as repulsed

by the idea of this union as you were."

She nearly choked on the bread. "How strange. I don't recall anyone threatening you with execution if you didn't agree to wed me."

"No one threatened you with execution," he scoffed. "You said you'd rather die than marry me. General de Valmiere took you at your word. My situation was different. I was given an order and I was honor bound to obey it."

"Another strange thing," she remarked with caustic wonder. "You seem honor bound to obey a foreign emperor, but you have no such loyalties to the country that gave you a life of happiness and plenitude. One would think you'd been raised by a pack of she-wolves rather than a loving father."

"I don't owe you an explanation for my actions any more than you owe me one for yours," he said through gritted teeth.

"No, you don't," she agreed as she reached across the tray for her wine goblet. She took a long draught of the ruby liquid before adding, "A very good thing, too. What possible reason could you give for bringing your homeland to the brink of ruin?"

He tossed the meatless bone onto the sterling dish with a loud thunk. "You haven't changed at all, have you? You still only see one side of an argument. I refute what I said before. Your father would be ashamed of you."

She rose and angrily brushed the crumbs from her skirts with the back of her hand. "What do you know about how my father would feel?"

"I knew your father very well, Chess. Perhaps even better than you did."

"I'd ask Papa his opinion on that matter," she retorted, "but as you know, he's dead now. Although I've been told he died valiantly, protecting the country and the people you abandoned in your quest for glory. So I suppose I'm meant to find solace in that fact."

"I'm so very tired of defending myself against your unfounded accusations," he replied with a deep sigh.

"Unfounded? No, Pietor. I accuse you honestly."

"You accuse me because you're still angry that I stopped writing to you."

The barb struck tender flesh, and she tossed her head to hide the pain. "I don't give a whit about some childish promise we made to each other years ago. I knew when you left here you would forget me. It didn't surprise me when you stopped writing. It took your sudden return to Simion with five hundred armed soldiers accompanying you to surprise me. What are a few old letters compared to the death and destruction of my home?"

With the stamp of her foot, she fled the Reception Room before the tears began.

♥

Two hours later, Pietor slowly climbed the staircase to the nursery. His mind fixed upon thoughts of his wife and her angry words in the Reception Room. He didn't know what to do about Chesna.

Throughout the day while he'd hidden behind the tapestries, he'd listened as she spoke to the women who came before her. He couldn't help but feel a sense of pride at the wisdom she had shown with each of them. Even the selfish Zora hadn't defeated her. The lazy wench had never seen Chesna's clever ploy until firmly trapped within it.

And that poor exploited Monika and her dastardly betrothed. Chesna managed to offer the girl some charity without stripping her of her dignity.

Yet when the women had departed, so had the judicious Chesna. In the blink of an eye, the wise advisor had become unreasonable and vulnerable. Emotions never before attributed to the unflappable Chesna now reared their ugly heads.

He entered their bedchamber, not the least surprised when he discovered the room unoccupied. He knew exactly where to look for her. Once again, he tiptoed into Zarek's chamber through the unlocked door. So she expected him to seek her out.

This time, however, she had curled up in the huge bed beside the child. Her arm wrapped around the boy's waist as if she could protect him from all harm, even in her sleep.

No doubt she had come here straight from the Reception Room. Still dressed in the gown she tossed on early this morning, she hadn't bothered to remove her shoes before lying down beside Zarek.

"Forgive me, Chess," he whispered against her ear as he bent to scoop her up. "You forgot our agreement."

Just as he had on their wedding night, he carried her through the playroom and into the other sleeping chamber before placing her gently in the center of their bed. He turned away only long enough to light the bedside lamp. When the room became illuminated in a soft yellowish glow, he sat on the edge of the bed, removed her shoes and hose, then unlaced her bodice. Even in the dim light, faint lines shimmered silver on her cheeks, the trails of her tears.

Poor Chess. Every day that passed bruised her spirit a little more. And he saw no end in sight to her torment.

While guilt stabbed his conscience, he pulled her gown down past her shoulders. He wriggled her arms out of the sleeves of her short-waisted blouse. As gently as possible, he pulled the blouse up over her head, silently praying his actions wouldn't rouse her. Thankfully, Chesna slept on. After slipping to the foot of the bed, he tugged at the hem of her skirts. The gown and petticoats slid off her frame with a whoosh. He tossed the garments into the chest in the corner while he pondered what to do with her next.

She wouldn't appreciate knowing he had stripped her completely while she was senseless. And frankly, he could live without the temptation of her naked flesh pressed against him in this soft bed. So he left her chemise on as a covering for her modesty and a protection for his sanity. Satisfied, he pulled the bedsheet up over her shoulders, lowered the lamp, and left the room. It would be a long time before he joined her tonight.

He reentered the playroom and dimly lit another lamp before sitting at her desk. What to do next? Sleep lay miles out of reach. Sighing with frustration, he moved to the large settee and sat down with the copy of *Antigone* that still remained on the table. He flipped through the pages quickly, trying to find the place where he'd left off last evening. A folded sheet of paper fell from the book and floated gently to the floor. Curious, he bent to pick it up, unfolded it, and scanned the contents with bewilderment. How had this letter found its way inside this book? And when?

Someone must have placed the damning document between the pages while he and Chesna were in the Reception Room today. If the letter had been tucked inside the book before this morning, he would have found it earlier.

His brain buzzed. Who would do such a thing? Who had access to the royal nursery?

Karol.

It could only be Karol. But why? And how had he found this letter at all? Only one man was privy to this information. And that man was dead. So how did Karol get his hands on it?

Pietor stuffed the letter into his pocket and rose from the settee. He would need to deal with this problem at once. He dared not wait until tomorrow.

16

There's a plot within the Opal Palace to kill King Jarek. I've written to your father, to warn him and to seek his counsel.

—August 18, 1805

Pietor found Karol alone, staring at the plates of armor lining the walls near the grand staircase. On catlike feet, he scaled the steps until he stood a breath away. If he'd meant to slip up on the older man unnoticed, however, he failed.

"I know you're there," Karol said without turning around.

"Ah." Pietor stepped up beside the older man. "And I suppose you know why."

Karol clasped his hands behind his back. "Where is Chesna?"

"Chesna is asleep. And I'm here because I received your message."

He turned then, eyes wide with feigned confusion. "Message? What message?"

Pietor kept his expression blank, his voice deadly soft. "The message you left inside the pages of *Antigone*. It was you who placed that letter in Bela's book, wasn't it?"

"I don't understand. What message? What are you saying about *Antigone* and Bela?"

Pietor's patience thinned to a hair. "Don't play the unwitting fool, Karol. I may have cried on your shoulder as a child, but those days are long gone. I could slit your throat before you even had the opportunity to see the blade coming toward you."

Karol's Adam's apple bounced on a strong swallow, but the man said nothing.

"I know you didn't wish for me to see it," Pietor pressed, "and I know you were the culprit who left the letter. You didn't expect me to look in that book, did you?"

At last, he let out a shuddering breath, and the veil of secrecy fled from his face. "H-how did you f-find it? Y-you don't speak Greek."

Pietor clasped Karol's shoulder, squeezed. "While I admit I've never been very good at it, Chesna has been teaching me the cursed language. And I'm always amazed when I can discover something interesting in my lessons. Although she isn't aware of what I found, and I intend to keep it that way."

"What do you want?" Karol grumbled. "It's late, and I'm in no mood for games, Pietor."

"It's very simple, Karol. I wish to know why you placed that particular letter inside that particular book."

"Because I wanted Chesna to know the truth about the man she married."

Pietor started in surprise, and his grip on Karol's shoulder faltered. "And you know the truth about me?"

"Yes." Karol took the opportunity to step backward out of reach.

"How long have you known? Who told you?"

"I've known since the very beginning. Bela insisted someone in the palace must know. Since he had no one else in whom to place his trust, he confided in me. I promised to watch out for Chesna if Bela should die."

Bela? Bela had trusted Karol with the truth? "Why?"

Karol shook his head slowly. "For her. For Chess." His gaze focused upward, as if he could see into the governess's chamber. "You have no idea how your disappearance devastated her. Even Bela didn't realize what would happen until it was too late. You were the spark in her life. When you stopped writing, she faded to a whisper of herself. Day by day, little by little, she slipped away from us. Bela was terrified your absence might actually kill her. He nearly broke down and told her the truth. Fortunately, he confided in me first. I counseled him to give her more time and find something else to occupy her. Since the queen was about to bear a child. Bela appealed to Jasia to assign Chess as royal governess. The ploy worked. And when Mikhail was born, he became her new spark, her only joy."

His words punched Pietor in the gut. "What made you decide Chesna should know the truth about me now?"

"Because it's obvious you still intend to keep your secrets," Karol retorted. "Chesna deserves to know what's happening beneath her very nose. If she knows the truth now, she may be prepared for the events yet to come."

With the speed of a panther, Pietor cupped his hand to Karol's throat, his voice inches away from the older man's ear. "If Chesna knows the truth now, she may as well be prepared for her death. And Zarek's too. Her ignorance is the only thing that keeps them both alive."

Karol's eyes widened, and understanding appeared to slowly permeate his brain. "I only s-sought to pr-protect her," he stammered.

"From her husband?" Pietor demanded. He didn't wait for a reply. "Have you hidden any other secret messages for my wife to find?"

"No."

"Are you certain?"

"Yes."

Appeased, Pietor relaxed his grip ever so slightly. "Listen to me very carefully, old man. You can't tell Chesna what you're uncertain of yourself. You know nothing, Karol, nothing at all. You don't understand what's happening here any more than she does."

"Bela told me all of it, Pietor," he insisted.

Pietor laughed, a mirthless sound in the dark hall. "Bela didn't know anything either, Karol. He relied on information from his spies. He saw nothing firsthand. Unfortunately, Bela can't help anyone anymore. As for Chesna, when the time is right, I'll inform my wife what I believe she needs to know. Until then, I would advise you to do and say nothing to arouse suspicion. The emperor does not take well to spies in his camp, Karol. He believes in swift and deadly punishment for those who dare to go against him. It would be wise of you to remember that."

Before Karol could form an argument, he disappeared up the stairs to his bedchamber. Convinced he'd made a lasting impression on Karol, he decided to attempt to sleep. Comfortably ensconced in their bed, Chesna still remained deep in slumber. With as little noise as possible, he quickly stripped out of his garments, tossed them into the corner chest and slid beneath the bedsheets.

He remained completely still, waiting for her to roll onto her side and snuggle up against him as she always did in her sleep. But tonight, she never moved. She may have been asleep, but her hostility toward him remained intact. She stayed as close to her edge of the bed as she could without falling over the side. When he reached to wrap an arm about her, she nearly tossed him off the bed with the force of her rebuff.

Closing his eyes, he allowed sleep to overtake him.

When morning came, the tensions between Pietor and Chesna became even more rigid. He rose first, but she came awake the moment he tossed off the blankets. Once again she averted her eyes when he left the bed to see to his personal needs.

"I trust you'll take care of my son today so that he's not abandoned to the servants." The coolness of her tone when she spoke left no doubt she considered him beneath contempt.

"I sincerely doubt Zarek considered spending the day with Karol as abandonment."

After he'd dressed, he left his wife to see to her own toilette and headed for Zarek's room. But when he and Zarek returned to escort Chesna downstairs for the morning meal a short time later, she was already gone. He poked his head into the empty room. Nothing out of place, everything in perfect order. Which meant Chess was seething.

Hoping to keep Zarek from learning about their disagreement, Pietor feigned indifference. "Your mama must be famished this morning," he remarked lightly. "She didn't wait for us before going to the kitchens."

Zarek giggled as he took Pietor's hand and dragged him out of the bedchamber. "Someone should punish Mama for her rudeness."

"Oh? What do you think someone should do to punish your mama?"

The child appeared thoughtful for a long time while they descended the staircase. "I don't know what to do. You should think of something. You're much better at punishing her. You've done it so many times already."

Pietor stopped dead in his tracks at the first landing of the grand staircase. "I've punished her? How have I punished her?"

"It all began when we forced her to marry you."

He had to take a deep breath, force an easy expression, to keep up the pretense they weren't holding a serious conversation. "*We* forced her to marry me? Who are we?"

Zarek looked at his feet and shook his head. "You and I forced Mama to get married. She didn't wish to marry you, but we left her with no choice."

"Don't blame yourself, Zarek. You had nothing to do with our marriage."

"Yes, I did. Mama had to marry you to protect me. She's always protecting me. She promised to keep me safe and she had to marry you to keep her promise. And ever since you married Mama, she's been so unhappy. Before you married her, Mama smiled all the time. Now, she only cries. But only when she doesn't know anyone's watching." He cocked his head to look Pietor in the eye. "You make her cry. And I don't understand why. She's very pretty and smart. Everyone thinks so, everyone but you. Why don't you like Mama?"

Once again, Pietor swallowed his guilt. If he continued this action much longer, he would weigh as much as his horse before a year had come and gone. Taking a large gulp, he sighed in defeat. "I told you, Zarek, I like your mama very much. But sometimes she makes me angry."

"Mama says anger is a wasted emotion unless it stirs one to action."

"Mama is absolutely right," he admitted.

"So why do you get angry with her?"

The boy knew how to strike a nerve. "I'm not certain. Your mama and I don't always have the same opinion on matters."

"You shouldn't get angry with her because she disagrees with you," Zarek persisted. "Mama's a very clever lady. If you knew what I know about her, you'd understand. And you'd know she's brave and smart, as well as pretty. She's not any of those nasty names you call her."

He flushed at the boy's look of disapproval and found himself sliding into the past. Suddenly he was the boy, and Zarek was his Uncle Jarek. The resemblance between this child and the king couldn't be denied, particularly when Zarek glared with so much displeasure.

"I agree. Your mama is all you say she is."

"Then don't call her names."

Pietor bit back a smile at Zarek's simple solution to his marital problems. Life certainly seemed easier when one was five years old.

"If you didn't call Mama names, perhaps she wouldn't cry so much."

"Perhaps," he agreed noncommittally.

"And we could all live together happily. Wouldn't that be nice?"

"Yes, I suppose it would be very nice."

Zarek smiled and walked toward the dining hall. "Do you know what else would be nice?"

"What?" Pietor asked as he followed along.

"If Napoleon Bonaparte's soldiers would leave here. If there were no soldiers here, perhaps you and Mama would find it easier to be nice to one another."

The child was wise beyond his years.

17

Chesna's emotional outburst after the Women's Council had left her bereft of all feelings except deep self-pity. She decided to avoid any contact with Pietor. During the daylight hours, she would stay in her little prison cell, which she had furnished with several candles, a blanket to ward off the damp chill, and her father's book for company.

She allowed only Karol access to her, but even he turned traitor on her by the second day of her self-imposed imprisonment.

"I don't understand why you can't at least feign a tolerance toward the man, Chess," he exclaimed while she ate the small luncheon Urszula had prepared. "For God's sake, whether you like it or not, you're married to the bastard."

"How kind of you to remind me." She dropped the stuffed prawn she'd been enjoying as if the morsel had suddenly burst into flames.

"Forget your misery and think. You have an advantage no one else in this palace has. He once loved you, and it's no secret you've loved him your entire life."

Her stomach curdled, and she shook her head. "You don't understand. The man I loved is *not* the man I married."

"Perhaps he feels the same way about you," Karol murmured. "When he left seven years ago, you were an innocent maid who fawned over him and adored him. Now, he comes home to discover you were his uncle's mistress, you've borne a son, and every word that spews from your lips is laced with enough hatred to poison the royal well."

"Even if I were to soften my tongue as you suggest, my other alleged faults can't be changed. I won't risk harm to Zarek for any reason. And certainly not to win over Pietor Gabris, the traitor."

"No, but if you convinced Pietor he'd won *you* over, he would probably relax his guard around you. And you might be able to learn something useful to us."

"By the rood, I may be my father's daughter, but I'm not a spy," she retorted. "If I were to do such a thing and be caught, it would mean my life. I can't take such a chance."

"I'd protect you, Chess."

She laughed bitterly. "How? You're no longer the prince's personal servant. You're a kitchen steward." On several deep breaths, she released her fear, but not her righteous anger. "The royal family entrusted that little boy to my care. What would become of Zarek should I be charged with espionage and then executed? And though some may consider it an honor, I don't wish to replace St. Ambrose as Amatia's patron saint."

Karol shot up and took the neglected tray from her lap. "You're a fool, Chess."

"Then you shouldn't feel the need to remain in my company, Karol." She waved him away. "Leave me."

Bowing, he clicked his heels together. "Madam." Without another word, he left the cell.

From that moment on, Karol ceased his visits to her dungeon cell. Chesna merely breathed a sigh of relief at convincing him to leave her be and returned to her father's book, but found no peace of mind.

♥

Pietor stayed busy training soldiers for their eventual advancement into Moscow. And now he had the added responsibility of keeping Zarek out of trouble. That meant he spent nearly every moment of his day with the boy. Aside from meals, baths, lessons and bedtimes, Pietor also took the boy riding and taught him fencing techniques.

At night, he and Chess still played their game of "who cared less." They slept in the same bed, but somehow she had erected an invisible wall, impenetrable to him. Chesna always retired first, and pretended to be asleep when he joined her hours later. No words or contact of any kind passed between them. Even in her deepest sleep, she never touched him or relaxed her position.

Despite the many inconveniences, Pietor enjoyed spending his time with Zarek. The boy exuded charm with his regal bearing, clever mind, and avid curiosity. In so many ways, Zarek reminded him of Chesna at the same age.

He'd only turned eight the week before his mother died. And his father—an infrequent visitor—appeared to tell him he'd live at Opal Palace from now on. Now, hours later, he stands on the shore of Lake Matya, planning to run away at the first opportunity.

A high-pitched voice comes from behind him. "You missed lunch."

He whirls.

A young girl, maybe four or five, balances atop a flat boulder less than a foot from him. Her long, tawny hair whips in the breeze, but she doesn't make any move to straighten the strands when they cover her elfin face.

"I don't care," he mumbles and returns his gaze to the crystalline lake.

"Prince Milos said eventually your hunger will override your anger, and then you'll see reason."

Rage spikes. He recalls the arguments overheard between his mother and his royal father in their little cottage in town. Mama always refused to allow him to have any dealings with royal intrigue. He frowns at the memories. "My father doesn't know me very well."

"Here." While he'd recalled those heated words overheard from his old bedchamber, the girl has sidled up beside him. She thrusts a linen-wrapped bundle at him. "I stole this from the kitchens."

Too engrossed in his anger to accept kindness from this strange child with vivid blue eyes, he ignores her.

But rather than pester him further, she simply places the bundle on the boulder. "I'll leave this here for when you're hungry."

With one sweep, he scoops up the bundle and hurls it

into the lake where it lands with a wet plop.

The girl never flinches. Instead, she bends, picks up a rock, straightens, and tosses the rock in the exact same location where the bundle disappeared. Ripples of water flow from that point of impact to the shore.

"I'm very sorry your mama died." Without another word, she skips away.

At first, he doesn't care that he might have hurt her feelings. Nothing matters but his own grief, his own loss. But after he misses dinner, someone knocks on his bedchamber door. When he answers, no one is there. Except a similarly wrapped bundle sits on the floor on the other side. This time, he swallows his pride, along with the roasted capon and honey bread tucked inside the linen.

For three days he avoids his father's plan to force hunger into overpowering anger—thanks to his little benefactress. She hasn't attempted to speak to him again after that initial meeting by the lake. But he's seen her several times since then, running barefoot through the meadow, lurking behind the grand staircase, and slipping out of the royal advisor's private study.

On the third day after his arrival at the palace, no bundle appears outside his door. And as he goes about his day, still scheming his eventual escape and pointedly ignoring the adults, he notes the girl's absence with growing concern.

Sunset has faded when he hears the panicked calls. "Chesna! Where are you?..."

"Captain Gabris!" Major Montfort's voice shattered the visions before he reached the conclusion of that memorable event.

Shaking off the vestiges of those long ago days, he offered a crisp salute. "Sir?"

"I would have a word with you."

"Aye." With a nod, Pietor gestured to the path winding around the edge of the lake. If they walked there, he might still keep an eye on Zarek, but ensure no eavesdroppers to their conversation.

"Excellent." Major Montfort began a slow pace on the barren strip of ground, but waited several minutes, putting plenty of distance between them and the soldiers, before he finally spoke again. "It's not a good idea to keep your wife in the dungeon."

Pietor bit back a sharp retort. "I'm not keeping her there, sir," he said blandly. "She stays there of her own stubborn will."

The major's brows drew together in a disapproving line. "Nevertheless the servants are grumbling. If the populace of this city learns Bela Dubrow's daughter is languishing in a prison cell, they'll not bother to ask if she's there of her own stubborn will. They'll take up arms and storm the palace to rescue her."

But Pietor waved a hand. "You and I both know Amatia is not known for its army, sir. We would defeat such an attack easily."

"That is not my concern, Captain. The emperor ordered General de Valmiere to seize Amatia with as little bloodshed as possible. Your wife's behavior could change a peaceful invasion into a full-scale war."

Too little sleep and too much pent-up frustration rose to Pietor's lips. "I don't recall a peaceful invasion, Major," Pietor noted dryly. "Many innocent people lost their lives on the day we arrived in Simion."

The major clasped his hands behind his back, the picture of nonchalance, but the air hummed with displeasure. "Some bloodshed is necessary and not unexpected in the overthrow of an inept government, Gabris. The deaths of the villagers were due to their own panic and not to our guns."

Sweat trickled down Pietor's spine, but he pressed on. "And the royal family, sir?"

"If the king had not died in the town square he would have died when we dragged him back to the palace. The emperor's orders were to gain Jarek's allegiance or execute him. You and I both know Amatia's king would never pledge his fealty to Napoleon. As for Bela Dubrow, he would have followed his king blindly. The Dubrows always did." He shrugged nonchalantly. "The only true tragedy was the loss of the boy, Prince Mikhail, but that was an unfortunate accident. Our soldiers had no way of knowing his body was lying beneath his father's when they attacked with their bayonets."

"Yes, sir," Pietor agreed, shaking his head in disappointment. "It is indeed a shame we don't have the boy at our disposal. He would have been the perfect pawn for the emperor."

"But we do have Jarek's bastard," Montfort concluded. "And this Zarek could prove even better for our purposes. That is, if you can win his mother over to our cause."

Pietor grinned. "Never fear, Major. When the time comes, Chesna will be a willing participant in our plans."

Montfort's corresponding grin nearly split his pudgy face in half. "I'm very glad to hear it, Captain. But just to be certain, you had best put an end to your wife's exile in the dungeon immediately."

♥

When Pietor reached the entrance to the dungeon, he threw open the heavy iron door with force. He winced as the thick metal clanked against the stone wall, disturbing the silence around him. On a deep breath for fortitude and calm, he descended the slippery staircase that would lead him underground to Chesna's hiding place.

After no more than a few moments down here, he could feel the dampness creeping into the marrow of his bones. His eyes didn't quickly accustom themselves to the darkness, and he waited at the bottom of the stairs for a while until he could discern more than gray shadows.

How could Chesna stand to spend all her time down here? The screeches and scratches of rats moved inside the walls, and the clicks and cracks of hundreds of beetles scattered over the ground at his booted feet. Somewhere in the farthest corner of the cellar, water trickled down the musty stones to splash onto the dirt floor.

Sometimes Chesna had more obstinacy than sense.

A quick movement on his right caught his attention. He whirled in surprise. An enormous rat, frightened by a strange human's entrance, glared with glowing yellow eyes before scurrying back into its hiding place, a rusty pipe set in the wall. Pietor suppressed a shiver of revulsion as he watched that skinny, hairless tail disappear inside the hollow aperture.

He had to agree with Major Montfort. Someone should convince his wife to give up her inanity and leave this hole in the ground. Chesna's stubborn nature would endanger her health. The little fool thought nothing of remaining in this dank and gloomy place in order to avoid a confrontation with him.

He continued walking down the narrow alleyway toward the cell she had appropriated. "Chess?" he called. When he didn't receive an immediate reply to his summons, he became impatient. "Stop playing games, Chesna. Come out here!"

He waited in the thick silence for a long time, but she said nothing.

No doubt she was too busy nursing her grudge to respond. Same old Chesna, as stubborn and as willful as a mule.

He would have to go into the cell and drag her out by her hair after all.

Muttering about her childish behavior, he strode toward her cell with grim determination. "Enough, Chess. You've had plenty of time to recover from your tantrum. Now it's time for you to rejoin the living."

When he stepped inside, he found Chesna curled up on her side on the cold hard bed, sound asleep. Unease crept into his veins. The light of two candles flickered on the cell walls. Dappled shadows danced sinuously over the granite like skeleton ghosts in a graveyard.

On the floor beside the stone bed sat a tray containing an empty plate and a half-filled goblet of watered wine.

"Wake up, Chess!" he shouted.

The sheer volume of his roar caused several more rats to scurry out of hiding in the walls, squealing and shrieking their own outrage. But Chesna never stirred. How could she sleep in this hellish place? He marveled at her resolve.

One enormous rat, clearly the leader of the group, slithered to the tray on the floor and knocked over the wine goblet, spilling the remnants into the dirt. Instantly several of the wretched creatures surrounded the tray, climbing over one another in a frenzy to reach their newfound feast. He turned his eyes away from the disgusting sight and back to Chesna.

"Come, my dove," he murmured in a much softer tone. "You shouldn't be sleeping down here with the rats. Why don't I carry you upstairs where you belong?"

He had to stifle a chuckle as he bent to scoop her into his arms. This had become routine for him, carrying his wife to bed as if she were Zarek. He rose slowly with his burden, jostling her only slightly as he straightened, but she never stirred.

"You must be exhausted, Chess," he whispered. "I would never have the mettle to let down my guard in this pit."

Step by step he carried her out of the dungeon and upstairs to the grand hall where Zarek waited with Karol.

"Mama!"

"Hush, Zarek," Pietor chastised him gently. "Mama's asleep. Don't wake her."

"She was asleep?" Karol couldn't keep the incredulity from his voice. "In the dungeon?"

"I know." Pietor grinned. "I'm just as amazed. But there she slept, on that slab of stone, as if she reclined in the finest featherbed. I've never seen anything like it. The rats inside the cell never gave her a second glance."

"Rats?" Karol made a grimace and shuddered. "Chess hates rats. She's been terrified of those vermin since childhood. Don't you remember the day Urszula inadvertently locked her in the root cellar?"

Zarek's eyes rounded with terrified curiosity. "Mama got locked in the root cellar?"

"A long time ago," Karol told the boy.

"How?"

"She was exactly the same age as you are now. It was mid-autumn, and Urszula had only recently stored the season's apples in the cellar. Mama wanted to surprise a special friend by having Urszula bake an apple tart for dessert that evening." He cast a glance over the boy's head, and a guilty flush heated Pietor's cheeks. "Unfortunately, your mama didn't tell anyone where she was going before she went into the cellar. She'd left the door open when she climbed down the ladder. But Urszula thought some negligent kitchen boy had forgotten about it and locked the door before your mama could climb up again."

Zarek shivered. "How long was she there? How did anyone find her?"

"We searched all day, until a few hours after dusk," Karol said. "We were all frantic with worry. Her friend finally found her early in the evening. When he opened the door to the root cellar, she was sitting on the uppermost rung of the ladder in the darkness. The rats had her pinned at the top. They kept climbing up the ladder to reach her. Your poor mama was terrified. But she'd watch their shadows and kick them in the head when they came close to her. She was so frightened she couldn't utter a sound and couldn't climb out of the cellar unaided. Her father had to carry her out to safety."

The memory came back into Pietor's mind, the frantic cries of the servants on that long ago day.

"Chesna! Where are you?"

The pale, wide-eyed little girl perches at the top of the ladder in the dark. Another rat dares to ascend toward her. Before anyone can shout an alarm, she swings her leg, her heavy black shoe connecting with the vermin's head. Clunk! On outraged squeals, half a dozen rats scurry downward.

"Chesna." Her father slowly, softly, gently scoops her into his arms and cradles her against his chest. He kisses the top of her head. "My sweet, sweet girl. You're safe now."

She clings to him, but her eyes—those blue, blue eyes still wide with her terror—focus on the boy who found her, Pietor, and never waver. She mouths the words, "Thank you," and purses her lips to blow a kiss at him as her father carries her away.

Later, when her father discovers why she'd gone to the root cellar, and for whom, he takes a switch to her backside for her interference between Pietor and Prince Milos. But the girl never cries, never whimpers, never blames Pietor for the punishment she receives. And when, after the beating, Bela Dubrow sends his daughter to her room without supper, it's Pietor's turn to provide a secret meal.

"She never went near the root cellar again." Karol's remark intruded into his memories, shattering the visions of their shared childhood subterfuge. "And she's been terrified of rats ever since that day."

Pietor shook his head. "Well, she was unfazed by their existence in her cell right now." He turned to the wide-eyed boy at Karol's side. "Why don't you help me bring Mama up to her bedchamber?"

Karol released Zarek's hand. "I'll go back downstairs to fetch Bela's book. She'd never forgive herself if she allowed the rats to chew up her last link to her father."

Once again, Pietor swallowed the lump of guilt that rose in his throat. He still had her mother's earrings in his pocket to remind him how much he'd have to make up to her. *If* she'd allow it.

"I doubt the rats will abandon their feast anytime soon," he said as he turned toward the staircase. "When I left the cell, they were too busy lapping up the spilled wine to care about anything as tasteless as a book."

Karol's next question stopped him in mid-stride. "Wine? What wine?"

"The wine you brought Chesna with her meal today."

Karol's moon face paled to a sickly white color. "I didn't bring Chesna a meal today."

An icy finger zipped up Pietor's spine. "You didn't bring her a tray?"

"I haven't been in the dungeon for several days now." He ducked his head. "Chess and I had a disagreement."

Pietor glanced down at the still sleeping woman cradled in his arms. None of this made sense. Chesna sound asleep on a stone bed in the dungeon, the rats scurrying about inside the cell with her, the empty tray and half-filled wine goblet on the floor at her side.

The icy finger became a fist that gripped him by the throat.

What if Chess's current slumber wasn't of a natural origin? Once born, the idea refused to go away.

"Take her," Pietor commanded and smoothly transferred Chesna to Karol's outstretched arms. "I need to return to the dungeon."

Karol shot a look toward Zarek who watched the exchange with curiosity. "What's wrong?" the boy asked, his voice trembling with his worries. "Is Mama sick?"

He forced a smile to his lips. "I think she's just tired. But why don't you go with Karol? You can stay upstairs with Mama until she wakes."

Karol took Zarek's hand. "Come along, boy."

Pietor watched them disappear before he sped in the opposite direction toward the door leading to the dungeon. He never stopped until he reached Chesna's cell and, there, received confirmation of his gruesome suspicions. Four of the rats lay dead beside the spilled wine. Two more convulsed in the throes of death nearby, their mouths foaming a mixture of pink and white.

Ignoring the rats' ghastly predicament, he picked up the goblet and sniffed, then held it up to the light of the candles. Inside the bottom of the cup, he discerned the remnants of some form of powder. He ran a finger along the particles and brought them to his lips. The acidic taste of the dregs caused him to retch. Still coughing, he raced from the cell and back upstairs with the goblet held tightly in one hand, Bela's book in the other.

He reached the third floor where Karol paced in the hall, his face etched with worry. "Where is she?"

Karol jerked his head toward her bedchamber. "Lying down," he replied. "What did you find?"

With shaking hands, Pietor showed him the goblet and the dark flecks inside. "The wine was poisoned. I think it's foxglove."

18

Pietor shoved the goblet and book into Karol's hand and raced past him into the chamber. "We mustn't let her sleep. We have to wake her. Now. Before it's too late. If it isn't already."

"What's wrong?" In the bed beside Chesna, Zarek shot up, eyes round and nearly white. "Is Mama dying?"

Damn. In his haste to reach Chesna, he'd forgotten Zarek.

"She can't die," the child insisted. "She promised she wouldn't leave me."

"Zarek," Pietor began. "Let me help her."

"No!" Zarek threw himself into the middle of the bed. He shook Chesna by her shoulders, rolling her back and forth across the pile of pillows. "Don't die! You can't die! You promised!"

"Karol?" Pietor glared at the stupefied servant until the man blinked and came back to himself.

"I'll take him." Karol strode to the bed and peeled the child out of the way.

"Mama!" The boy struggled to break out of Karol's grasp, arms outstretched. When Karol pulled him tighter against his chest, Zarek used his feet. Quite successfully. One swift kick connected with the man's most sensitive area. Crumpling at the waist, Karol released the boy.

Pietor sucked in a sharp breath in empathy.

Zarek attempted to scramble back toward where Chesna lay, stone still and silent, but even in his bruised state, Karol managed to clamp a hand on the boy's shoulder and whirl him around again.

"No, Zarek," he ground out. "Allow Pietor and me to help your mama. She won't die. I promise."

Pietor studied Chess's ashen complexion and prayed they'd find a way to keep such a promise. Hands trembling, he pulled her into a sitting position. But the moment he removed his hold from her shoulders, her head lolled to one side, and her upper torso slid away. Quickly, he whipped the pillows and bolsters around her into a soft retaining wall.

Once certain she'd remain upright, he placed his ear to her chest. The rise and fall of her breasts brushed whisper-soft against his cheek. She breathed. Short tiny gasps—barely enough air to satisfy a mouse—and long intervals in between.

With tentative fingers, he forced her eyelids open. Pinpoint pupils stared back. Shudders racked him. Those miniscule black dots dampened any spark of hope her shallow breathing had elicited.

He slapped her cheeks.

Once.

Twice.

Nothing. Not a sound or reaction came from Chesna. She might as well have been a rag doll for all the outrage his actions wrought.

Pietor's brain buzzed. How could he reach her? By God, he had no experience with poison. And he trusted no one else to assist them. What in the world could he do?

For starters, he'd get her moving. Lying in the bed would no doubt guarantee her death.

"Karol," he called softly. "Help me get her up."

Both Karol and Zarek rushed toward him while Pietor grabbed Chesna's wrists and yanked her forward. She slumped, arms dangling over his shoulders. His guts twisted at her lifelessness. *Please, Chess, don't give up on life just yet.*

"Take her left side," he ordered Karol.

"What can I do, Pietor?" Zarek asked.

"Talk to her."

With Karol's help, he pulled her to her feet. She swayed,

and he gripped her tighter. Meanwhile, Karol stepped back to stand beside Zarek.

The boy hovered nearby, hands wringing. "I don't know what to say."

"Say anything you can think of, lad," Pietor advised. "We have to wake her. Say anything at all, but say it loud enough for her to hear you."

He then shifted his position slightly so that he stood by Chesna's side, her arm around his shoulder. His hand wrapped her waist to keep her from sinking to the floor. By kicking his foot gently behind her knees, he propelled her limbs to move.

"I'll fetch some water." Karol grabbed the large pitcher from atop the bedside table and sped out of the room.

"Mama, can you hear me?" Zarek demanded as he walked alongside them. "Wake up. You must wake up this instant. Don't sleep. If you sleep now, you'll leave me. I didn't grant you permission to leave me yet. You promised to care for me until I didn't need you anymore. Tell our Lord He must wait for you. He took everyone else from me. He can't have you, too."

Pietor paid scant attention to the boy's cries. His heart, pounding in his ears loud as cannonfire, drowned out most sound. Except the words she'd tossed at him in a fit of pique.

God cursed me the day He sent you back to Amatia. I hate you. I will never forgive you.

By God, what had he done? He should have heeded Karol's advice and told Chesna the truth. What if she died hating him? Cursing him?

He set his lips in a grim line. No.

She had to live.

"Don't die, Mama. Please. I need you." Zarek's plaintive cries cut through Pietor's panicked haze.

He paced the room with Chesna hauled up against his side, clumsy yet determined. Zarek was absolutely right. She couldn't die. But not because Zarek needed her.

He needed her.

"Wake up, damn you!"

Of course, she remained unresponsive. Same stubborn Chesna.

"Please wake up," Zarek called. "Please, please, please..."

Long minutes elapsed, minutes that seemed like days to Pietor's tortured mind. Back and forth, he forced her feet across the floor, stopping only to slap her cheeks, check her breathing, and then continue the traverse.

All the while, Zarek shouted his demands. "You can't leave me. I forbid it."

"Is she awake yet?" Karol entered the chamber with the pitcher. A dozen rags dangled from his fist.

Pietor shook his head. "Start praying, Karol," he said. "If we don't wake her soon, she'll never survive."

If his ear hadn't been so close to her cheek as he walked with her, he would have missed the sound, her barely audible moan. But he hadn't missed it. The soft response raised hope in his heart, and he instantly stopped walking to watch her face. How long now before she opened her eyes? How long before he could be certain the danger had passed?

Another murmur erupted from her lips.

"Keep talking, Zarek," Pietor exclaimed. "She's starting to stir."

"Mama! Mama! Wake up!" Zarek shouted at the top of his lungs. "Open your eyes! Please!"

Pietor moved his hands from her waist to her shoulders and shook her violently. "Please, Chess, open your eyes."

Her head rocked back and forth, and her thick lashes fluttered, but she seemed incapable of opening her eyes. Instead, she opened her mouth and vomited all over the floor.

Zarek sidestepped the deluge, but Pietor never had a chance. Pink slime soaked his trousers from thighs to knees.

He didn't give a damn. His only concern was Chesna.

"Good girl." He sat her down on the bed and knelt beside her, his relief escaping in one long whoosh of air. "Good girl. You'll be all right now."

He signaled to Karol, who filled a goblet with water and handed it to him. Pietor placed the rim of the goblet against her lips and forced a few drops into her mouth.

Immediately, she coughed violently. She pushed the

goblet away, sputtering and gasping for breath. Finally, she collapsed against the headboard, breathing deeply, but with her eyelids still sealed.

"Open your eyes, Chess," Pietor ordered her in a much softer voice. "Open your eyes and look at me."

For the first time since he'd come home, Chesna did as Pietor demanded without any argument at all.

Her lashes quivered against her pale face, and at long last, her beautiful wildflower eyes opened. "Wh-what happened?"

Pietor looked up at Karol and shook his head. Not yet. He couldn't tell her the truth yet. He still had to digest the gruesome details himself. "You were ill, Chess," he said with more calm than he felt. "Something you ate made you ill."

Karol raised a querulous eyebrow, but he never gainsaid the statement. Nor did he expound upon it. He simply stood, hands clasped behind his back, silent.

Unfortunately, Zarek had no such self-control. "We had to wake you, Mama," the boy announced as he crawled onto the bed and nuzzled into her shoulder. "You might have died, but Pietor saved you. He walked with you until you were better."

Chesna looked up at Pietor, brow pleated in confusion.

"Zarek is exaggerating." He shrugged. "You were ill, that's all."

"What did I eat that made me so ill?"

"I don't know." To avoid her curious stare, he rose and moved away from the bed. "I need to wash up and change my trousers." He cast a warning glance at Karol and Zarek. "Wait here. Quietly."

♥

Chesna's head swam. She'd been ill? How ill? And for how long? Why didn't she know? According to Zarek, she nearly died. But Pietor insisted he exaggerated.

Absently stroking Zarek's curls, she tried to conjure up a memory. Unfortunately, she couldn't recall anything of substance. She remembered putting on this sunny yellow gown this morning. Her fingers picked at the folds in agitation. Was that this morning? Or had so much time passed that the dress had come back from the laundry and someone else dressed her in the last garment she remembered wearing? Needing answers, she turned to Karol to determine the truth, but the old man's expression remained inscrutable.

As if he sensed her burning desire to question him, he suddenly turned away and busied himself with the ewer at her bedside. "I'll see to the floor."

Embarrassment seared her cheeks.

"I can do that, Karol," she told him.

"You will remain where you are until Pietor returns," Karol replied gruffly as he scrubbed the pink slime off the carpet with a wet rag.

The silence in the room slowly lulled her, and she allowed her eyelids to drop.

"Stay awake, Mama," Zarek shouted near her ear.

On a screech, she opened her eyes.

When Pietor finally did reenter the bedchamber a short while later, he strode straight to her bedside, sat on the edge, and placed a hand on her forehead. With his hand lingering on her brow, he leaned forward to stare into her eyes.

"Your pupils still look small." He frowned, but removed his hand and stood. "Chess, I know you feel quite drained right now, but you mustn't fall asleep."

The power of suggestion worked against her, and she issued a very unladylike yawn. "But I'm so tired. Why can't I sleep?"

"It's too soon for you to sleep."

Too soon? What in the world had happened to her? "If I've been so ill, don't I need sleep to get well?"

"No, you don't," he insisted, arms folded over his chest in a posture of authority.

Enough mystery. She needed answers. And Pietor would have to provide them. "How ill have I been? And for how long? Exactly what happened to me?"

Karol caught her attention when he rose from the carpet and cleared his throat. "Chess, who brought you a tray today?"

She blinked, tried to push aside the veil shrouding her

brain. "Tray?"

"The tray in the cell," he elaborated.

A tray in the cell. In the dungeon. So she *had* remembered dressing this morning. She hadn't lost any time. "Urszula sent Monika to the cell with bread and cheese and watered wine. She knows her bread and cheese is my favorite." She studied the two men who stared at her with such intensity. "You don't think the meal is what made me ill, do you?"

"Perhaps," Pietor answered noncommittally.

Ridiculous. "I've been enjoying bread and cheese since I was a child. Why would I become ill all of a sudden?"

Pietor sighed and turned to Karol.

Karol simply nodded. "We have to tell her the truth. She should know, Pietor."

Chesna's gaze swerved from Pietor's face to Karol's then back to Pietor's again. "What is the truth?"

Pietor lowered his voice. "Someone tried to poison you, Chess."

Zarek gasped.

But Chesna shook her head. She couldn't have heard him correctly. "Poison?"

Pietor nodded.

"Why would someone poison me?"

"That's what we want to know," Pietor told her. "I found you in the dungeon, sound asleep. There were rats in the cell with you."

"Rats?"

Shivers skittered across her flesh. She'd shared her cell with rats and hadn't noticed? Impossible. But...

Her throat tightened.

...Poison?

"Karol carried you up here," Pietor continued, "while I returned to your cell to fetch your father's book. The rats had knocked over your wine goblet and were dead on the floor."

The wine. She remembered now. "I only took a few sips. The wine had a bitter aftertaste. I thought it was sour."

"It wasn't sour." Pietor scowled. "I found foxglove dregs in the bottom."

But that would mean...

No.

"Urszula would never harm me." The words left her mouth the moment they popped into her head. "Nor would Monika." No one in the kitchens, as a matter of fact. "It must have been one of your soldiers."

Pietor's lips twisted in a grimace. "No, Chess. No one under General de Valmiere's command would dare such a thing."

Chesna bit back an angry retort. Pietor was still loyal to the monsters? Even now? "What if the general ordered someone to kill me? Perhaps he learned I'm Bela Dubrow's daughter and he felt threatened by me. Perhaps that Major Montfort."

Pietor shook his head. "Major Montfort sent me to fetch you from the dungeon. He worried your continued imprisonment might incite a riot. And the general knew who you were from the start. If he wanted you dead, he would have had you executed when he first arrived at the palace. Rather, he placed you and Zarek under my protection. That's why we were married."

"Our marriage had nothing to do with protection," she retorted. "We were married so you could influence my child."

Pietor gestured to Zarek with a curt nod of his head. "Not now, Chess. We'll discuss this later."

A heated flush crept into her cheeks. They shouldn't involve Zarek in their arguments. "I'm sorry," she mumbled.

"Listen very carefully to me, Chess," he told her. "Someone is plotting to kill you. And we need to find this culprit before he tries again."

She attempted to argue, but he raised a hand to cut her off.

"Your days in the dungeon are over. I must know where you are and whom you are with at all times. Together we'll find out who's behind this attack."

Suspicion coiled around her heart, and she blurted, "How do I know you're not plotting to kill me?"

"You don't," he admitted with a shrug. "But I'm asking you to trust me."

Her chest constricted. "How can I trust you? After you've already betrayed me a thousand times over?" She shook her head. "I dare not trust you again."

He knelt beside her then, one hand before her face, palm outward. "I swear on the soul of my late mother. I *will* protect you, Chesna."

Their solemn vow. Her heart thudded, but her mind tumbled. The last time he'd made such a promise, he'd broken the oath within months. Could she put her pure faith in a man with a dark past? Did she have a choice?

Finally, she placed her palm flat against his. "And I swear on the soul of my late mother. I'll trust you, Pietor."

19

Zarek lifted his head from Chesna's shoulder and kissed her cheek with a great deal of exuberance and moisture. "I'm so glad you didn't die."

"I made you a promise." She fought the urge to wipe the wetness from her face. "I won't leave you until you no longer need me."

"Chess?" Pietor still knelt at her side. "Do you feel strong enough to stand up?"

Did she? "I believe so."

"Move slowly," he advised. "You'll still be weak and you may become dizzy if you move too quickly."

Easing out of Zarek's grip, she flexed her feet, and sidled to a sitting position. A little shaky, but manageable.

When he extended his hand, she placed her fingers into his clasp. He grasped her around the waist for additional strength. A jolt ripped through her, and she gasped. The heat of his palm branded her like a glowing fireplace ember. Eyes wide, she raised her head to meet Pietor's steady gaze.

"I know." His whispered words tickled her belly. "I feel it, as well."

"Wh-what do we do now?"

Both eyebrows rose at her question.

The fiery heat sizzled from her waist all the way up her neck and over her cheeks. "I mean, about me. That is, about the villain who tried to poison me."

"Nothing," he said as he helped her to her feet.

She swerved to glare at him. "Nothing? But, you said we needed to find the culprit before he tried to kill me again."

"I changed my mind." He had the nerve to grin.

"How comforting," she snapped. Was this a ploy to lull her into a trap? Did he already plan to betray her? Again? She cast a worried glance at Karol, but he looked away from her. Due to guilt? Was there anyone in this blasted palace she could trust implicitly? Besides Zarek?

"Trust me, Chess." Pietor's reply refocused her attention on him. "The best way we can find our villain is to do nothing right away. That will make him wonder how you managed to elude his plans for you. And his failure to kill you the first time will make him wish to try again."

"So we're going to allow this fiend another chance to kill me?"

"No!" Zarek scrambled over the bedcovers to wrap his arms protectively around her waist and bury his head in her stomach. "No! I won't let anyone harm her. She's all I have left. You can't let him kill her."

"Hush, Zarek," Pietor and Chesna said simultaneously.

"I won't allow any harm to come to her," Pietor added. "It's merely a ruse to flush the villain out of hiding. He's bound to slip up due to eagerness, and we'll neatly trap him in our web when he does."

Zarek raised his eyes from Chesna's stomach to look into Pietor's face. "You promise you'll protect her?"

Pietor nodded solemnly. "I promise you, Zarek. Nothing will happen to your mama. I give you my word." He turned back to Chesna. "Why don't you wash up and change your gown? We'll wait for you right outside these doors."

♥

Pietor had been absolutely right about one thing. The poison still swam rampantly through Chesna's blood. If she moved too quickly, she became lightheaded. She had to do everything slowly or dizziness overcame her. Thus, she required nearly an hour to wash her face and hands, clean her teeth, and change her gown. After each activity, she sat for several minutes and took gulps of clean air before moving again.

When she finally left the bedchamber and entered the playroom, she came upon Pietor at once. He paced like a caged madman, running his fingers through his thick black hair.

Her heartbeat sped up. Zarek! Where was Zarek? Had something happened to him? Oh, God, no!

Her gaze quickly scanned the room and came to rest on the child's golden curls. He and Karol sat on the floor playing with blocks, unfazed. Still, Pietor paced, ground-eating strides that would take him over the mountains to Russia if he'd stalked in a straight line.

"Pietor?" she asked hesitantly. "What is it? Is something wrong?"

He turned in her direction, and his posture visibly relaxed, as if his bones had suddenly softened. "No, Chess, nothing's wrong," he said on a sigh. "Everything is as it was."

"You look angry," she noted.

"You took a little longer than I anticipated." His easy smile renewed the dimpled cheeks she'd thought long gone with his youth. He clasped her hand and led her farther into the room. "I was worried about you. I thought our poisonmonger might have succeeded after all."

His concern seemed a far cry from the animosity she'd noticed in him in the last few weeks. Perhaps almost dying had some benefits after all, she thought with a rueful smile. Or perhaps, the poison had addled her mind into seeing things that didn't truly exist.

Zarek popped up, face etched with worry. "You're not still sick, are you, Mama?"

"Of course not." She forced a carefree-sounding laugh. "It would take more than a little poison to kill me." She tilted her chin a bit higher and puffed out her chest. "Don't forget. I'm a Dubrow. We don't die easily."

Pietor raised her hand to his lips, kissed her fingertips. Tingles rippled through her arm, straight to her rapidly beating heart.

"You're a Dubrow and a Gabris now," he remarked. "That makes you doubly stubborn and twice as hard to kill. I don't think I've ever been happier with your obstinacy. Our murderous scoundrel is bound to kill himself trying to assassinate you."

Her life had certainly taken some strange turns in the

last few hours. Someone had tried to murder her and had very nearly succeeded. Her savior turned out to be a man she considered her enemy. And she planned to allow the attempted killer to try again. Even odder to her way of thinking, her near death brought the old Pietor back to her. He sounded caring and funny and attentive, just as he had in their earlier days together. She stifled a sigh of confusion. What kind of game did he play? And was she his pawn? His rival? Or his partner?

"So what do we do now?" she asked.

"Today, nothing." He frowned. "But I do expect you to remain up here for the rest of the day for your own safety. Unfortunately, I have to report to Major Montfort."

Apprehension chilled her blood. "You're not planning to tell the major what happened, are you?"

The creases around his lips deepened with his transfer from frown to scowl. "Truth be told, I'm not certain. I firmly believe the fewer people who know what's occurred today, the safer *you* are."

Warm relief rushed through her. Something about the puffy-faced Major Montfort raised hackles on her nape. Several times she'd caught him studying her when he thought her involved in some detailed task. He never spoke to her, but his black, soulless eyes—on memory alone—set the fine hairs on her arms dancing with alarm. She shivered.

Pietor must have misinterpreted the cause of her reaction because he immediately removed his jacket and tossed it around her shoulders. His scent enveloped her, earthy and sweet.

"What shall we do with you now?" he said, his breath wafting near her ear to reawaken the shivers, but in a more pleasant fashion. "You need to rest, but I can't risk you falling asleep just yet. If I allow you go to bed, will you promise to stay awake?"

Craning her neck toward him, she arched a brow. "For how long?"

"Until tonight."

"Hours in bed? Alone? With nothing to do?" Seconds after the words left her lips, the hidden innuendo struck her brain, and she winced. Heat flooded her face, hot enough to set the room ablaze.

His knowing smile tingled all the way down to her toes. "I forgot. You're accustomed to more activity."

Her breath left her lungs in one sharp gasp, heat and tingles forgotten in the icy splash of his insult. She shrugged off his coat and allowed it to fall to the floor. Blast him!

Karol, fists balled, took a threatening step forward. "By God, Gabris, I'll kill you yet, you young whelp."

Pietor simply waved a hand, then bent to retrieve his jacket. All the while, his expression remained bland and inscrutable. "I'll allow Zarek to remain with you this afternoon. He'll only be in the way on the training field anyway."

The insult he'd uttered still stung, and acid dripped from her lips when she retorted, "Your generosity overwhelms me."

Zarek, on the other hand, voiced enough enthusiasm for all of them. "I get to stay with Mama?" With a gleeful shout, he skipped around her. "This will be so much fun. We'll play Cassino, and Graces, and The Elements..."

While the boy spun, he listed dozens of various games. Thanks to his constant rotations and his ambitious list of activities, the room's colors smeared in Chesna's vision. Icy chills coiled around her skin, freezing her to the spot.

"Chess?" Pietor's voice echoed in her head from some distant time or place. "Chess? Can you hear me?"

A high-pitched ring drowned out anything else he said, and she closed her eyes against the strident wail. The room seemed to cave in, suffocating the breath from her lungs. Equilibrium failed, and her toes curled in an effort to grip the floor. To no avail. Blindly, she reached for an object—any object—to hold onto.

Her fingers found a solid mass, a wall that must have popped up from the floorboards. Her heartbeat slowed, the black veil of nothingness threatened to drag her under. Before panic stole the last of her faculties, she flung her arms around the top of the invisible wall and held on tight. A hearty breeze whipped through her, and she swayed like a twig. With the force of the wind, her grip faltered. While her hands scrambled for purchase, she snapped and plummeted.

Something snagged her before her bottom crashed to the ground. Strong arms wrapped around her, buffeting her from the storm that tried to sweep her into oblivion. She clung to this unknown lifeline, digging her fingernails into the rippled texture of whatever held her upright.

She opened her mouth to scream, but her chest constricted from the lack of air, leaving her to gasp for breath.

"Breathe, Chess." Pietor's voice, tender yet stern, reached through the noisy maelstrom. "Breathe. You can do it."

She struggled to heed his advice, to gobble up any air to fill her lungs. Oh, God, if she didn't find relief soon, she'd die. The pain inside her rib cage intensified, wringing her from the inside out. Pinpoints of light danced before her closed eyelids. The icy claw of death gripped her heart and squeezed.

"Slowly, my dove."

Slowly? How could he expect her to breathe slowly? Her lungs threatened to burst with their need. She gulped again. Nothing.

A mouth pressed to her lips. Pietor's. Did he really think to kiss her now? Of all the inopportune times...

But, no. Air pushed into her throat. His air. One puff. Then a second. And a third. Her head pounded with sharp intensity. As if his actions reminded her lungs how to function, she felt her chest expand. Breaking away from him, she pulled air into her mouth. Slowly. Gradually. Until she finally found her natural rhythm.

When she finally focused again, her gaze met Pietor's terrified expression. "Chess?"

She inhaled deeply, exhaled deeply. "Yes. I'm all right now."

Her fingers curled into his shoulders deep enough to draw blood. His hands wrapped her waist, keeping her crushed against him. Memories assailed her, afternoons in the Amatian Forest, beneath the dipping boughs of ash and pine trees, her bodice unlaced, baring her to Pietor's gaze, to his touch...

Shaking away the visions of the past, she tried to pull

out of his grasp.

Pietor simply tightened his hold. "Obviously there's still too much of the poison in you to consider you out of harm's way." Although the worry lines fled from around his eyes, his voice remained somber. "To hell with Montfort. I'm staying right here."

"No." She held up a shaky hand. The longer he remained, the harder it would be for her to think clearly. She needed him gone—needed peace. And with her breasts pressed to his chest, a slow ache bloomed inside her, hardly an easy road toward peace. "Go. I'll be fine with Zarek."

"Oh?" He arched a brow. "You think your son will know what to do if you stop breathing again."

"He might not," Karol interjected gruffly. "But I will."

Pietor whirled, never losing contact with her hips. "And you think I'm going to leave my wife alone in our bedchamber with you?"

Oh, for heaven's sake...

Before exhaustion claimed her entirely, she broke away from Pietor's imprisonment. "Karol can stand guard outside the nursery. If anything happens to me, Zarek will fetch him." On legs that trembled beneath her gown, she stumbled to her bed and climbed onto the mattress. "I will remain here. Awake." As if to emphasize that point, she propped the pillows behind her, and folded her arms over her chest.

He matched her glare, gray eyes hard as steel. She refused to flinch, would show him no more vulnerability. Already he'd seen her at her worst. The poison must have affected her mind because she'd let down her guard. A mistake. But with Karol's stern countenance to remind her, she wouldn't repeat her error.

Despite the strain to her muscles, she stiffened her posture. Her gaze fixed on Pietor's sharp eyes, never blinking. Bolstering her position, Zarek and Karol moved to stand beside the bed. Karol's hand protectively clasped her shoulder. Zarek tried, bless him, to appear imperious rather than frightened. But his thin frame shuddered, and she fought the urge to pull back the counterpane and invite the child to snuggle beside her.

At last, faced with this stony wall of resistance, Pietor

relented on a sigh. "I'll return as soon as I'm able."

She waved him off. "Don't hurry on our account. We'll be quite all right without you."

And she silently promised to mean it.

20

Pietor paused in the armory of the grand vestibule. The old weapons had fascinated him as a youth. Whenever he clashed with his father, he'd find his way to this alcove. Surrounded by shields and swords, he'd close his eyes and imagine himself as a warrior, free from Prince Milos's influence. When he was young and naïve, the life of a soldier seemed glamorous and exciting. Even when he'd left the University of St. Petersburg to follow Bonaparte, ideals of glory clouded his mind from the ugliness of war. He'd never realized the waste, the destruction, the stink of death. Now, he doubted he'd ever fully erase those sensory details from his mind. Yet, while he'd seen his comrades fall too many times to count, today's events brought death far too close for his peace of mind.

Chesna.

The fine hairs on his arms danced in static air. By God. Every time he recalled how close he'd come to losing her forever, his heart stuttered.

Hadn't Father Grigory tried to warn him? Before his marriage, during his confession to the old priest, Pietor had disclosed all. Barely three months into his education in St. Petersburg, he'd stumbled onto information that could ruin Amatia. With no one else to trust, he'd contacted Bela. To be fair, Bela had offered him a choice. But in his heart, Pietor had always known what he had to do. The decision changed his life forever. And Chesna's.

Father Grigory had listened carefully, never giving away

his thoughts in action or expression. When at last Pietor had finished, the old man simply commented, "Our lives often take crooked paths before we find our way home again. The road is set with traitors and thieves. Let no one waylay you, my son. May our Lord watch over you and keep you safe."

That was all.

If only Father Grigory resided in the palace! But, no. He remained at the Church of St. Ambrose, protecting the souls of the dead and directing the souls of the living.

He cast a glance at the staircase, as if by force of will, he might see inside the nursery, might know she was all right. She'd looked far too pale when he'd left her. But her anger at him, her uncertainty regarding his trustworthiness, and his duties to Major Montfort compelled him to leave her in the care of a five-year-old boy and a servant who might have shifted loyalties years ago. Only time would tell. Had he placed her life in jeopardy by leaving her in the wrong hands?

She'd nearly died today. Because of him. Because she'd married him. Guilt tore his insides to shreds. He really should push the general to move on toward Moscow. The longer he remained here, the more danger surrounded Chesna. He couldn't bear to lose her. To never see her smile again? Never watch the flash of anger light her eyes? Of course, he considered with a grimace, when she learned the truth about him, the rage in her gaze would no doubt blaze enough to incinerate the thousands of acres in the Amatian Forest.

His gaze scanned upward to the arched ceiling and the gilt-painted angels above him. *Please, God, keep her safe.* The angels simply smiled down, saying nothing, providing no clue as to what might happen next. An icy finger trailed up his spine, leaving goose flesh in its wake.

Dammit, he should be up there with her.

How could he possibly expect a little boy to protect her? But he had no choice. Zarek was the only person in the entire palace he trusted implicitly. Ironic, he thought, as he turned away from the arsenal around him. Because Pietor was the one person in the entire palace Zarek could *never* trust. And as long as Chess attempted to protect the boy, she could never trust her husband.

"Gabris!" de Valmiere's shout drew him forward with a start. "There you are." The general, pipe stuck between his teeth, scaled the stairs toward him. "Where's the boy?"

"Napping, sir," he lied.

A billow of headache gray smoke swirled and tinged the air with sweet tobacco. The smell reminded him of the sour-sweet wine Chesna had expelled all over his trousers and the floor. Again, his gaze strayed to the upper floor.

As if reading his mind, alongside the general, Major Montfort nodded, one sooty eyebrow perched in a dubious arc. "And where's your wife?"

He turned, pasting a blasé expression on his face. "Currently locked in our chamber until she learns to accept who's lord and master." Envisioning Chess's violent reaction to his statement, he squelched a wince. Then again, in his book of sins against Chesna, this particular remark barely registered a footnote.

Their dark expressions were a stark reminder he could trust neither officer with his concerns about Chesna. For them, Chess's death would be a convenience, a way to keep Zarek in line without his mother's influence.

Montfort clapped a hand on his shoulder, effectively drawing him into the French web once again. "A far better place to keep her than the dungeon, Captain."

Picturing the dead rats, Pietor stifled a shiver. "Indeed, sir."

"I trust you'll have her in hand before we set off for Moscow," the general remarked.

Tread carefully. Don't appear too curious. Pietor nodded. "Do we know when that will be, sir?"

"Soon," the general replied and clamped on his pipe as if to prevent any additional information from leaking through his lips. "We'll need to cross the Carpathians before the snows set in."

Pietor didn't bother to mention that when the Carpathian Mountains weren't snowy, rain often fell steadily in its place. "And when we leave, I can promise you my wife will be well aware of her new place in this palace." As well as in his heart.

Because the time had come to tell her the truth. After

all, Chess was a grown woman, logical and clever. Yes. She'd understand why he'd done what he'd done. She wouldn't like it, of course. In fact, he anticipated she'd be furious when he told her.

But first he planned to do a little digging into the identity of their poisonmonger.

♥

To his vast surprise, Pietor managed to keep Chesna in bed for two full days. During that time, he attempted discreet inquiries about the kitchen staff and the new servant, Monika. Nothing leaped out at him as suspicious.

By the afternoon of the third day, his logical and clever wife threatened to tie him to the bed to play Graces with Zarek while she fought with his soldiers in the courtyard.

"Very well," he said with mock defeat. "But you'll stay with me all day, madam," he warned.

"If agreeing allows me out of this chamber," she replied, "I'll agree to spend the day with General de Valmiere, discussing the finer points of Napoleonic rule."

Between her words and her expression of pure joy, he laughed. "Nothing quite so dire, Chess. I promise."

"Good. Because I really didn't want to see General de Valmiere." As if she had springs on her feet, she bounded out of the bed. "What shall we do this afternoon?"

"We'll go to the kitchens first," he replied. "I want to see the reaction of the staff when you stroll in showing no ill effects from your poisonous snack. I doubt our scoundrel will react strangely and give himself away, but it's worth a try."

An hour later, the kitchens bustled with activity. Dozens of servants worked hard to have a splendid meal prepared in time for this evening's dinner. Pots and pans clanged. Laughter and chatter mingled with the sweet aroma of cherries and the hearty smells of roasting meat.

Pietor remained at Chesna's side. She still looked far too pale to his way of thinking. And once or twice, she'd stumbled on the stairs. He'd caught her each time, used the opportunity to study her eyes, to ascertain the pupils increased in diameter. They strolled through the kitchens as nonchalantly as possible, nodding a cursory hello here and stopping to taste a bit of something there. Very few heads looked up at their entrance and those that did showed no obvious surprise at her appearance.

"Chess? Pietor?" Urszula lifted her gaze from the large pot simmering upon the fire. "What brings you here? Was there something you wanted?"

"Could I trouble you for a special dinner request for Chess and me?" Pietor asked. "We'd hoped to go riding this afternoon and I'm not certain we'll return in time for this evening's meal."

"Of course." Urszula wiped her hands on her apron. "I'd be happy to prepare a meal for you to take with you. Was there something special you desired tonight?"

"Indeed there is, Urszula," he whispered, rubbing his hands together in feigned malicious glee. "But my appetite isn't whetted for food. What I desire is to gain a certain female's compliance and have my way with her. What would you suggest to aid me in my cause?"

He shot a heated look at Chesna, who blushed profusely and stared at her feet in embarrassment.

Urszula laughed. "You always were a delightfully naughty boy." She tweaked his cheek with a pair of pinched fingers. "I have a few stuffed quails roasted. Would that be enough to satisfy your appetite?"

"Your quail with sage and chestnut stuffing?"

Urszula's stuffed quail had always been his favorite meal, and his mouth watered at the mere memory.

"Sage, chestnuts, diced apples and raisins," she elaborated. "The very same way you've always liked it."

"It's a pity I'm already married." He placed his right hand over his chest. "Your delicious meals could easily win my heart. But I'd swear my undying devotion to you if you'd consider preparing an apple tart or two for our dessert."

"You still have a taste for those tarts, eh?" She shook a finger. "You may have grown quite a bit on the outside, but you haven't changed at all on the inside. You're the very same charming boy who drove my kitchen maids to distraction with your antics."

He opened his eyes wide in mock innocence. "Antics? Me? Never."

"Ha!" Urszula retorted. "Poor Agata received many a beating for purposely burning meals on your account."

"I never asked Agata to burn a meal for me," he denied, but he couldn't suppress a guilty grin.

Urszula smirked. "How strange. Agata always burned the spinach with wild rice, but never burned a fruit filled tart in all her days."

"Coincidence," he remarked with a wave of his hand.

Urszula shook her head, but the smirk remained. "So you'd like stuffed quail and apple tarts."

Pietor stole another glance at Chesna, who still stared at her feet as if she'd suddenly grown extra toes. "And your oat bread with maple butter?"

Urszula followed his gaze and leaned closer to whisper, "How about a little bread and cheese?"

"No!" His shout snapped several heads in their direction. He had no intention of allowing Chess near bread and cheese again until their culprit was caught. On a calming inhale, he added in a much softer tone, "No bread and cheese. And no watered wine. We'll have cider to drink."

"If that's your wish." She shrugged. "But if you ask me, you'll get farther in your pursuits with wine than with cider."

"No wine," he repeated firmly. He changed the subject before she became suspicious of his requests. With a slender finger he pointed to the long table where several kitchen maids pitted cherries. "And some of those, if there are any left."

She folded her arms over her ample chest. "Are you riding a horse or is the horse riding you? Do you think you've requested enough food to appease you?"

"I have a very healthy appetite, Urszula," he said with another wink in Chesna's direction. "I haven't had a decent feast since I left Simion and I need to sate myself now."

"Sounds more like gluttony to me." She sniffed. "Stuffed quails, oat bread with maple butter, cherries, apple tarts, and cider. Will that do?"

Ignoring the sweat that drenched her from hairline to the hem of her apron, he pulled her into an embrace and kissed her cheeks with loud smacks. "It will more than do,

Urszula. It sounds delicious." He glanced again at Chesna. "Don't you think so, my dove?"

Chesna looked up from her feet only briefly to nod in his direction.

"Shoo, then," Urszula pushed Pietor away. "And I'll prepare a perfect meal for you in no time."

"You'll make all the food yourself, Urszula?" he asked. At her questioning look, he added hastily, "No one prepares a feast the way you do."

"I give you my word I'll see to the entire meal with my own two hands. Now, go! I have a great deal of work to do."

♥

An hour later, Chesna followed Pietor to the mews.

Over one shoulder, he carried a large sack filled with linen-wrapped delicacies. Despite the smells of dung, straw, and horseflesh, the aromas coming from inside that sack tantalized.

Pietor's stomach growled like a hungry bear, and Chesna flinched, instantly on guard.

"I beg your pardon," he mumbled.

But she couldn't care less about his rumbling stomach. Other more pressing concerns ruled her thoughts. "Are you certain we shouldn't take Zarek with us?" She craned her neck to look back at the ivory walls of the palace. "He's in danger as well."

"No, he's not. No one has tried to poison him," he replied. "Never fear. Zarek will be quite all right with Karol to watch out for him."

"You don't understand," she argued. "I promised my father I would always keep him safe. It's not Karol's responsibility. It's mine."

Pietor stopped in mid-stride. "What did you say?"

She flushed. How could she make such a devastating slip? "I said Zarek's not Karol's responsibility, he's mine."

"Before that," he directed. "What did you say before that?"

"That Zarek is in danger, as well," she replied, pinning her gaze to the ground.

"After that. After, 'Zarek is in danger,' but before.

'Zarek's not Karol's responsibility.'"

She lifted her head to look him squarely in the eye. Let him call her a liar if he dared. "I said I promised Zarek's father I would always keep him safe."

For the briefest of moments, the silence between them deafened. But at last, Pietor nodded and resumed walking. Chesna breathed a tremendous sigh of relief and whispered a thank you heavenward.

Meanwhile, Pietor headed for the stall where a fine white gelding waited. "You remember Columbidae," he said as he brushed the horse's long nose with the flat of his hand.

Chesna ran an affectionate hand down the silky mane. "I remember his name isn't Columbidae. This horse's name is Dove," she said. "I should know. I was the one who named him before I sent him to you for your twenty-first birthday."

"I remember. Very clever of you to name my horse for the nickname I gave you. Did you hope it would keep me from forgetting you while I was away?"

Yes. But of course, her ploy hadn't worked.

"I named him Dove because his coat was such a fine white, like the wings of a dove," she lied. "Why did you change it?"

Another way to forget her?

"Because Dove is hardly a suitable name for a soldier's steed," he grumbled as he secured the saddle. "When I left St. Petersburg, I changed his name to the Latin form, Columbidae. I told my comrades it was Amatian for 'Freedom for all.'"

"And they believed you?" She couldn't suppress a snicker of disbelief. "Your comrades are such fools."

"No, they're not fools. They don't have your flair for language is all. Never mistake a lack of education for a lack of danger, Chess. The most ignorant animals in the world are also the most ferocious."

Dove snorted, as if to confirm Pietor's statement. Chesna glared at the beast. Even his horse had turned traitor while in St. Petersburg.

"I don't need you to teach me about danger," she retorted. "Since your return to Simion, I've been fired upon

169

by Napoleon's guns, threatened with execution if I didn't marry you, and fed poisoned wine. I've learned quite a bit about ferocious animals in the last month or so."

"I should imagine you have."

"Indeed."

She leapt over a pile of straw, intent on retrieving her mare, but he grasped her by the wrist, yanking her back. Her slipper skidded on a wet spot, and she tumbled against him. He captured her easily, just as he had each time she tripped on the stairs earlier. But because this time she faced him when he grabbed her, she wound up plastered to him, breasts to chest, lips separated by a mere breath. His arms tightened, pulling her closer. Her blood sizzled, and the fine hairs on her arm danced in anticipation.

Dove whinnied.

Pietor blinked twice and then took a step backward, his arm still around her waist. "You're still too weak to ride alone. I don't want you to tumble out of the saddle because you don't have the strength to hold onto the reins. I've already told you I don't intend to let you out of my sight. So we'll ride Columbidae together."

"I'll ride with you, but we'll ride *Dove*," she insisted, pulling out of his grip. "I don't know any horse named Columbidae."

"Then we'll ride Dove together," he amended.

Her brain fuzzy from either poison or Pietor's presence, she allowed her tongue free rein. "This isn't a trick, is it? You're not planning to drag me out into the woods, kill me, and leave my body somewhere for the vultures to feed upon, are you?"

He flinched as if she'd struck him. A flash of pain crossed his features, and he sighed. "That's exactly why we need to ride."

"Why?" On shaky legs, she took a step backward. Did she really guess his true motives? Had she inadvertently walked a straight line into his trap?

"Because there are things we need to discuss," he bit out. "Alone."

Alone. Shivers prickled her flesh as he strode past her, leading Dove from his stall. Alone, so no one could hear her scream? His insistence that she not ride her mare might be, as he'd said, due to her recent poisoning. But what if he wanted her to ride with him to lessen her chance of escape?

Her fears must have shown on her face because he softened his expression and his tone. "Keep faith with me, Chess. Please. I know you think I have no right to ask, but please grant me this one boon."

The plea touched her heart, and she nodded— hesitantly at first, but soon with more conviction. This was Pietor. Despite their differences, he would never harm her.

Would he?

No, she told herself firmly and promised to believe it.

Once they were outside the stables, he bent to give her a leg up into the saddle. After she settled her skirts, he mounted behind her.

"Shall we begin with a ride around the lake?"

His hot breath tickled her ear, and she shivered. Here she sat sidesaddle on Dove. Pietor's thighs rubbed against her calves. His arm gripped her waist, and she had to fight the urge to lean back against his chest for support.

"Chess?" he prompted. "Does a ride around the lake sound pleasant to you?"

His closeness left her too shaken to speak, and she nodded. He clucked the reins, and they headed off toward the farthest end of Lake Matya where the water bordered the dense Amatian Forest. The sun's rays broke in and out of the trees, dappling light and shadow on his face as if some invisible sprite drew attention to his strong chin, straight aquiline nose, and that regal brow.

Once they reached the clearing, Pietor pulled Dove to a halt. He dismounted first, then placed his hands upon Chesna's waist to assist her out of the saddle. Instantly, that familiar heat from his palms seared her.

If Pietor had the same reaction, he hid it well. His face never registered any emotion. "I don't know how you feel," he said as he placed her on the ground, "but the delicious smells coming from inside our dinner sack are making me lightheaded."

Is that how he felt? Hungry? Nothing more? She kicked an errant stone with her toe, wishing it was his heart. Everywhere she looked was a memory. And all he thought about was his stomach.

"Shall we eat here?" His cool conversational tone sent a spike through her spine.

If she spoke her wishes aloud, she'd spew bitterness and he'd discern her true feelings. Instead, she nodded.

He settled the bag on the ground near a fallen log at the edge of the forest. But Chesna remained rooted, silently hoping the ground would disappear beneath her feet and catapult her into some bottomless pit.

Shadows of the past locked within the trees around her screamed the truth, a truth she didn't want to face.

At the tender age of five, she'd first met a brooding boy by this lake's edge, a boy who'd just lost his mother and hated the world. His melancholy touched her, and after their first conversation, he'd stolen her heart. Twenty years later, he still had her heart. He'd *always* have her heart. And he didn't care.

"Chess? Come sit down." He patted the rough surface of the log in invitation.

On hesitant steps, she walked toward him and sat. While Pietor busied himself with Urszula's culinary efforts, she looked up at the cloudless blue sky then down again at the scenery around them.

If she ignored the enemy encampment, which lay to the east, civilization seemed miles away. Behind them, thick leafy trees held branches that reached high enough to touch heaven. The lake's aqua surface shimmered beneath the rays of the sinking sun. Beyond the lake, far off in the distance, the range of purple and white mountains speared the sky, a spiny backbone between Amatia and Napoleon's ultimate goal, Russia.

A late July afternoon in Amatia meant no breeze. Not a sound broke the humid stillness except the buzz of insects. Air, stagnant yet sweet with the scent of ripened fruit, lingered on her tastebuds to whet her appetite.

"Are you hungry?" Pietor handed her a thick slab of oat bread with maple butter.

"Mmm-hmm," she admitted and took a healthy bite from the bread. Her tastebuds popped at the sweet treat, and she reached for a handful of cherries. With a little food in her belly, she found the courage to ask the question burning in her mind. "Pietor? Who do you think tried to kill me?"

"I wish I knew." He held out a joint of quail.

That quickly, her appetite fled, and she held up a hand to decline his offer.

He quirked a brow, then bit into the quail himself, chewed, swallowed. "Unfortunately, our visit to the kitchens did nothing to confirm or deny any suspicions I might have had."

"But you believe it was one of the servants at the palace," she persisted.

"I'm not certain what to believe anymore."

Confusion muddied her thoughts. "I thought you suspected one of the kitchen servants. Isn't that why you flirted so outrageously with Urszula? To find out what she might know about the culprit?"

He tilted his head, stared at her hard, a smug smile playing around his lips. "You sound jealous."

"Of Urszula? Ridiculous." A heated flush crept into her cheeks. The sun. The sun burned far too hot here in the afternoon. "I'm merely curious about why you behaved so strangely while we were in the kitchens."

His gaze held hers for a long uncomfortable minute while she steeled herself not to squirm. Finally, he returned his attention to his meal. "Well, at first I thought it must be someone who worked there. It made sense, don't you see? The culprit must have access to your food in order to poison you. But now I'm not so certain. Our visit there only proved how easy it would be for anyone to slip in, tamper with the food on your tray, and slip back out with barely a notice from the other servants. Everyone is far too busy with their chores to pay attention to what anyone else does."

"Wonderful," she remarked acidly. "So we still have no way of knowing who would wish to poison me."

He leaned closer, picked up her hand, squeezed her fingers. "Think, Chess. Think about everyone with whom you've come into contact recently. Has anyone seemed angry or secretive around you?"

She narrowed her eyes, tried to focus on every person she'd spoken or dealt with in the last several weeks. But, by the rood, she'd spoken to *so* many people! Between the

Women's Council and the funeral and the French invasion, where would she possibly start?

On a deep sigh, she shook her head. "I honestly don't know. If I believe you, someone whom I've known all my life wants me dead. I have nowhere to turn and no one in whom I can trust. I'm surrounded by enemies on all sides. Do you have any idea how that makes me feel?"

For a long moment, he said nothing.

She watched the sunlight play upon the surface of the water, glistening like diamonds atop the bright blue surface.

"Yes," he said at last, never turning his gaze from their surroundings. "I do know how you feel."

"I doubt that," she retorted.

He finally faced her, eyes alight with a glint of silver. "Ask me why, Chess."

She blinked. "What?"

"Ask me," he repeated. "Ask me why I stopped writing, why I abandoned you, why I've come back with an army intent on destroying Amatia."

Her throat tightened, and her mouth dried to dust.

"You've wanted to know from the moment you clapped eyes on me in the grand hall that morning. And now, I'm willing to tell you. All you have to do is ask me."

The intensity of his expression rang alarm bells in her head. Did she want to know? Yes. No. Both. Her belly flipped. "Maybe—"

"Ask me, Chess," he urged.

Her lips formed the syllable, but her tongue refused to allow the word to escape. Finally, on an exhale, she pushed out the question, a whisper of air. "Why?"

"Because I was working with your father."

21

Burning fury infused Chesna from head to toe, and she shot up from the log to glare down at Pietor. "You're a spy?"

Her shout startled a nest of starlings from a nearby tree. Pietor, the lying scoundrel, had the nerve to duck at their sudden squeals. If only she could command them to peck out his eyes and pull out his tongue. "Why didn't you tell me?"

While the birds flew off in a huff, he raised a hand against her righteous outrage. "Hush, Chess."

"I will not hush. Not until you answer my questions."

He shook his head. "No."

"No?" Her hands fisted at her sides.

"Not yet."

"Oh?' Blood pounded in her temples as she struggled to rein in her runaway temper. "When? If not now, when? When I'm dead?"

"Chess," he said, his hands extended in supplication. "I'm sorry. But I can't tell you anything more right now."

"Why not?"

"Because it doesn't concern you."

She gasped. "Are you mad? How can it not concern me? You were spying for *my* father."

"Keep your voice down." He swiveled to study their surroundings. "I would hope we're alone out here, but we still have to be careful."

"I don't care if Napoleon Bonaparte himself hears me," she retorted. "I'd like to scream the trees down on your deceitful head."

He had the audacity to sit there, placid as the lake, while she seethed. And much as she wanted to scream the trees down, his calm response stole her fury. More's the pity. She preferred rage to tears. Her emotions churned faster than a spinner's wheel, and she sank onto the log to regain her balance.

"I don't understand you anymore," she said with a deep sigh. "A long time ago, you confided everything in me. Then after a few months in St. Petersburg, you disappeared. And now you've returned—a stranger."

"It was never what I wanted, Chess."

Her heartbeat slowed, and the pain of devastating loss crushed her. "I wrote you so many letters, asking what I did to anger you, why you suddenly stopped writing. And you never once answered. You forgot all about me. Just as I always knew you would. All for some misguided quest for glory."

"That's not true. I didn't intend to become involved in espionage when I first left Simion. My main goal was to complete my studies and return to you, as I'd promised."

Tears skimmed her lashes, and she blinked to remove them. "What changed your mind?"

"One night, at a student rally for Napoleon, I stumbled onto some very crucial information." He held up a hand to stem her interruption. "Don't ask me for the details. I can't tell you. At least, not yet. All I can say is that it wasn't something I could ignore or walk away from."

"All those years I thought you hated me, or found someone else to love, or *died*! And the entire time, you were in contact with my father, but ignoring me. Why didn't you just tell me the truth?"

Pietor shrugged. "Your father forbade me."

"My...?" She longed to deny it, couldn't bear to think her father could betray her so horribly. But, her father always put Amatia first. As he'd often told her, *Sometimes, a select few must suffer great pain to improve the lots of the masses.* Before now, however, she'd never been part of the select few. Desolation swept over her. She folded an elbow, perched her chin atop her fist. "Papa never understood how much I loved you."

"He understood all too well how we felt about each other," Pietor replied softly. "But my information was bigger than us. Bigger and more dangerous. He didn't wish for my activities to somehow cause you harm."

A bitter laugh burst from her lips. "And your sudden abandonment didn't cause me harm? You broke my heart!"

"Maybe," he admitted with a frown. "But that pain was temporary. Once you realized I was truly gone, you made a new life for yourself. That was what your father intended. Bela knew if my secrets were discovered, innocents would die. Therefore, the fewer people who knew the truth, the safer we all were."

She remembered the shadows in Prince Milos's eyes, the times she'd sought him out to learn if he'd had any news regarding Pietor's whereabouts. And all the times the prince would sigh and shake his head in despair.

"What of *your* father?" she pressed. "Did *he* know what you were about?"

Pietor's eyes flashed steel. A trick of the light?

"No," he bit out.

Her brain buzzed with questions, each one louder than its predecessor. "Why didn't you tell me the truth when you returned to Amatia? My father was dead. Your loyalty to him was at an end."

He shook his head. "My loyalty was never to your father. My loyalty is to Amatia. Your father's death didn't release me from my duty. All it did was remove the one person from my life who knew the truth. And since the danger still exists, it was better if you despised me."

"Why?" Dizziness assailed her again—her constant companion lately. She clutched at the folds of her gown, seeking something tangible and logical to hold onto. "I don't understand any of this. Why would you want me to despise you?"

"For my own protection," he admitted. "I'm a decorated officer in the French army and a sworn enemy to Amatia. If you were to look at me as anything else, General de Valmiere or one of his underlings might become suspicious."

"You might have confided in me," she said with a toss of her head. "Do you have any notion how it feels for me to know you didn't trust me? All these years..."

Pietor reached out a hand to chuck her chin, but she pulled back.

"No."

She couldn't allow him to touch her. Not yet. On trembling legs, she rose again and headed to the edge of the woods. When he tried to follow her, she waved a hand. "Stay there. I want a few moments of privacy."

♥

Chesna walked deep into the forest before turning and heading back to the lake. She looked to her right as she entered the clearing, but the thick copse of trees directly in her line of vision made it impossible for her to see where Pietor sat. That satisfied her. If she couldn't see him, he couldn't possibly see her.

Her mind flitted from one thought to another like butterflies flying from flower to flower in the meadow. But her thoughts were not as bright and beautiful as butterflies.

Pietor was a spy. He hadn't fallen in love with someone else. No, he'd turned his back on her for the good of the country. As a Dubrow, Chesna was raised to understand such sacrifice. To understand, appreciate, and feel proud that Pietor had shown such devotion to Amatia.

But she didn't understand, appreciate, or feel proud. She felt...

...jealous.

In fact, she hated Pietor for his choice—hated her father, too. Hated them both for every day she'd spent not knowing, for every sleepless night, for every tear she'd shed.

A primal need to shriek her outrage roared through her like a bolting stallion. But she didn't dare, not with Pietor so close. Then again, if she didn't vent her frustration through voice, the tears would come.

Pietor. A spy. And he hadn't trusted her enough to tell her the truth. Yet, he expected her to place blind loyalty in him.

Of course, for the moment, she had no choice but to trust him. She'd given her word to do so, swearing on the soul of her late mother. Meant for only the most serious of promises, their special oath grew from secrets whispered in their innocent childhood years. Secrets she still kept to this day.

But there were other secrets, too. Secrets she hadn't shared with him. Could she blame him for his deception while still deceiving him?

She had to keep her faith with him. But that little voice of doubt niggled her brain, refusing to stay silent.

On a disgruntled sigh, she walked to the lake and knelt at the edge. Hands cupped together, she scooped up fresh water to apply to her cheeks and forehead. The coolness soothed her tensions. A water turtle popped toward the surface, no doubt intent upon basking in the late afternoon sun. She leaned closer to touch its hard shell. Why couldn't people have such armor to protect themselves? Particularly to protect their hearts?

With no warning, a tremendous weight pressed against the back of her neck and plunged her face into the water. She struggled against whatever held her under, but could not raise her head. Her arms windmilled. Her legs flailed. To no avail. Dull thuds echoed in her ears, the sound of her hands hitting the lake's surface again and again and again.

The water quickly filled her nose and inched its way toward her brain. Her head throbbed. Clawing for a hand hold, her fingers found a patch of reeds. But when she gripped them, the brittle stalks broke apart, fragile and useless. Her chest burned for air.

The weight on her neck pressed her deeper beneath the surface and her forehead scraped the gritty bottom of the lake.

Help. Oh, God. Someone help me. Pietor!

But because of her stubborn insistence on gaining some privacy from Pietor, he couldn't see her from behind the copse of trees. Unlike the poisoning incident, there would be no timely intervention. If she didn't raise her head out of the water soon, she'd be dead.

Fight back, her brain screamed over the frantic drumbeat in her skull. *You must protect Zarek. Without you, he'll become easy prey.*

And Pietor! Pietor would never know how much she'd loved him, that she still loved him, that she'd never stopped loving him.

She should relax, conserve her air and her energy. Although she tried to make her legs and arms stop thrashing, sheer terror urged them to fight harder against whatever held her pinned beneath the water.

The throb in her head intensified to a fiery burn, only matched by the pain in her chest.

Oh, God. She was going to die.

Just as her body began to accept her fate and stop struggling, the weight suddenly disappeared from her neck. Still crouched on her knees and elbows, she hoisted her face up out of the water and gobbled air until she choked. Coughing and sputtering, she crawled away from the edge of the lake on trembling limbs.

At the first line of trees leading to the forest, she collapsed, face down, on a bed of pine needles.

Only then did she hear the voice call, "Chesna!"

22

"Chesna!" the voice called again.

Pietor.

"Chesna!" And Karol.

Blessed relief poured through her. Alive. She was still alive. Water rose in her throat and a violent fit of coughing shredded her already too-raw throat.

Barely alive, she amended. But alive, nonetheless.

"Chesna!" Pietor burst from the line of trees and collapsed at her side. "Oh, God, Chess, I'm so sorry."

"You should be, Pietor," Karol grumbled as he came into view from the other side of the clearing. "What happened? I thought you were going to watch out for her."

"Not...his...fault," she managed. Her throat opened, ready to retch, but she swallowed hard. One vomitous episode in front of these two men would suffice for a lifetime.

"Tell us," Karol demanded. "What happened?"

"I was...bending...over the lake." The coughing overtook her again, her face inches from the ground as she choked and gasped for air. Pietor knelt closer, but she waved him off in case she lost control of her stomach. She had to keep him out of firing range. "Someone pushed something heavy against my neck."

"What was it?" Karol pressed.

"I don't know. It might have been a hand. The weight forced my head under the water."

"Did you see anyone nearby?" Pietor asked. "Or hear

anything?"

She shook her head. "It happened too quickly."

Karol turned accusing eyes to Pietor. "Where were you while she was fighting for her life? Again?"

Pietor pointed to the heavy trees that blocked him from their picnic spot. "On the other side of the clearing. She wanted a few moments of privacy, and I gave it to her. Why are *you* here? I left you to take care of Zarek while we were gone."

"I came to find Chesna. It was time for Zarek to say his prayers, and he wanted her to hear him."

"Please," she murmured as she struggled to rise. "Take me home." She faltered yet again, almost spilling into Pietor's lap.

And once again, he managed to catch her, cradling her close enough that his heartbeat echoed her own as he assisted her to stand. She steadied herself by wrapping an arm around his neck for support. Concern etched his brow. His warm hand cupped her nape, fingers kneading her sodden hairline.

"Ahem!" Karol cleared his throat, his frown emanating disapproval in steady rays. "Zarek is waiting, Chess."

Shakily, she unwound her arm from Pietor. "Zarek needs me," she mumbled, her senses in an eddy. "I must go."

"Very well," Pietor said. "I'll bring you back to the palace."

But Karol reached out, grabbing Chesna's hand and yanking her away from her husband's side. "No, *I* will bring her back to the palace."

Pietor pulled her back against him. "Don't be ridiculous. My mount is tethered near those trees." He pointed again at the copse. "I could have her back at the palace in no time."

Karol nearly dislocated her shoulder on his next tug. She cried out, but neither man heeded her.

"Or you could leave her to die," Karol suggested.

Pietor inhaled sharply. "Are you accusing me of having something to do with what happened to my wife?"

Simultaneously, they dropped their hold on her to clench fists at their sides. Meanwhile, Chesna, left to flounder on her own, fought the waves of dizziness drowning her sense of balance.

"No, I'm accusing you of neglecting her so that her assailant could attempt to kill her again," Karol said through gritted teeth. "If I hadn't walked in this direction from the forest, her attacker might have succeeded while your back was turned. Luckily, the villain heard my approach and was frightened away."

"How do you know he was frightened away by *your* approach?" Pietor retorted. "Did you see her attacker?"

"No." A flush crept into Karol's cheeks. "I saw no one."

Chesna's gaze swerved back and forth between them, which only made the world tilt at a more acute angle.

"I find it very strange you happened to be strolling through the forest when someone tried to drown her. It's quite a coincidence, isn't it?"

"Is it?" Karol folded his arms over his chest and glared at Pietor, hostility like fire in his eyes. "You were the one who discovered the foxglove in her wine goblet. And I arrived here in time to find you kneeling over her at the edge of the lake."

"You dare to accuse me?" Pietor demanded.

"You dare to accuse me," Karol countered.

Finally, Chesna's perilous sanity could take no more. "Enough!" She stumbled between the two combatants. "I'll settle this right now. I'm taking Dove and riding back to the palace. You two *gentlemen* will walk there on your own. Perhaps the evening air will cool your tempers."

Satisfied she'd silenced them both, she staggered back to the tethered gelding and, with her strength already waning, managed to slowly ride the beast home.

Outside the mews, she dismounted and tossed the reins to a stable hand, with a quick murmur that Dove be returned to the stall assigned to Captain Gabris.

To avoid the scrutiny of leering French soldiers in her current state of dishabille, she slipped inside the palace through the rear entrance. While her slippers squished along the way, she dragged herself up the servants' staircase to the royal nursery. She reached the top landing and nearly upended Irina, on her way down with a bundle of linens in her arms.

"Chess?" the kitchen servant asked in bewilderment. "What happened to you?"

Chesna picked at the sodden folds of her gown. "I fell in Lake Matya."

"Oh, my," Irina gasped. "Were you hurt?"

"Only my pride," Chesna replied with a grim smile.

"Perhaps you'd like me to send up some of the kitchen boys to fill you a hot bath."

Chesna's patience, dangling on spider's silk, finally snapped. She shook out her head, allowing water droplets to splatter Irina's face and bodice. "Don't you think I've had enough water for one day, Irina?"

Face flushed, Irina dropped her gaze. "I-I'm sorry. I didn't think."

On a sigh, Chesna touched the older woman's forearm. "No, Irina. I'm sorry. I shouldn't have snapped at you. I've spent the last several days..." She bit off the rest of her statement, that she'd spent the last several days fighting to stay alive, and replaced the words with, "I'm very tired."

"Change out of that wet gown," Irina ordered softly. "You'll catch an ague if you're not careful."

An ague. Thank God she was too drained to laugh.

"Would you like me to have a tray brought up for your dinner?" Irina offered.

"No," she replied. "Thank you. I've already eaten tonight."

"Very well, then." Irina took the first step down. "Get some rest. Amatia needs your strength right now."

With a weary nod, Chesna turned and headed toward the nursery. Exhaustion stole the last of her energy as she entered the playroom.

"Mama?" Zarek's imperious voice called from his chamber.

"Yes, my darling."

"I'm waiting for you to hear my prayers."

"In a moment," she said. "I need to change my gown first."

Once in the privacy of her chamber, she managed to pull the wide strips of her bodice off her arms, but the under blouse clung tightly to her drenched frame. As if removing the skin from an apple, she peeled the sleeves away from her arms and then wriggled out of the blouse, petticoat, stockings and chemise. Stripped, she tossed all the soggy items into the cedar chest.

"Mama!" Zarek's demand rang in her ears. "I'm waiting."

"Just a few more minutes, Zarek," she called back with forced calm. "I'm changing my gown. I reek of horses after my ride with Pietor."

She'd never before lied to him. Guilt pierced her conscience, but she reminded herself that telling him the truth would only upset him. She didn't want to give the child nightmares. Quickly, she changed into a fresh gown, tied back her wet hair, and headed for Zarek's room.

She found him sitting up in bed, arms folded over his chest and an expression of supreme impatience on his royal face. "Shall I begin now?"

"Of course." She sat on the bed's edge and forced one last indulgent smile for his benefit.

And so he began. Chesna listened intently as he intoned his prayers, asking for God to watch over all the people who loved him, whether they were dead or alive. But tonight, Zarek added something new.

"Please, dear Jesus, help Pietor keep my new mama, Chesna, safe from the terrible person who wishes to kill her. I need her with me. You must not take her yet. Amen." He beamed. "All done."

Discomfort tickled her spine, but she leaned forward and kissed him goodnight. "I wish you sweet slumber," she murmured against his forehead.

He snuggled down beneath the bedsheet. "And you as well, Mama."

A nice wish. But with all the ugly thoughts racing through her mind, sweet slumber was impossible. She rose from his side and quietly left the room.

Pietor entered the palace with Karol still beside him. Neither had spoken since Chesna left them at the lake. When they reached the grand hall, they separated. With a terse nod, Karol strode toward the servants' quarters.

Meanwhile, Pietor climbed the staircase leading to the nursery.

Inside their chamber, Chesna, scrunched on the sill near the open window, dozed. She jumped awake at his entrance, her formerly relaxed posture turning rigid.

He approached her slowly, taking in the dark circles under her eyes, her pale complexion, the slight tremor in her hands. "How are you feeling, Chess?"

She sighed. "Considering all I've been through lately, I think I'm holding up quite well. How are *you* feeling?"

"Foolish for letting you out of my sight again," he admitted.

"Don't feel foolish. You couldn't know our poisonmonger would try again so soon."

"I should have. It's one of the reasons I took you to the lake."

"Strange. I thought you took me to the lake to tell me the truth about why you stopped writing to me."

Her brittle tone raised the hackles on his nape. If anyone stood beneath that window—a strong possibility— her comments would carry straight down. At least she spoke in Amatian, making them less likely to have their conversation understood. Still, they were never completely out of danger here.

"Not now, Chess," he whispered with a meaningful nod at her position.

But she was either too upset or too exhausted to heed his warning.

"If you didn't want me to question you, you should have kept your secrets to yourself," she retorted. "After all, years passed me by without a word from you."

He sank into the nearby chair. "I've already explained why I couldn't tell you."

She shook her head, her brow furrowed. "But even since your return, you've kept the truth from me. Until today. So, why? Why tell me at all? I've spent the last hour trying to figure out your reasoning. What am I missing?"

Her eyes pierced his soul, demanding the truth. Hell, she'd earned the truth. "These last few days'..." He swallowed the dread that rose in his throat. "...*events* made me reconsider."

Understanding eased the lines from her forehead. "You mean, in case I died."

A flush of shame infused him from head to toe. But he wouldn't deny her statement. "I owed you the truth," he murmured.

To his surprise, she nodded, a satisfied smile on her wan face. "So then I owe you the same."

"Chess," he began, but she cut him off with a quick hop from the sill.

Her legs wobbled slightly, and he reached out an arm to steady her, but she managed to straighten on her own. "I want no more secrets between us."

"You have no secrets from me, my dove. I know all there is to know about you."

Her eyes narrowed. "You may think you know me, but you don't."

Relief eased the tension in his shoulders. With one outstretched arm, he scooped her off the floor and pulled her into his lap. When she struggled to break away, he wrapped his hands around her waist to keep her put. "Believe me when I say that I know all your secrets. All of them."

She stiffened. "No, you don't."

"Yes, I do."

She shifted on his lap so her gaze met his. "No, Pietor, wait. I'm not talking about secrets from our childhood. I want to tell you things you couldn't possibly know since you went to St. Petersburg."

"You mean…" He nuzzled the crook of her neck, reveled in her clean, sweet scent. "…how you didn't eat or sleep for two weeks after I first left Simion? Or how your father obtained a position for you with Queen Jasia's retinue to help you forget me?"

"No."

He pulled away slightly to study her through narrowed eyes. "No?"

She dismissed his knowledge with a wave of her hand. "I wrote you about all that. Even if you didn't answer me, I assume you read my letters."

"And I know you read the ones I sent to you. In fact, I know you kept every word I ever wrote, until the day you realized I'd stopped writing to you. And then you burned every word I ever wrote in a tremendous bonfire in the meadows. It took fourteen servants to put out the blaze before it reached the forest."

A rosy blush bloomed in her cheeks. "Servants' gossip."

He bit back a chuckle. She still didn't believe him? Very well. He could supply all the details she'd need to see the truth.

"I know the queen trusted you implicitly and that she called you, 'Little Sister.' I know it was your idea to begin the Women's Council. You saw the hundreds of women clamoring to get close to the queen on her Coronation Day and suggested she might want to ask her new husband for several days a year to address the concerns of the female population. I know that, at every Women's Council meeting, you remained behind the curtain, dispensing advice to the queen as to how to handle each problem placed before her."

Her eyes widened, and her blush deepened to scarlet.

"I know in the last four years, six men have asked for your hand in marriage, but you turned them all down."

She sat bolt upright now, eyes rounder than the ancient shields in the grand vestibule. "How could you...?"

"I may not have written to *you* in the past several years, but your father and I communicated often. He wrote me about everything you did."

"Papa told you everything about me?" She leaned closer to repeat in a shocked whisper, "*Everything?*"

Pietor nodded.

Frowning, she shook her head. "He might have been my father, but he had no right to betray me that way."

"He had every right. I asked him, Chess. No. That's not quite true. I *begged* him to tell me. I needed to know you were well and happy."

"But I wasn't happy." She turned to stare out the open window, her tone mournful in her confession. "I was miserable. I thought you hated me. I never understood why you suddenly stopped writing, why you forgot me as if I were nothing more than a piece of dust that caught your eye and then floated away."

With two fingers on her chin, he redirected her teary gaze toward him. "I never forgot you. I promised you I wouldn't. I wrote you almost every day in the letters I sent to your father. Everything I did, everyone I met, and why I'd suddenly disappeared from your life. I didn't know if you would ever see them, but I needed to try to explain things to you, and hope someday, you'd know the truth."

"I never knew..." she murmured. "Papa never showed me anything."

"No doubt, because it wasn't safe for either of us. It still isn't. We can't know what truly lies in the hearts of others, even those we've known and trusted all our lives." He grimaced.

"So many secrets. And I've never noticed anything..." She shook her head slowly, and he sensed the doubts assailing her.

"There's still one secret of yours we need to discuss," he said with mock severity.

She tensed, eyebrow arched. "Oh?"

"Yes," he crooned in her ear. "I know your father ordered you to do everything in your power to protect Prince Mikhail from the French invasion. So you renamed him Zarek and have been raising him as your son."

23

Shock propelled her to her feet, but Pietor pulled her onto his lap again.

"You *know*?" The words erupted from her desert dry mouth as a harsh whisper. "How?"

A smug smile spread across his face and prickled her nerves.

"Because I know *you*, Chess. I already knew you were Mikhail's governess, and I knew you'd protect the boy with your life. Your father would expect nothing less from you. You were the one who pointed out the boy's likeness to King Jarek. A blind man could see the resemblance." He lifted her left hand, kissed the third finger where the gold band encircled her. "Your wedding ring gave me all the proof I needed."

On a gasp, she yanked her hand away, instinctively covering the telltale symbol in the folds of her skirt. "You recognized the ring?"

He laughed. "Do you really think me so oblivious? I know the Amatian royal signet ring. My father would allow me to wear his occasionally, but never in public."

"So I have no secrets from you? None at all?"

"Well, you may have one or two I've yet to figure out." He gripped her more tightly, as if he could squeeze the truth from her.

"Such as?"

His eyes hardened to flint. "Such as, when have you ever seen a grown man nude? And when has anyone made you melt with just a look from across a room?"

For what seemed like the first time in ages, Chesna smiled with real joy. "Why, Pietor. You sound jealous."

"Don't be absurd."

The smile broadened, and her heart lightened. He still cared about her. If his obvious jealousy didn't tell her so, the way he held her—with such ferocity—spoke volumes. His fingers lightly brushed her arms, invoking memories of long ago summer days when he'd trace her skin with the same lazy, sensual touch.

"You haven't answered my questions. Where and when, Chess?"

She shrugged. "From Karol."

"Karol?" He snorted. "Why in the world would Karol tell you about nude men and melting looks?"

"He didn't—not really. I mean, he tried to explain to me what I could expect from you on our wedding night, but..." She broke into a fit of giggles. "Oh, you should have heard him stammering and stuttering about urges and wifely duties. If not for our days in the forest, I wouldn't have understood a word."

"The nude men, Chess?" His brow furrowed, and a frown etched apostrophes in the corners of his lips.

She sobered at once. "I've only seen one nude man." Heat rushed into her cheeks. "You."

A curious mixture of relief and arrogance lit up his face. "And the looks that made you melt from across a crowded room?"

"I overheard Urszula talking one day. She said Karol could make her melt with a look from across the kitchens. Can you believe it? Urszula and Karol. Isn't that the most unusual pairing?"

"Never mind Urszula and Karol," he growled.

♥

For weeks, Pietor had endured sleepless nights of cold sweat and gritted teeth. He'd lain beside her and struggled against his need to touch her flawless skin. Now, he had the opportunity to indulge at least a few of his fantasies. The urge to savor the woman whose taste had lingered in his soul for nearly a decade almost overrode common sense.

Almost.

Be careful, his conscience warned. For his own sake as well as hers, he would have to maintain some self-control. When he drew her softness against him, every muscle hardened to hot steel. In contrast, she melted.

She sighed, a sound full of expectation, promise. And surrender. Slowly, like a drop of dew on a window, he rolled a fingertip down her cheek and jaw line. She shivered. The perfume of her skin, honeysuckle-sweet, enveloped him. The fire in his blood blazed higher.

While his palm cupped her chin, he used his thumb and forefinger to part her lips. With a slight tilt of his head, he covered her mouth with his own. She tasted like sunshine, warm and dizzying. The flames in his veins jumped in a frenzied dance. His heartbeat thudded.

When he'd kissed her on their wedding day, he'd managed to keep his passions at bay through anger, conscience, and sheer force of will. But in this one moment, seated on his lap in the plush armchair, Chesna broke through all his defenses to meld with him—one entity, one heart, one soul. He gave all of himself to her. And though she took him in, she gave herself in equal amounts.

For the last seven years, he'd starved for her, suffocated on her loss. But now he breathed her in, felt himself expand, relax, and still want more. His tongue swept inside her mouth, deepening the kiss. Pleasure rippled from the top of his spine to the cleft of his back, satin-soft but more powerful than a thunderstorm.

She moaned against his mouth, pressing closer, almost feeding herself to his hunger. Somewhere, somehow, logic returned to whisper new warnings in his brain. This was madness. With just a kiss, she'd transformed him from a rational man to a quivering lump of clay. He ran his hands through the tumble of silken honey curls that fell around her like a curtain. She reciprocated, her fingers skidding through his scalp. Desire warred with common sense but finally, he settled his hands on her shoulders and reluctantly released her lips from his.

Awareness came slowly for her. She blinked once, twice. Then, eyes closed, she bent backward far enough to crack her spine, no doubt to allow him access to her throat and bosom. God, how she tempted! On a deep sigh of regret, he kissed her eyelids one at a time.

At last, she opened her eyes. Confusion clouded her face. "Why did you stop? Did I do something wrong?"

He stifled a chuckle. "No, my dove. You did everything right."

"Then why did you stop?"

Need burst inside him, a hunger to possess her. He shifted in the chair, sought some release from her sweet torment. "God, Chess, you're the most alluring woman I've ever known. But if I don't stop kissing you now, I won't be capable of stopping later."

She grinned wickedly. "Good. Because I don't want you to stop. So...kiss me again." Wrapping an arm around his neck, she pursed her parted lips a whisper away from his mouth.

"No," he said firmly and peeled away from her, nudging her off his lap. "I can't."

♥

"Do you want to drive me mad?" Frustration exploded from her mouth in a foot-stomping outburst. "Damn you, Pietor, make up your mind about us. I love you!"

From the sudden way his mouth dropped open, she surmised she'd surprised him.

He scrubbed his slack jaw. "*Do* you?"

She collapsed at his feet and wrapped herself around his legs, her head pressed to his knees. "I've always loved you. From that first day when I risked Urszula's wrath—not to mention your father's—to feed you, you've been the dearest person in my life. The only man I'd ever love. And well you know it. So kiss me and don't stop."

He shook his head. "I can't, Chess."

She opened her mouth to argue, but his upraised hand cut her off.

"I love you, too. Surely you believe that now. And I want nothing more than to throw you onto that four-poster bed and kiss every inch of the flesh I bare as I remove your garments, piece by piece."

Her flesh crackled. Did he want her permission? Didn't

he understand how much she desired him? How long she'd waited? She sighed. "I've waited far too long and I'm far too old to play the trembling virgin, Pietor. I may be a maid, but that doesn't mean I don't feel the same urges as you. I don't want to wait any longer to consummate the pledges we made. And what's more, there's no need for us to stop. We're officially married, our union sanctified by Father Grigory with a half-dozen witnesses. So kiss me again, and let's follow that kiss to its natural end."

To her surprise, no relief etched his features. If anything, the worry lines in his brow deepened. "I desire nothing else as much," he murmured while his fingertip kissed a gentle line down her cheek. "But I can't make love to you."

Realization struck hard, and she gasped as she clutched his hand in a desperate grip. "Oh, God! You've been hurt? That's why you've avoided the marriage bed? All those insults about tasting your uncle's leavings? You were trying to hide the truth from me." She rose, tugged at him to follow her. "It doesn't matter. We can simply lie together in the bed. Perhaps, we can find a way to—"

He laughed. "Sweet Chess, you can still surprise me."

She drew back, hands fisted at her sides. "I show my concern for you and you mock me?"

"No." His tone grew tender, a husky promise of love. "Never. Forgive me for laughing at you. I'd almost forgotten how candidly you see the world."

"I-I don't understand."

"Then allow me to elaborate. There's nothing physically wrong with me. I can't make love to you *because* you're still a maid."

Heat seared her cheeks all the way to the hairline. "But, I waited for you. As I promised I would." Tears of frustration and confusion stung her eyes, and she rubbed them away with her fists. "Even when I had no way of knowing if you'd ever return, I never went back on my word. I couldn't give myself to anyone else until I knew for certain you were out of my life forever. And so I waited for you."

"I'm thrilled you waited for me. Thrilled, touched, honored, and so damn in love with you I ache with the need to make love to you night and day. But, for now, we have to continue to wait."

"What on earth for? I've waited forever for you. I'm tired of waiting."

"Chess, my dove, please. Listen to me. The Opal Palace is not the safe haven we thought it was when we were children. There are some very dangerous people residing within these walls. And not all of them wear uniforms. I'm not merely speaking of the scoundrel who's made two attempts on your life, though we must certainly add him to the list of scurrilous villains in our midst."

Exhaustion, emotional and physical, took hold and refused to let go. The tears broke through her carefully constructed dam and flooded her cheeks. "I still don't understand what any of this has to do with you and me finding pleasure in our rekindled love." But she did know. She sighed her disappointment. "Papa always tried to convince me to accept one of the gentlemen who had asked for my hand, but I wouldn't. I swore on the soul of my late mother I would wait for you. And so I waited. And waited. *And waited.* And now, we're to be punished because I'm not who your general and his men think I am."

His frown deepened. "I'm sorry, Chess. You began the charade that you're Zarek's mother. Which led to your marriage to a French soldier."

"Not just any French soldier." She stabbed her index finger toward him. "You."

"And I thank God every day for that boon. Though I'd swear poor Bela, God rest his soul, must have interceded on our behalf. But even Bela couldn't clear all the obstacles for us. You can't be Zarek's mother if you're a maid. Isn't that why you tried to keep me from bedding you on our wedding night? To prevent my learning the truth?"

"But you *know* the truth."

"And General de Valmiere does not. We may have sorted out our own differences today, yet nothing else has changed. You know how servants gossip."

"Zarek." An invisible icy hand clutched her heart, and she shivered. "We have to protect Zarek."

"And ourselves."

On a sigh heavily laden with regret and wistful, wicked wishes, she nodded in surrender.

Pietor loved her. He hadn't forgotten her. The rest could wait.

24

Pietor lay beside his wife in their bed and cradled her close. Thank God she'd seen reason. He should have realized she would understand the ramifications. He'd always admired her clever mind, her grasp of politics and history, her logic. "Have you ever considered espionage, Chess?

She shivered against him. "Good God, no. I wouldn't make a good spy. I'd be found out too quickly."

"I disagree. You have a way of calling attention to yourself, yet distracting your enemies from learning anything of import from you. I've watched you again and again these last few weeks—how you protected Zarek from the general, your work on the Women's Council, even your subterfuge with me—you have a chameleon aspect to you. Only the best spies do. Your father had that talent. No doubt, you absorbed a great deal of skill from him without ever realizing."

"Perhaps," she replied noncommittally as she snuggled closer to him. "But I could live without such talent."

He kissed her forehead. "You're not enjoying this adventure?"

"No, but thank you all the same. This isn't a game, Pietor. Every day I grow more aware that my actions affect lives, one very important life in particular. I'll see this subterfuge through to the end because my father would expect nothing less. But once Napoleon Bonaparte has been sent packing from our peaceful province, I don't want any more intrigue in my life."

He stiffened at the passion in her tone. "There will always be intrigue around the throne, my dove. You know that."

"I know," she replied, "which is why I decided long ago we should live in America."

Hope sparked, and he pulled away to study the intentions in her eyes. "You'd be willing to leave Amatia?"

"Not now," she said on a husky sigh. "Not while Zarek needs me."

Zarek. Of course. The hope that had temporarily lightened his heart disappeared. Zarek would always remain the one blight on any golden future for them.

Her fingers trailed his jaw line, traced the edge of his face, grabbed a hunk of short hair, and yanked. "Pay attention, Pietor."

"Ow!"

While he rubbed his abused scalp, she smiled. "Eventually, Zarek will no longer need me. And when that day comes, I'll go to America, provided my husband and our dozen children are with me."

"A dozen?" He quirked a brow. "Shouldn't we have *one* first?"

"We can start with one. But I want a dozen in total. Neither of us had a sibling. I want a large family so none of our children ever feel alone. And we're already years behind schedule, thanks to *your* espionage adventures. But now that you're home again..." She let the thought trail off and sighed happily.

Pietor didn't share her joyous view of the future. "Both your mother and mine died in childbirth, Chess," he reminded her.

"As did poor Queen Jasia." She shook her head. "But I won't."

No, he supposed she wouldn't. Death had already tried to steal her away from him twice. Without success. The Chesna he knew would not relinquish her life easily. Of course, should she ever attempt to surrender, he'd take up the sword in her defense.

"By the way, Pietor," she murmured. "Once Bonaparte's men have been defeated in Moscow, there'll be no more intrigue or espionage for you, either. You won't leave me a young widow with a dozen of your children to care for."

He couldn't fight the smirk that twisted his lips. "Are you saying you couldn't keep twelve of me in line?"

His gaze swept her swollen lips, tousled hair, and the loosened strings of her bodice—when had *that* happened?

To his delight, her cheeks pinkened and her glare softened to the adoration he recalled from their youth. She pressed against him, head tilted, staring into those silver eyes alight with magic in a shaft of moonlight. "I love you, Pietor Gabris."

"I love you, Chesna Gabris." His index finger traced her lips with a slow, deliberate touch.

"I've never stopped loving you," she countered.

"Not even when I'm wearing a French army uniform?"

"I far prefer you without any garments at all to the garb of a French soldier," she replied with a grimace. "But even then, you're not ugly. I love you regardless of what you wear. Besides, it won't be for much longer now. Once de Valmiere and his soldiers have left for Moscow, you and I will finally have peace in our lives. Knowing my subterfuge is temporary, I can carry on feigning hatred toward you for a while longer."

His heart sank. Why did he have to tell her now? But to avoid the truth would be the worst kind of betrayal. He inhaled deeply before plunging into the thick of battle. "You're forgetting one thing, my dove. When de Valmiere and his soldiers leave for Moscow, I'll be going with them."

The color drained from her face as she pulled away from him, sitting up. "No."

He shook his head. "You must have realized—" But, no. Why would she? She had no idea why he'd begun this charade. Didn't know the threat to all she held dear.

She folded her arms over her chest. "I won't allow you to go."

"It's not up to you, Chess."

Her eyes glittered like a cobra's just before it strikes an unwitting victim. "Still chasing after glory, Pietor? When will you have had enough of your mock heroics? When you're dead? When *I'm* dead? How much more blood must spill before you'll give up your games of espionage?"

"I've already told you," he said softly. "My continuing this intrigue has nothing to do with mock heroics or glory."

The first tear escaped, slipped down her cheek. "Then why?" Her voice cracked. "Why must you continue?"

"I can't tell you." Not now, when she was already overwrought.

Her spine stiffened as if he'd slapped her. "I see. Even now, you don't trust me." She dug for her shoes among the bedclothes, found one, slipped it on her right foot with the ferocity of a Valkyrie.

The tears fell in earnest now, sliding down her face like spring rain.

"Please don't cry," he said.

"I'm not crying," she retorted, but she quickly averted her face to stare out the window at the ash trees cloaked in shadow. "Only cowards cry. And I'm not some weak-minded child to use female hysteria as a weapon. I'm a logical, rational person."

"Then you know that I must go to Russia."

"And *you* know as well as I that Napoleon Bonaparte's armies will be defeated in Russia. He cannot hope to prevail against the tsar's forces. Don't you understand? If you go to Moscow, you may very well die there."

He placed his hands on her shoulders. Her tremors radiated through him. "I will come back to you, Chesna. I promise you." Leaning forward, he placed his palm before her face. "I swear on the soul of my late mother, I will return to you."

She stared at his hand with open disdain, and then shrugged out of his hold. After two wobbly steps away from him, she swayed before falling to her knees. "I lost you once," she whispered hoarsely. "And it nearly destroyed me. I can't bear to lose you again. Please don't leave me again."

He knelt beside her, cupped her chin in his hand, and locked his gaze on hers. "After all we've gone through to be together again, do you think I want to leave? I've never wanted to leave you. Not for St. Petersburg, not for the French army, and not now."

She yanked out of his grasp. "But you did leave me for St. Petersburg." She punched the floor. "You did leave me to join the French army." Another punch. "And now you'll leave me to go to Moscow." And once again.

Before she used her fists on him, he grasped her hands to stem the tide of her anger. "I have to see this game through to the end, regardless of the consequences. It's my duty."

"It's idiocy," she snapped. Slowly, she rose, looked down upon him with derision. But her voice when she spoke again, was softer than kitten's fur. "If you leave Simion with your French army, I won't be patiently waiting here at the palace for your return, Pietor. Make this choice very carefully. Go away again, and don't expect that I'll be standing at the threshold with open arms when you finally decide to give up your foolishness and come back to me. Come home in a coffin, and I won't be here to bury you."

He narrowed his eyes. "Are you threatening me, Chess?"

She laughed, but the sound held no humor. "No, Pietor, I don't make threats. I make promises."

Color high with her fury, she turned on her heel and fled out the door.

Quick on her heels, he followed her down the hall and to the stairs until she reached the bottom landing. When she stood in the foyer, he grabbed her arm and turned her to face him. "Dammit, Chesna, I will have the final say."

A pair of sentries near the double-doors that led outside turned and gawked. One poked the other in the ribs. "That's her."

She ignored them and focused her fury on her husband. "Then you'll have to find someone else to argue with. Because I refuse to continue this discussion."

With her chin high, she stormed past the gawking armed guards and pushed out the door.

♥

Chesna managed to keep her inner turmoil in check with fisted hands and ramrod posture. The sentries on duty flashed tight lips, no doubt in an attempt to hold back their smirks. With an impudent head toss, she marched straight out to the meadows. Despite the cloak of evening, reminders of her helplessness assailed her. Tents, soldiers, garbage, and buzzards all loomed in the shadows. Nowhere to run.

God, how she wanted to cry. Instead, she fisted her hands until her fingernails dug deep enough to draw blood. Focused on the pain in her palms, she forced herself to think of simpler days. Unfortunately, the most blissful days of her life had always included Pietor. Damn him!

The hair on her nape rose seconds before he touched her shoulder. The air thrummed with violent energy. A red mist floated before her eyes, washing the soldiers and tents with imaginary blood. Every nerve inside her stretched taut as she struggled to hold the tears in check. She didn't turn to face him.

"Dammit, Chess," he muttered, his voice an angry bee in her ear. "Why must you be so difficult?"

Without moving, she replied, "I'm not being difficult. You are. I'm trying to stop you from getting yourself killed."

"You're behaving like a spoilt child."

She whirled to face him then. "I am not." Hands still balled into tight fists, she swiped at her cheeks.

"Yes, you are. A grown lady would use a handkerchief." He flashed a grin no doubt meant to charm her.

Charm had disappeared from her moods years ago, never to return. "If you find this impasse humorous," she said with frigid control, "you're a fool."

He took her trembling hands in his. But she yanked away, slamming her knuckles on the lintel behind her.

She ignored the pain, too intent on the desolation in her heart. "Seven years," she stated flatly. "Perhaps for you, our separation was easy. A lark. After all, you knew where I was, what I was doing. You knew I was safe. You knew I was *alive*. I had no such consolation. I've lived in an agony of uncertainty since your last letter." The tears flourished, and she blinked to banish them. "When weeks passed with no word from you, I thought I had done something to displease you. Weeks turned to months, and I assumed you'd fallen in love with someone else. Then months became years. All I could think was that you'd died. And I found myself enshrouded in this half-life, as if I'd been wrapped head to toe in some strange mourning veil."

His face clouded. "I'm sorry, Chess."

She slapped his shoulder, spitting fire. "Dammit, I don't want your apologies. I want your promise that you won't go to Moscow." Pride no longer mattered—if indeed, it ever had. The realization pounded her into the ground, and she sank into a puddle of skirts, hands outstretched in supplication. "Please. We've only just found each other again."

"For God's sake," he exclaimed, taking a step back. "Get up before someone sees you."

She touched her head to his boots. "Don't make me watch you ride away from me again."

"Don't ask me to make a choice."

"Because you'd choose Amatia over me. Over us."

"No," he replied softly as he lifted her to her feet. "I need to protect Amatia from Napoleon's greedy ambitions before I can devote my life to you and our dozen children."

Rage bit her heart, tearing off pieces slowly, painfully. "I don't care one whit about Napoleon's ambitions." She yanked off her slippers and hurled one toward his sanctimonious head.

Pietor easily sidestepped the missile.

"He can set his sights on hell, if that's his wish," she continued. "I just want him to leave us alone."

She drew back her arm to fling the other shoe, but his quick grip on her waist halted her forward momentum.

"This is why your father insisted you remain ignorant of my situation," he said. "He knew you'd become too emotional."

Kicking and thrashing against him, she allowed her fury full power. "I'd wager neither my father nor you could have survived what I've suffered through these last few weeks."

"You're right." He released his hold on her waist, then took her hand and gently kissed her knuckles. "Come along, Chess. Let's go back up to bed."

A scream of frustration swelled inside. Did he think to cajole her into blithely accepting his decree? With a deep, painful swallow, she pasted a sultry look on her face. Allowing her slipper to dangle from her fingertips, she rose and slinked toward him.

Lips pursed, she bent close enough to his ear that he

might hear her every inhale and exhale. "Go to the devil."

In a wide arc, she slapped the back of his head with her shoe. Her spine snapped to rigid, and she turned away from his outraged expression. "Right now," she said as she strode away from his odious presence, "I feel the dire need for a bath. Afterwards, I plan to sleep in the nursery with Zarek. I suggest you bar your bedchamber door if you don't wish your compatriots to know you weren't able to beat me into submission tonight."

25

In the morning, Pietor woke up alone. Chesna's side of the bed remained empty and cold. No creases in her pillow, no scent of her skin in the air. No surprise, he thought as he swung his bare legs off the mattress. His obstinate wife would grant him no quarter.

He understood her anger, if not her behavior. After all, he didn't have rocks for brains. Much of what she railed about last night struck fertile ground and took root. He *had* sentenced her to a half-life, what with his sudden and complete disappearance.

He'd never made peace with the thought she might fall in love with someone else. Thus, he'd kept her beholden to him on the slim hope they might one day be reunited. Perhaps, in hindsight, he should have released her from the promises they'd made before he'd left for St. Petersburg. Or found a way to contact her, despite Bela's demands. To be honest, growing up in Opal Palace as the only son of a prince hadn't exactly prepared him for the possibility he couldn't have everything he wanted, regardless of time and distance. Or that his wants didn't necessarily take precedence over someone else's feelings—not even those of the woman he purported to love beyond measure.

But he'd learned his lesson. Too many years in Napoleon Bonaparte's army had removed any lingering feelings of entitlement. Except, however, where Chesna was concerned. She was *his*, dammit! Had been since that first afternoon at Lake Matya when she'd brought him a meager bundle of food from the kitchens. He'd tried to deny the power she held over him, had attempted to lose her memory in other women, in warfare, in espionage. Always, his thoughts—his *heart*—cried out for her. As the years had passed, his need had never weakened, had in fact, intensified. Until their reunion here, drenched in the blood of people they'd both loved, had tainted his dreams with stark reality.

She loved him. He'd never doubted the depths of her feelings for him.

He sighed. Poor Chess. No matter how painful she found the realization that he'd leave her to travel to Moscow, he'd suffer more. Having only rediscovered her, he dreaded the day he'd march away from her. Again. Risking death for an ideal that, quite frankly, turned his stomach. Again.

On a growl, he shoved thoughts of his demise into the darkest corners of his mind. He'd faced his mortality often over the last several years. Their marriage only made the end more disheartening.

After he'd washed and dressed, he slipped into the nursery. Zarek slept in his draperied, immense royal bed. Chesna, always the loyal subject, had curled up on the floor, the slipper she'd slapped across his head now wedged beneath her ear as a makeshift, shabby pillow.

Conscience warred with justice. He should wake her. God knew she'd eaten barely enough to sustain a sparrow lately. And a lot of the food she'd swallowed hadn't stayed in her stomach for long. Not to mention, sleeping on the floor would leave her stiff and sore.

Drawing on old memories, he considered his late father's method of dealing with stubborn children. Withhold food to weaken a stubborn will. Effective, but cruel. Pietor had no intention of starving Chess to regain her cooperation, the way Prince Milos might. No. Before heading to the dining hall, he'd stop in the kitchens and make sure Urszula hand-prepared a meal for her. Since he couldn't be certain their poisonmonger wouldn't make another attempt, this plan actually worked in his favor.

Besides, his obstinate bride was no child, easily swayed by an empty stomach. She'd see reason on her own. Soon enough, her aching muscles would dictate she return to sleeping in a bed. *Their* bed. Beside him. Where she belonged.

Leaning over the royal mattress, he clamped a hand on Zarek's shoulder and gave him a rapid shake. The child's sooty lashes fluttered, and he sat up with a wide yawn.

Pietor pressed a finger to his lips. "Not a sound," he whispered. "Mama's asleep."

Zarek leaned forward and rubbed his fists over his eyes, then stared at Chesna's place on the floor. "Don't wake her. She cried herself to sleep last night."

Guilt heated the back of his neck. "I know."

"I thought you might." That cool, royal countenance flickered over Pietor's face, as if scanning him for physical flaws. "Do you know why?"

Unbidden, his gaze dropped to the carpet. Incredible. In an instant, beneath that intense scrutiny, Pietor went from hardened soldier, *man*, to cringing fool, *child*. "We had a disagreement," he murmured.

On a sigh, Zarek threw up his hands, then slapped the silken sheet. "Have you forgotten what I told you about Mama? How clever she is? How you should heed her advice? What did you say to her now?"

Royal blood or no, unless the boy suddenly donned a priest's collar and stole, he would not bare his sins to a five-year-old.

"I'll apologize to her later," he said instead.

While he slid out of bed, Zarek cast another glare in Pietor's direction. By God, the child's frown could freeze the sunburned meadows. "See that you do."

All through the morning meal, Pietor watched the servants closely for any suspicious activity. His focus honed in on Monika, the newcomer. He considered her arrival— less than a week before the first attempt on Chesna's life— too much of a coincidence to ignore. This morning, she fawned over Zarek, who was seated on his right. The pretty blonde took every opportunity to hover near the boy, constantly filling his plate or goblet. If she continued indulging him much longer, the child would waddle away from the table like a stuffed goose.

Around him, the officers discussed strategy and their plans to move on toward Moscow in hushed tones over the soft clink of silverware on plates.

"Tell us, Gabris," the general's voice boomed from the head of the table. "What happened between you and your wife last night?"

Lost in the flurry of different conversations, as well as his own thoughts, Pietor whirled to face the general. Meanwhile, his brain scrambled to catch up. "Sir?"

"The night sentries reported a disturbance between you and your wife. Care to elaborate?" His eyes glittered like onyx.

All attention swerved to him, and silence reigned at the dining table. Even Zarek wore an expectant look.

Pietor forced his body to relax, despite his stiffened spine. "Nothing to elaborate on, sir," he replied blandly. "She dared to challenge my authority and was suitably punished for her actions."

"By...?" The general leaned forward, as if he hoped to hear details before anyone else.

"After a good solid reminder about who was master in our marriage, she slept on the floor."

"Like a dog?" Major Roucher exclaimed then burst out laughing. "Splendid work, Gabris. Splendid, indeed."

"Indeed," the general agreed. "And now I'd like to discuss another issue with you. I've received word from Grand Equerry General Armand de Caulaincourt. We leave for Moscow in three days' time. What do you think about taking the boy with us? As a bargaining chip."

"To Moscow?" Bile rose in Pietor's throat, and he swallowed hard.

"Bah!" Montfort cut in. "Bargaining chip or no, he'd be a hindrance. A five-year-old boy on campaign? What's next? Babes in nappies? With wetnurses?"

"Your opinion has already been noted, Montfort," the general barked. "I'm asking Gabris what he thinks. After all, he's spent the last few weeks in endless company with the child."

Pietor stole a glance at Zarek, noted the boy's sudden

pallor and terrified eyes. The same horror whirled in his head. "I'm not sure what you mean by bargaining chip, sir."

"Major Roucher suggested we bring him with us so that when we drive Tsar Alexander to his knees, we can toss the child beside him. Kill two birds with one stone, if you will."

To stifle the outburst of rage welling inside, Pieter bit into a strip of crisp bacon. "To what end, General?"

"Why, to make his humiliation complete," Roucher retorted. "What better way to prove King Jarek's failure to protect his province than to drag his only living issue kicking and screaming through the streets of Moscow?"

Oh, dear God, no! Chess would never let them take Zarek. She'd kill the boy herself first. Or die trying. An icy fist clenched his stomach, twisted.

The bacon reversed direction, but he swallowed hard and maintained his banal tone. "You'll forgive my impertinence, sir, but I grew up in the foothills of the Carpathians." *At least, for the first eight years or so.* "Those mountains are treacherous—even in the summer. I don't doubt we'll lose some hardened men on the journey to Moscow. And now, you wish to risk the life of this *very special* pawn to gloat at the end of the game?" He cast a meaningful glance at Zarek, who sat stock-still, eyes round and unblinking.

de Valmiere appeared to digest this opinion, along with an enormous slab of hamsteak. While he stuffed his cheeks like a squirrel storing food for winter, deafening silence reigned at the table. Finally, he chewed, swallowed. "An excellent point, Gabris." He pointed his knife, dripping cream sauce, at Montfort. "More convincing than *his* argument. But then, Montfort hates children."

"Who doesn't?" another officer chimed in.

While around the table, chuckles and guffaws erupted, Pietor seized his opportunity. Rising, he bowed first to the general, and then to the majors. "By your leave, sirs. It's time for the boy's lessons."

The general, still consumed with laughter, waved a beefy hand in dismissal.

Montfort stayed his exit with a quick grip on his sleeve. "A word, Gabris," he murmured around a bite of sausage. "One night's sleep on the floor like a dog is enough humiliation for the daughter of a man still revered within these walls. Don't overstep your influence. With mere days until we leave for Moscow, we can't afford for you to lose your focus right now. Do I make myself clear?"

Despite a dozen different emotions tumbling inside his skull, Pietor managed to remain calm. "Yes, sir."

Pulling out the boy's chair, he helped Zarek to stand. On a nod, he strode with the boy from the dining hall. Neither spoke until they reached the grand vestibule.

"Pietor?" Zarek whispered. "Should I be afraid?"

Keeping his gaze on the array of shields and spears on the walls, Pietor replied, "Your father would counsel you to remain courageous, but keep your senses alert to danger. I would add one further caveat to that advice. No matter what happens, until your life is secure again, trust no one except the one you call Mama."

Zarek tilted his head, his expression perplexed. "What about you, Pietor? I can trust you, can't I?"

"God, no," he growled. "I'm the *last* person you should ever trust."

26

Late morning sun blazed across Chesna's swollen eyes, and she cupped a hand over her brow to shield them from the blinding light. She'd spent the night on the floor in the royal nursery, stewing over the stubbornness of men— particularly the man she'd married. For hours in the dark, her mind concocted arguments, sane and logical, to dissuade him from his reckless intentions. Now, she needed to confront him again, somehow make him see reason.

Despite stiff limbs and an aching back, she pulled herself into a sitting position against Zarek's footboard. Her muscles screamed in agony. She barely remembered falling asleep, what with her eddy of thoughts to drown out slumber. Yet, morning had clearly arrived, ready to punish her with another day.

What kind of torment would the next several hours bring?

"So," a feminine voice said from the doorway, "it's true then."

She looked up into the sharp eyes of Irina. Wonderful. Only awake a mere moment, and already trouble sniffed at her heels, a hungry wolf intent on her destruction. "What's true?"

The serving woman tiptoed into the nursery, a bundle of linens tossed over her arms. "That your husband beat you last night and made you sleep on the floor like a dog."

Outrage stole her breath, but not her voice. "Who told you such a falsehood?"

Irina placed the clean sheets at the foot of Zarek's bed.

Zarek's *empty* bed. "I overheard Captain Gabris in the dining room boasting to the officers."

Chesna felt the insult like a slap. Her cheeks burned with humiliation. "H-he s-said that?" Hands gripping the post of the royal bed, she pulled to a standing position. No child's head lay upon the satin pillow. She whirled to face Irina again. "Where's Zarek?"

"With the captain, as always. It's nearly mid-day. You missed the morning meal. Would you like me to bring you something?" Irina took a tentative step closer and brushed a lock of hair from Chesna's face with a tender touch.

She flinched away from the sympathetic tone, raised a hand. "Don't, Irina. Please."

A frown marring her features, Irina pulled back. "I'm sorry. How badly are you hurt? Should I send for the physician?"

Hurt? Physician? What exactly was Irina saying? Something about Pietor telling the soldiers he'd beaten her? She couldn't think. Needed to clear the fog in her brain and study this latest information with clear common sense. Had Pietor really uttered vile lies to his compatriots? How had he known she'd slept on the floor?

Zarek. Pietor must have come into this room to fetch Zarek this morning. Or Zarek had gone to Pietor when he woke and mentioned she'd slept on his floor.

Unless Irina concocted this story? But if so, why? What could Irina possibly gain by making her believe Pietor would debase her for the delight of his superior officers? Nothing.

No. One look at the concern in Irina's sharp gaze conveyed the truth of the matter.

Shame heated her flesh from the inside out. Why? Why on earth would he humiliate her in this manner? Yesterday's events replayed in her mind. Logic hastened to remind her of their heated debate in front of the night guards. Obviously, the general or someone else at the table, having learned of their disagreement, demanded details this morning.

But, honestly. Her husband couldn't devise a more credible excuse than that he beat her and made her sleep on the floor? A better tale would have been that Zarek awoke from a nightmare and she remained in his chamber to comfort him. Anyone with sharp eyes would notice she didn't bear a mark upon her person, which would immediately brand him a liar.

By God. Her husband must be the world's worst spy. How in the world had he managed to avoid discovery all these years with such transparent veils as his disguise?

His words tolled like church bells in the steeple of her memory.

You have a way of calling attention to yourself, yet distracting your enemies from learning anything of import from you. I've watched you again and again these last few weeks—how you protected Zarek from the general, your work on the Women's Council, even your subterfuge with me—you have a chameleon aspect to you. Only the best spies do.

Strange how he didn't follow her example. Unless...

Suspicion coiled in her belly. What if she were the fool? What if he'd lied last night to gain her cooperation? To lull her into trusting him and only him? After all, what exactly had he told her yesterday? A few facts he might have learned from casual conversation with any servant?

Except for the information about Zarek. But if he recognized her wedding band as the royal signet ring, he could have easily pieced together the child's true identity.

In fact, he'd held so much back. But she'd urged him on, clinging to him with her need for his love, for the attentions of a man who'd once written sonnets to the hue of her eyes.

Oh, God. Had she fallen prey to a few pretty words and some echoes of long-gone love? Like the same pathetic child who'd doggedly adored him from their very first meeting?

She sank to the floor again, and a groan of despair escaped her tight lips.

"Poor chick," Irina crooned and settled beside her with a swish of muslin skirts. "They married you off to a monster. It's my fault. I'm so sorry."

Chesna barely heard Irina, couldn't register the apology, with her brain's reproof ringing in her ears. She'd played into his hands, offering herself *and all her secrets* like a collapsed dam. Then, in her supreme moment of stupidity, she'd relinquished her bedchamber and slept on the nursery floor!

Oh, how he must be laughing at her this morning. Besotted fool! Lovesick idiot!

"...and I can help you." Irina's last statement broke through her self-recriminations.

What? What did Irina say now? She blinked, shook her head slowly. "I'm sorry. Help me? Help me do what?"

The serving woman leaned closer, eyes feverishly bright. "To escape. You and Zarek. You have to leave the palace before he kills you. Both of you."

Escape?

Too many sleepless nights, too many attempts on her life, too many lies wrapped around her brain, making clear thought impossible. "I-I'm not certain I understand."

"Zarek is half Lithuanian, Chess," Irina hissed. "You and I could smuggle him out of the palace, bring him to his grandparents. They'd keep him safe."

"Are you mad?" Chesna scooted away from Irina's dark whispers and stopped only when her back painfully met the corner of the bed's hand-carved mahogany column. "Even if I were to consider such a scheme, how on earth would we slip away from de Valmiere's guards unnoticed? Not to mention the trip to Lithuania. I sincerely doubt we'll be able to travel in the royal coach. Two women and a five-year-old child walking hundreds of miles? With no escort? No protection? No money?"

"We'll steal the coach," Irina suggested. "And I hid some of Jasia's jewelry before the bastard French found it. The queen would want us to use her gems to keep her son safe." Her voice buzzed in Chesna's ear. "We could be gone before first light tomorrow. Let them think we're fleeing to Tsar Alexander for aid. Surely the others here will help lead them off our trail. For heaven's sake, everyone in the palace wants to protect you and Zarek."

No. Not everyone.

Memories of her brushes with death clogged her mind. Opal Palace was not the same safe home she'd always known. Danger lurked at every turn. Hadn't Pietor warned her? Or did he simply want to leave her with no one to trust? No one to trust except for him?

She rose on unsteady legs. Doubts assailed her,

constricted her breathing, paralyzed her from taking any action.

How on earth could she know what was truly in Irina's heart? Or anyone else's, for that matter? Even Pietor's? Where could she find the truth?

I wrote you almost every day in the letters I sent to your father. Everything I did, everyone I met, and why I'd suddenly disappeared from your life. I didn't know if you would ever see them, but I needed to try to explain things to you, and hope someday, you'd know the truth.

Of course. Papa's letters. An excellent place to start.

"Irina," she said. "Forget your ideas of escape. Zarek's place is here, where his father and grandfather and great-grandfather ruled. General de Valmiere and his men won't remain in Simion much longer. They've set their sights on Russia. Somehow, I'll find the means to keep Zarek safe until they leave."

Irina stood, smoothing wrinkles from her skirts with her palms. "But at what cost, Chess? What if your husband beats you to death? Where will Zarek be then?"

To appease the older woman, she smiled, but couldn't force any warmth into the expression. "In that respect, allow me to ease your troubled mind. Pietor may do many things to hurt me, but he won't kill me."

I'll kill him first. Especially if I discover he's played me false. Again.

"If you'll excuse me," she added, "I should dress and go about my duties for the day." Hands fisted at her sides to prevent Irina from seeing them tremble, she strode from the nursery.

The moment she stepped into her own chamber, she headed straight for the jewelry box atop her armoire. Scattered among the simple bits of gold, she found what she needed. Soon, she hoped, she'd have the answers she sought.

She'd barely left the doorway when she practically fell over Irina who was leaving Zarek's room.

"Chess?" Irina stopped short. "Is something else amiss?"

She cleared her expression to reveal nothing of what went on inside her head. "No. With Zarek spending all his time with Pietor, I find myself with empty time on my hands. If you'd like to leave the linens outside the door, I'll see to setting my chamber to rights."

"Nonsense." Irina shifted the bundle of linens she carried and, with a hand wrapped around Chesna's upper arm, attempted to drag her back into her room. "After what your husband put you through last night? You should rest. In fact, let me straighten your bed first. Then you climb between clean sheets while I tidy up."

Chesna held back. "I...um, that is..." The older woman's kindness overwhelmed her, and words failed.

Irina clucked her tongue. "Just look at those shadows under your eyes. I'll wager you haven't slept well since they married you to that beast. You put yourself in my care for a while."

The offer tempted sweeter than Eve's apple. But Chesna dared not surrender to the lure. With time running out, she couldn't afford to spend the day in bed. She had other sins to commit today.

Like espionage.

♥

Pietor had hoped to see Chess when he brought Zarek to the nursery for his nap after lunch. If for no other reason than to ease his conscience about letting her sleep on the floor all night. Instead, he ran into someone else, who was leaving the boy's chamber as they entered.

"Karol!" Zarek raced to the red-haired servant and captured him by his narrow hips.

Karol's eyes widened in horror as he stepped out of the boy's exuberant embrace. "S-sir, please." He took another step back and caught Pietor's scrutiny. Instantly, his expression turned to stone-wall. "Gabris," he grumbled.

Pietor mirrored the expression, but in his gut, rage simmered in a pool of mistrust. "What are you doing up here, Karol?"

"I wanted to talk to Chess."

"Oh? Planning to disclose more secrets?" He thrust enough steel into the questions to get a porcupine's back up.

"Of course not," Karol snapped. "I saw her earlier and remembered something I wanted to discuss with her. I came up here, assuming I'd see her. But apparently she hasn't returned to the nursery yet."

Without another word, Karol strode down the stairs.

Suspicion whispered in Pietor's ear, but he forced his questions about Karol's true motives into the back of his mind. First he'd see to Zarek's nap, and then he'd pursue his own intentions. For now, Karol would remain low on his list of suspects—mainly because Bela had placed so much trust in him.

Nudging Zarek toward his own room, Pietor dared a sweeping glance into the doorway to the governess's chamber. He didn't need to step inside to know his wife lingered nowhere nearby. Disappointment sank his spirits. The soft wood furnishings and pale colors reflected less light without her presence. Her scent, sweet and innocent as honeysuckle, barely tinged the air, like a long held memory. And who knew more about long-held memories than he?

Zarek perched on the edge of his bed and kicked off his shoes with matching thuds. "Where's Mama?" A slight catch in his voice suggested growing concern.

Pietor tread carefully, both physically and verbally, as he neared the boy's bedside. "She missed both the morning and afternoon meals. I wager she's in the kitchens convincing Urszula to prepare her something to keep her belly full until supper."

The boy tilted his head, giving Pietor the royal scrutiny once again. "Truly?"

Damn. Apparently his longing to see his wife affected him too deeply to hide. Somehow Zarek sensed the lack of confidence in his statement.

"Truly," he said with more conviction than he felt. To refocus the boy's attention, he flipped back the bedsheet and slapped a palm on the feather pillows. "Get some sleep. I'm sure your mama will be back before you wake again. And I promised you a fencing lesson after supper. But only if you take your nap now."

Stripped to his underdrawers, Zarek scrambled into the bed and pulled the sheet up against his chest. "Very well. *If* you read to me first."

Pietor stifled the urge to roll his eyes or make excuses. The future king of Amatia would brook no argument. Although time poured through his mental hourglass at an alarming rate, he loosened his posture and feigned complete ease.

"Very well." He phrased his reply with the same authoritative tone the boy had used. "What shall I read?"

"*Antigone*. In Greek, of course."

He stretched a hand to the bedside table and lifted the book to leaf through the pages. "Of course."

27

After fumbling through another excruciating translation of *Antigone*, Pietor strode to the other bedchamber. The room was immaculate. And empty. On a disgruntled sigh, he stepped out into the hall. What to do? He should seek out Chesna. They still had a great deal to discuss—most importantly, his plans for the next several weeks. Besides, he didn't like her roaming the palace alone with a would-be assassin lurking nearby. But, other responsibilities tugged at his conscience.

In the meadows, the general and his henchmen put the troops through their paces to prepare for the upcoming trek across the Carpathians. Which meant now was probably the last chance Pietor would have to search Bela's old rooms without risking discovery. He'd waited too many years for this day, for a chance to glean any information that could help lead him to the identity of the traitors inside this place. He couldn't allow this opportunity to pass.

Perhaps, if he didn't tarry too long, he might be on the fields before Major Montfort noted his absence. Or he might persuade the major he was delayed due to some difficulty with Zarek.

On the other hand, Chess's continued distance itched his spine. Dammit, he shouldn't have left her asleep when he took Zarek from the nursery this morning. Then she would have broken her fast with everyone else, and he would have some peace of mind right now.

He stood at the top of the stairs and considered his

destination. Bela's study? Or search for Chess? But was she really in any danger? Surely she understood the need for caution around the rest of the palace.

No doubt the tale he'd woven for Zarek came a hair's breadth from the truth. She probably woke on the floor in the nursery—stiff and hungry. Since she hadn't opted for a more comfortable bed, she must have gone in search of food. And during that time, apparently she and Karol had disagreed again. If he knew his wife at all, he understood that after any heated disagreement, the last place she'd seek refuge was the first place anyone would look for her.

Decision made. He'd risk a quick visit to the study, in the hopes he could find the information he sought quickly. Then, he'd fetch his wayward wife from wherever she'd hidden herself and continue their discussion. To hell with the rest of his unit. He'd suffered through enough battle exercises. And no one in a French uniform knew the Carpathian Mountains better than he did.

Once on the second level of the palace, he crept through the vestibule and down the long hall. Intent on his goal, he ignored the portraits, the armory, the chatter of servants in the distance. Senses on full alert, he slipped into the last room on his right and closed the door with a light snick. Even before he turned, the hairs on his nape alerted him to her presence. And then that sweet scent of honeysuckle tickled his nostrils. Tension melted, but suspicion flourished in its place.

"Chess?" he hissed into the darkened room. "Where are you?"

Nothing stirred.

"I know you're in here." He allowed frustration to lace his tone. "Don't make me rip this room apart to find you."

On an exasperated sigh, she crept out from beneath the hand-carved desk in the corner. Rather than the guilt he expected from her, she propped her fists on her hips and glared unflinchingly at him. "How did you know I was here?"

He ignored the question, unwilling to admit he'd stumbled on her completely by accident. "What in blazes are you doing? You do realize if anyone else had caught you in this room, you'd be tossed into the dungeon before you'd have a chance to voice any explanation."

She gave him a disgruntled look. "I should imagine you might suffer the same fate. Why are *you* here?"

"I've been looking for you."

Her disbelief erupted in a snort of expelled breath, and her jaw released its hold. "You tiptoed in on cat feet, Pietor. Which tells me you hoped to be alone in here. But somehow you knew I'd hidden behind the desk once you closed the door." With one finger dancing over the barren desktop, she inched sideways, out of reach. "What were you really looking for? Shouldn't you be with my son?"

"Your son is napping. A fact you'd well know if you were in the nursery right now, where you should be." He closed the gap between them in two strides, trapping her between his expectation and the mullioned window. No escape. "You missed the morning and afternoon meals. And you're far too thin as it is. I want your word that you'll go straight to the kitchens and have Urszula give you something to eat. Something heartier than bread and cheese."

"How did you—?"

He cut her off with an upraised hand. "By Jove, Chess, you look like I could blow you over if I whistled."

"I don't—"

Again, he thrust the hand forward to halt her argument. "After you eat," he continued as if she hadn't interrupted, "heed your son's fine example and take a nap. Not on the floor, but in our bed. Where you belong." The image flared his desire, made him painfully aware of her nearness, the soft scent of her skin, the curves at her hips, the swell of her bosom. A slow ache built in his mid-section, and his center throbbed with need.

He ran a gentle fingertip down her arm, and she snapped away as if he'd burned her.

"I appreciate your concern, Pietor, but you should worry more for your own welfare than mine. After all, you intend to ride away from me one of these coming days. And you and I both hold little hope you'll return alive."

Reality slammed him out of his dream world. So she knew about the general's plan. Still, that didn't explain the icy rage she blasted at him.

"Then satisfy a dying man's curiosity," he stated flatly.

"Tell me why you're in here."

"This was my father's study, a room where he spent a great deal of time." She flipped a golden tress over her shoulder, and he instinctively rubbed his fingertips—as if he'd touched the silken hair himself. "I was hoping to find some truths in here."

He bit back a laugh. How ironic. Despite all their years of separation, they were still of like mind in so many ways. "I thought you were content to leave the espionage to me."

"Perhaps you thought once you managed to manipulate me into sleeping on the floor like a dog, I'd blindly accept your version of the truth. Because you've always been so honest with me."

Gripping her wrist, he studied her a little more closely. Had hunger driven her to madness? But no, her eyes, though spitting sleet, appeared lucid. "I've never lied to you, Chess."

Her quick, deep inhale suggested she intended to argue, but he pressed his fingers to her lips.

"Listen to me. I've kept things from you—for your own safety. But I swear, no matter what you might have heard to the contrary, I have *never* lied to you."

God, how she wanted to believe him! The little girl who'd always loved him longed to believe they could conquer their enemies together. She would fight all the demons in hell with the old Pietor at her side. This new Pietor, this spy, this French soldier, still filled her with doubt, despite his pretty words and gentle manner.

"I need you to stay strong, my dove," he whispered as if he sensed her thoughts.

The tone of his voice, a soft caress, was probably meant to muddle her thinking.

"Promise me you will leave this room this instant, go straight to Urszula for a hearty meal, and then upstairs. I want you to get some sleep. In our bed."

The demand roused her ire. Did he think he was the only one who could dictate terms? She folded her arms over her chest. "And I'll do as you say only *after* we discuss your plans to abandon me for Moscow."

"There's nothing to discuss, Chess. I'm still beholden to Major Montfort, General de Valmiere, and Napoleon Bonaparte. To refuse to go to Moscow would be seen as an act of desertion, which would only *guarantee* my death. Until I'm officially released from service, where my superior officers command, I go."

A cry of frustration escaped her self-control. "Why aren't you beholden to me? You married *me*."

"Only because the general ordered me to."

His harsh admission sliced her heart in half. Her knees buckled, but she hugged herself tight enough to crack her spine. "And if the general had ordered Major Roucher to wed me, you would have allowed it?"

A guilty flush stained his cheeks, and she needed no other answer.

"Very comforting, Pietor."

He had the nerve to throw up his hands in defeat. "What did you expect me to do? Declare to the general that I'd been in love with you most of my life and wouldn't allow any other man to touch you? How could I? Do you have any notion of the general's first idea for Zarek? I walked in to find him planning the boy's murder."

Chesna gasped as chills rippled down her spine. "W-what? I don't understand."

"You established the boy as yours. And de Valmiere knew who you were. He saw you as a threat to the easy transfer of power he'd anticipated in Amatia. The general, Major Montfort and Major Roucher were discussing ways to be rid of both you and Zarek when I walked into the grand hall."

Her mouth dried to dust, but she rasped, "What did you do?"

"I told them about Amatia's ascension laws, suggested they'd be better served by using Zarek as a political pawn. They agreed, but only if your influence on the boy could be diminished."

"By marrying me off to one of the general's trusted men."

"Lucky for both of us, Montfort pointed a finger in my direction as a potential bridegroom," Pietor concluded.

"After reminding Roucher he was already married."

"You mean...?" Acid roiled her stomach. "That glutton actually...? And you would have...?" The acid rose, searing her throat, drying her mouth and tongue. The urge to retch overwhelmed her, and she turned away from him. Strong sunlight transformed the usual colorful gardens outside the window into a sheet of white. "How could you?" The words came out a rasp. "You would have sacrificed me to save yourself?"

"Never. But I didn't believe a marriage between us would benefit Zarek. Or us, for that matter. I'm still not certain it was a wise choice."

His breath brushed her nape, but she refused to face him. Couldn't bear to see whatever emotion he expressed. Pity? Resentment? Disgust?

"Please, Chess. Trust me."

At last, she leveled her attention on her husband. The intensity of his mercurial eyes sparked in her belly.

"Chess." He leaned forward until she could almost taste his lips on hers. "If I don't come back from Moscow—"

"Don't." Yanking her wrist from his grasp, she sank against him. "Don't say anything."

Gently, he nudged her away. "Go. Before someone finds you in here."

"What about you?"

"I'm hoping your father might have left a message for me here, and this is my only chance to search." With a heavy sigh, he shook his head. "Hopeless, I know. Even if your father had been foolish enough to leave anything behind, the general would have discovered it by now."

Perhaps.

Or perhaps not. The tiny key tucked into Chesna's bodice burned like a brand. *Not yet*, she told herself. *Not until you're absolutely sure you can trust him.*

♥

Food held no sway over Chesna. Regardless of Pietor's directives to the contrary, her stomach would have to wait until her heart was appeased. In the doorway to her chamber, she paused to catch a steadying breath. Nerves jumped and skittered beneath her flesh but she still managed to register how well Irina had put her room to rights.

The bed was made, down pillows aligned and fluffed, waiting for someone to sink into the feathery softness. As alluring as the bed looked, she had no intention of heeding her husband's demand—not yet. Her brain would not rest until she found some answers.

Surely, her father had kept some of the correspondence he and Pietor had shared. And if he did, knowing Napoleon's eyes had turned toward Amatia, Papa would have found a way to inform her.

She waited at the window until Pietor came into view outside. Assured she had some time to herself, she again headed downstairs to her father's study. The hall was clear, and she slipped inside like smoke. The room was dim, but she needed no light in here. She knew every fiber of carpet, every inch of furniture, and every book on the shelf. Of all the rooms in the Opal Palace, she'd spent most of her time in this one, listening to her father, watching her father, and learning about Amatian royal business from her father, day after day.

On instinct, she headed straight for the massive desk and crawled beneath. Due to the darkness, she struggled to fit the key into the nearly invisible lock on the inside panel. Eventually, metal slid into metal. With hope rising, she pulled open the secret door. She prayed as she reached inside and felt around. Her fingers brushed velvet, and she smiled. Just as she thought.

Papa had left answers to her questions.

She could hardly believe her luck. After stuffing the cloth-covered missive in her bodice, she relocked the desk's hidden door and ran her hand around the seam to be certain the niche could not be discovered. Satisfied, she crept from under the desk and slowly opened the study's door. Male laughter tickled her ears, and she quickly—quietly—closed the door again.

She waited, her heartbeat pounding against the velvet bundle, until the laughter and voices died down. At last, quiet resumed its place in this part of the palace, and she tiptoed from the room to the staircase. Giddy with excitement, she raced up to her chamber, eager to read whatever information her father had hidden away for her.

28

Once inside her chamber, she locked the door and settled on the bed atop the quilted counterpane, her back ramrod straight against the pillows. With shaking hands, she removed the packet of papers from inside the velvet.

The very first letter, written in Pietor's familiar scrawling script, cracked her heart in half.

Dear Chess,

How I wish I could tell you why I haven't written you in many months. And it may be many months before I am able to write to you again. Please know that I have not forgotten you. There is no woman in St. Petersburg, painted or otherwise, who could steal my heart from my sweet dove. I pray for a speedy end to what is occurring here so that I might fly back to your side. Wait for me. I beg of you.

—September 3, 1806

Tears sprang to her eyes, but she sniffed them back as she fumbled with the thick, yellowed pages in search of the catalyst that persuaded Pietor to join Napoleon Bonaparte's army as a spy. Perhaps, later, she might indulge her heart's desire to immerse herself in every word Pietor had written for her. But not now. Now, impatience pushed her fingers faster, eyes scanning minor details about the sights of St. Petersburg, his studies, and the continual plea that she wait for him as she'd promised she would before his departure from Simion.

Do you recall how you often dreamed of life in America? Dare I hope, if I asked, you would accompany me to that foreign land? Forever?

—November 21, 1806

Yes. Of course. If he had to leave Amatia, she'd be right by his side. No matter where he went, she'd follow. Surely he understood that. Love like theirs deserved to grow in a new world—safe from intrigue and espionage.

"Mama?" The plaintive cry from the room opposite her chamber snapped her back to reality.

Zarek. By Jove. Her heart split down the middle: one half devoted to her husband, the other to the child she'd loved since the moment of his birth.

She couldn't leave Zarek. She'd promised to stay with him until he no longer needed her. Which explained why Pietor attempted to keep her at a distance after their marriage. Particularly since he knew Zarek's true identity.

"Mamaaaaaa…" The whine behind the words brought Chesna to her feet immediately. Zarek never whined unless he didn't feel well.

"Coming, Zarek." She reorganized the letters, slid them into the velvet sack, and stashed them in her armoire—with a promise to find a much better hiding place as soon as she'd seen to whatever ailed her boy.

When she reached his doorway, she registered the pained expression on his face, the lines in his forehead and the way he squinted in the dim light from the adjacent window.

"My head hurts, Mama."

She sank onto the bed beside him and placed a kiss on his forehead. Cool flesh touched her lips, and she drew back to look more closely at him. No fever, but his pupils were smaller than usual in his silver eyes.

"Close your eyes and I'll rub your temples until you fall asleep again," she suggested.

"No." He struggled to sit up, folded the sheet over his waist, and crossed his arms over his chest. "My head hurts too much to sleep."

"No doubt your head hurts because you haven't slept

enough."

He peered at her more closely through his squinting eyes. "Does *your* head hurt?"

"N-no." Did he see something on her face? "Why?"

"You didn't sleep well last night. And I wonder, does your head hurt?"

She stifled the relieved sigh rising to her lips and offered a comforting smile. "No."

"Then perhaps my head hurts because I've slept too much."

On a giggle, she threw her arms around him and squeezed. She'd missed his clever mind, missed their hours together, his endless questions, and quick wit. Soon the French would leave this place and she would have her prince back.

Except...

Her happiness withered and died like a fragile crocus caught in late frost. When the French left Amatia, Pietor would go with them. Quite possibly, he'd die before he returned to her.

♥

After an hour of drills and weapons inspections, Pietor went straight to the kitchens. As expected, Urszula confirmed his suspicions that Chesna had not appeared there in search of food. He ordered a meal prepared—by hand by Urszula—and carried it upstairs himself on a tray. If necessary, he'd sit beside her and force feed her every drop of the hearty beef broth with plump dumplings. Beside the bowl of soup sat a think chunk of brown bread slathered with honey.

But when he reached the governess's chambers, he saw no sign of Chesna, although the creases in the counterpane suggested she'd lain atop the featherbed recently. He knew exactly where to look next. He returned to the nursery. Sure enough, he found Chess, asleep, beside her charge. Zarek, however, sat alert and ready.

With a smile, Pietor placed the tray on the bedside table, then pointed a finger at the boy. "*You* were supposed to sleep."

"I did, but I woke with a headache. Mama came to rub my temples for a while. She fell asleep, so I let her alone."

"You didn't tell her about the general's discussion, did you?"

Chesna rolled over and opened one eye. "What discussion?"

Damn. His brain scrambled for a lie.

Before he could devise a credible story, Zarek blurted, "The general wants to take me to Moscow."

"No!" Both eyes opened wide as Chess bolted upright and grabbed the boy to shield him in her tight embrace. "I'll take him to Lithuania first."

"Lithuania?" Pietor blinked.

Of course. Queen Jasia had come from Lithuania. Just like her father, Chess would leave nothing to chance. She'd already begun making plans to take the boy and run. Foolish. She'd get them both killed.

"You will not take him on that campaign to death, Pietor," she said, her tone iced steel. "If you wish to die for the glory of France, I can't stop you. You will not drag my boy with you."

He wished he could reassure her. Perhaps, though, she'd better prepare herself for any eventuality. "The decision's not mine to make, Chess," he replied. "I did, however, give sound advice to the general against such an idea, but ultimately, the choice is his."

"And once again, you'll stand by and let such an atrocity happen? Why? How can you convince yourself any harm to Zarek would be for Amatia's benefit?" Arms still clutching Zarek in a near death grip—a hold the boy emulated on her as well—she leaned forward. "How long do I have?"

He knew what she asked. How long to put her plans into action and gain a head start. "Three days. But if you're thinking of escaping with Zarek before we leave, I beg you to reconsider. The general won't let Zarek go that easily."

She clutched the boy tighter and shielded his head in her bosom. "Neither will I."

"Your father charged you with keeping him safe, Chess. If you attempt to hide him or slip away, you'll surely get him killed."

"And the trek to Moscow won't?"

He inched to the bed, sat on the edge, and took her hand, which allowed Zarek to wriggle out of her death grip. "So let's work together, Chess. Let me help you find a better solution."

"Not unless you tell me the truth, Pietor. All of it." His lips tightened, and she slapped the coverlet. "What do I have to do to get you to confide in me? Why won't you let *me* help *you*? Don't you see? If we keep fighting separate battles, we'll lose everything."

She was right. No argument, no doubt. Perhaps he should have told her from the start. But now, before any more could possibly harm them, now they had to stand united. All of them. Even the boy. His king and sovereign.

Picking up the tray, he said, "Eat, Chess. And while you eat, I'll tell you all you want to know."

♥

Chesna considered arguing about the food, but quickly reconsidered. Regardless of what Pietor told her, she'd need her strength for the battles yet to come. To show full cooperation, she lifted the bowl to her lips and sipped the savory broth.

"How much does he know?" Pietor jerked his head at Zarek, who sat wide-eyed and alert beside her.

"I know you're my cousin," the boy replied. "And you and Mama used to be friends. A long time ago."

"We're still friends, Zarek," Chesna said, picking up the bread and dragging a finger through the puddle of honey.

Zarek, arms folded over his chest, shook his head. "Friends don't make friends cry."

"They do when there are misunderstandings," she replied and licked the sweetness off her fingertip. "That's why we're going to talk now."

Zarek narrowed his eyes at Pietor. "But you told me not to trust you."

"You did?" The bread fell from Chesna's fingers onto the bedcovers, leaving a smear of sticky honey on the silk.

"I did. I told him to trust no one but you. All the more reason why you need to understand all the ramifications between us."

She rubbed her napkin against the stain, for no other reason than to keep her hands from shaking. "Very well."

"I was only in St. Petersburg a few months when I was approached by an agent of Napoleon Bonaparte's. He found me at the university, knew me by name, knew who I was, where I'd come from. My father..." The last two words came out a croak, and he stopped, looked out the window, and cleared his throat.

Chesna grabbed his sleeve. "What, Pietor? What is it?"

"My father had conspired with Bonaparte to remove King Jarek from the throne," he said, his tone a husky whisper. "And replace him. With me."

Zarek gasped, and Chesna sucked in a sharp breath. "But, that's impossible. Your mother..."

"Under Amatian law, I could never sit on the throne because my mother was not a royal, which was why my father never tried for a coup on his own. Instead, he struck a bargain with Bonaparte. In exchange for an easy surrender in Amatia, I would be named grand duke after the invasion. King Jarek, Queen Jasia, and any issue from their union were all to be cut down, eliminated. Your father, as well. Everyone but me. And, I think, my father assumed he would also survive the onslaught unscathed. I've no doubt Bonaparte ordered differently."

Recalling the surprised look on Prince Milos's severed head as it rolled near her feet, she shivered.

"And that's when I contacted your father."

She jerked her gaze away from the imagined sight on the featherbed and looked up into Pietor's mercurial eyes.

"Bela offered me a choice. A new name and a new life in a new place, or the opportunity to discover who else was involved in this treasonous plot by working for him."

Chesna's heart cracked as she remembered the passage she'd read in his letter. "I don't understand. Why didn't you choose the new life? You and I could have gone to America, the way we'd always planned. Bonaparte would not have found you there."

He shook his head. "I couldn't take you with me. Together, we were too well known. Had I chosen to flee, your father would not allow me to have any ties that could connect me to my true identity. Remember, you aren't just some Amatian peasant's daughter, unknown and powerless. You're Chesna Dubrow, a direct link to a past I had to leave behind, with a father who has the trust of the king. I couldn't take the chance someone somewhere might recognize us and use you to force me onto the throne. We were lost to each other, Chess." Sighing, he faced her, his expression wounded. "Do you understand that?"

She swallowed hard, envisioning the repercussions, one tragedy at a time. "Yes." She didn't like it, but she was her father's daughter, the last of the Dubrows. The safety of the royal family would always take precedence over her happiness.

"I chose espionage. Left the university, took on my mother's name, Gabris, and joined the French army as a former Amatian, sympathetic to Napoleon's cause. I had hoped that, if I stayed near Amatia, if I waited, if I survived..."

"We'd somehow find a way to be together." She cradled his hand, rubbed his knuckles across her cheeks. "And at last, we are."

"But it's dangerous for you and Zarek to remain with me, particularly Zarek."

Realization chilled her blood. "Because Napoleon only needs one grand duke in Amatia."

Pietor nodded, but the frown pinched deeper lines into his brow. "The treacherous plot originated here in the palace, Chess. And my father could not have acted alone. Nor could he have orchestrated the attempts on your life from beyond the grave. He had to have others working with him, others who are still scheming to make his dream reality."

"People who will kill to put you on the throne." The air left her lungs, and her statement came out no louder than a harsh whisper.

"Despite the fact that I don't now, nor have I ever wanted the throne." Pietor knelt at the side of the bed and bowed his head toward the young boy. "I pledge my fealty to you, sire, before God and my wife as witnesses. No matter what happens in Moscow, I will not return to Amatia to place you or your reign in jeopardy. Pietor of the royal house of Zenovia is dead."

The gasp escaped before Chesna could stifle her shock. She veered her attention to Zarek's wide-eyed countenance.

"And your wife?" he asked pointedly. "What will become of her?"

The crack in Chesna's heart deepened and cut clean through. But her pain did not diminish her obligations. "She'll stay with you, Your Majesty."

"No." Once again, Zarek folded his arms over his chest. "This, I cannot allow. Think, Mama. No one is more clever than you. Surely you can devise a way to remain with your husband yet keep your vow to me?"

Oh, to be a child where anything is possible. "I-I don't know."

"You have three days to do so."

29

Chesna stared out the bedroom window. A brown skylark danced in the leafy branch of an ash tree. A female, no doubt, waiting for the song of her mate from on high. Why did females always wind up waiting for the males? Sometimes in vain?

Three days. Three days to find culprits Pietor and her father had sought for years. Of course, she had an advantage the males did not. At least one of the villains was currently trying to kill her. Then again, she *hoped* the same monsters were involved in both treasonous activities. And that she'd succeed before they did.

By Jove, how she missed her father's solid, wise presence now. A wistful sigh escaped her lips.

"Chess?" Pietor's question intruded into her thoughts. He stood by the door that led to the hall, Zarek at his side. "Are you listening to me?"

"Yes," she lied. What exactly had he said?

"I mean it, Chess. Don't go off alone with anyone, no matter how long you've known them or how quick the errand. Your dearest friend could be the deadliest enemy. Trust no one." He sighed, and his stiff posture melted. "I don't suppose I could convince you to stay in this room?"

"No. Three days, remember?" She rose from the bed with a frown and strode toward her husband. "Don't fret, Pietor. I'll be careful."

He wrapped an arm around her and yanked her toward him until his lips were a breath from hers. "See that you are. I love you, Chess. I never stopped loving you."

His mouth claimed hers, connecting them heart to pounding heart. The cold chill of fear evaporated from her bones. Love's heat enveloped her, wrapped her in its warm glow. He broke away, drew a tender finger over her flushed cheeks.

"Trust no one," he repeated. Releasing her, he turned with Zarek, and they left the nursery.

Chesna stood, dizzy with Pietor's kiss. And his love. He still loved her. Three days. Somehow, she would find the answers. Their love had survived separation, treason, and a foreign invasion. She wouldn't surrender now. Time to stop mourning the life she once lived and forge a new one.

Imagine. Prince Milos a traitor to his own brother! What a stark reminder that no one was above suspicion.

She could trust no one to be who they claimed to be. The most trusted friend could be a spy. Pietor was certainly proof of that. Who, among the palace's many residents, might be working for Napoleon? And how on earth could they narrow down their vast list of suspects?

Her best option was to investigate everyone closest to her and Zarek. The culprit had to have access to the innermost workings of the royal family. What better place to start her search than in the kitchen? And she had the perfect excuse to be there. First, she'd return the tray from her meal. Then, she'd ask for help to replace the stained coverlet on Zarek's bed. One at a time, she'd eliminate suspects until she had her answers.

♥

Despite the noisy bustle as servants prepared the evening meal, Urszula caught Chesna's entrance within seconds of her arrival. Wiping her hands on her stained apron, she strode forward with the tray from her meal. "Chess, you didn't have to bring that down. I would have sent Irina upstairs."

"I wanted to thank you. The meal was delicious, as always." She leaned closer to whisper for Urszula's ears only. "Unfortunately, I ate in Zarek's room, and I dropped the bread on his coverlet. I need to replace the linens while he's occupied with Pietor."

Urszula looked around at the frantic maids, the flour flying in the air, the pot bubbling over and spilling into the fire. Irina suddenly appeared from the other end of the crowd and removed the cover from the simmering pot.

"Hmmm..." Urszula stroked her chin. "I really need Irina's help to keep order in here." She scanned the tables where the younger maids chopped herbs. "Why don't I have Monika help you?"

At the mention of her name, the pretty blonde jerked up her head. "Chesna? May I help with something?"

Before she could argue, Urszula replied, "Go with Chess. She needs help with Zarek's bed."

Irina turned. "What happened to Zarek's bed?"

Urszula grinned like a drunken woman. "Chesna claims she dropped bread on the coverlet and now needs to change the linens. All I know is I sent her husband up with a tray for her, and she returns the tray much later. I think it's safe to say that she and Pietor have called some kind of truce to their bedroom warfare."

A flurry of giggles erupted from the young girls at the table. Chesna needed a moment longer for the innuendo to become clear. When she finally realized what Urszula had intimated, fire crept up her throat and cheeks.

"Judging by that blush," Urszula cackled, "I'd say I'm right. You and Pietor are happy again at last."

Trust no one. Any one of the multitude of people crowded in this service area could be a traitor. She had to tread lightly. Forcing a frown, Chesna grumbled, "Oh yes, of course. I'm deliriously happy to be tied for eternity to a man who turned his back on me and all we believe in. Do you really think so little of me? Do you forget the blood that spilled in the streets those weeks ago? My father's blood. The king's blood."

Urszula blanched the color of the flour. "Forgive me." She dipped her head. "I should have realized your marriage would still be a sore subject for you."

"A sore subject?" She tossed back her head and laughed bitterly. "Oh, Urszula, I do love your choice of words."

"I must confess I don't understand your continued

enmity toward your husband," Irina interjected as she stepped toward them. A wooden spoon in her hand dripped brown gravy, and she set it down on the sideboard before the drops hit the floor. "I would be more than content with a husband like your Pietor." She sighed in an exaggerated fashion. "I believe he's the most handsome man in the French army."

"A husband should have more to recommend him than a pretty face," Chesna retorted.

"Oh? Such as?"

"A husband is more than a man to warm your bed, Irina," she replied. She thought of Pietor, the man who'd loved her. Who would love her always. Her heartbeat tripped. "He should be a dear friend, someone a woman might confide her secret dreams and deepest fears to without being laughed at. A husband should turn your emotions upside-down and inside out just by his mere presence in the same room. He should be a man who makes you feel strong yet vulnerable, serene yet giddy, prudent yet flighty, and confident yet apprehensive, all at the same time."

She paused.

Both women stared at her with expressions of wary skepticism.

Immediately, she realized her error and amended it as best she could, making her tone and her posture more confrontational. "When it comes to marriage, ladies, a woman should never settle for a pretty face. Beauty fades over time, but true love is eternal."

"Oh, Chess." Irina shook her head. "We're speaking of marriage, and you're speaking of true love. The two don't usually go hand in hand, you know."

"Perhaps not, but they should, Irina."

"Bah!" Irina scoffed. "You've always thought too much for your own good. All those men you turned down over the years. You have no idea how fortunate you are to have a husband at all. If I could, I'd trade places with you in the blink of an eye."

"Really?" Urszula's brow puckered with deep lines. "I've never heard you speak of a husband before, Irina. I always thought you were happiest serving Queen Jasia."

"I loved Jasia as if she were my own daughter," Irina replied softly. "But I loved a man once too. And because of who he was and who I was, we could never wed."

"Who was he?" Urszula urged. "Was he someone here in Amatia? Or did he live with you in Lithuania?"

But Irina clamped her lips and shook her head. "No, Urszula. I will not appease your curiosity. I shouldn't have spoken of him at all. All you need to know is that he's gone now and so is Jasia. So where does that leave me? I'll spend the rest of my life alone."

"My life isn't all sunshine and happiness because I'm a married woman, Irina," Chesna replied. "I know scores of women who would trade places with *you* in the blink of an eye if they had the opportunity. Sometimes it's better to have fond memories of a man you loved than to live with a man you despise."

Monika pulled a stack of clean dishes from the sideboard. "I agree. I thought I loved my Oleg until he betrayed me. Now I'm grateful I learned the truth before I was tied to him in marriage."

Chesna smiled. "It sounds as if you're ready for us to summon Oleg to the palace."

"Indeed, I am, Chesna."

"Then we'll have to see to it at once."

Urszula waved a hand at Chesna. "Go. Whatever the reason, go upstairs and see to Zarek's bed. But don't tarry, Monika. I still need you here."

Chesna looked between the women uncertainly. She had promised Pietor to remain with many people and not to be distracted by a mundane task or a simple errand into following one person anywhere alone.

But her logical mind trusted Monika. The young jilted woman couldn't possibly be their poisonmonger. She was too sweet, too fresh-faced and too ingenuous for such an intrigue. Besides, she'd never known Prince Milos.

"Come, Monika," she said firmly. "While we're replacing the linens, we'll plot our revenge against your Oleg."

"Wonderful." Monika giggled and followed Chesna out the arched doorway.

Chesna felt a momentary glimmer of doubt as they left Urszula and the others in the kitchens, but she pushed it away impatiently. Pietor's dire warning was making her mistrust her own instincts. What could possibly happen to her if she were alone with someone as open as Monika?

Monika followed Chesna up the stairs, down the long hall and into the royal nursery. She chattered lightly, already scheming with ideas for making Oleg pay for his bad behavior.

"We should summon him to the palace under the pretext that he's receiving something special," Chesna suggested. "An honor of some sort, perhaps."

"And once he's here in the palace, I'll have my opportunity to confront him."

"Slow down, Monika," Chesna admonished as she opened the door to Zarek's bedchamber and walked inside. "If you truly wish to achieve satisfaction from your enemy, you must be patient. Bide your time until the moment is right to strike."

Monika nodded, but confusion wrinkled her brow. "What do you suggest, Chess?"

"I'm not certain yet," she admitted as she stopped before the bed and bent to remove the linens. "Tell me more about your former betrothed, if you will. What's he like?"

"Oh, Oleg is a very handsome man. All of the ladies in my village find him so. My friends were so envious of me when they learned Oleg had asked for my hand. I suppose that's why I said what I did in the kitchens a short while ago. I agree with your thoughts on the matter, Chess. A pretty face is never enough to count on in a marriage."

"I've always believed marriage is not something to be taken lightly," Chesna told her. "So many women place themselves in loveless marriages and subject themselves to becoming little more than slaves in their own homes simply to avoid the stigma of spinsterhood. It's such a shame."

Monika pulled down her side of the crimson coverlet. "I suppose some women would disagree with us. Did you see how angry Irina became during our discussion?"

"Yes." Chesna yanked on her side of the large quilted bedcover. "I must confess I found it a bit unsettling. Irina has never spoken so passionately about marriage before. I wonder who she loved who would hurt her so badly."

"I can't wait to get back to the kitchens now," Monika said with a smirk. "No doubt, Urszula will have the whole sordid story out of Irina by the time I return."

"I'm not so certain about that." With the coverlet in a scarlet heap on the floor, Chesna strode to the linen closet for another. "I've known Irina since she first came to Amatia and in all that time I've learned very little. She's always been tight-lipped about herself."

"I should imagine she hasn't had an easy time in life," Monika replied. "It takes a great deal of courage to leave behind everyone and everything you know to travel to a foreign land. And if she also left behind a man whom she loved to come to Amatia and serve Queen Jasia..."

While Monika efficiently replaced the counterpane on the boy's bed, Chesna tossed the dirty linens into the cedar launder chest in the corner of the room. "Tell me more about your former betrothed."

"Oleg's our village's apothecary. He's a wonder with herbs and poultices. Some days when he'd come to our house to walk out with me, he'd escort me through the woods that bordered our town. I'd help him dig up certain plants or fungi for his medicines."

"He sounds very romantic." Chesna had to bite back a smirk.

Monika simply smiled. "I know how ridiculous it seems, but I was young, and I thought I loved him. I was deeply interested in anything he told me, regardless of how macabre it sounded. He explained about poisons that could kill a man in many different ways. There were some plants that could be ground into a powder and mixed with food or wine. A person would die within a few bites or sips without tasting anything amiss at all. And did you know that the bark of certain trees could be boiled in liquid to become a poison for weapons? Many soldiers in the armies of ancient times would dip their arrows into the liquid before a battle to kill their enemies."

As Monika kept up her lighthearted chatter about poison and death, a deep sense of unease creep into Chesna's bones. Never before had she heard anyone speak of grisly subjects with such abject calm. Every sentence Monika uttered chilled Chesna's blood another degree.

Had Monika's sweet face and innocent demeanor misled her? Was Monika the poisonmonger they sought? Had she played right into the villain's hands? Pietor had warned her not to be alone with anyone. How could she have been so foolish? To be duped by Monika's act of the helpless, jilted female.

Well, she wouldn't allow Monika to gain her objective without a fierce fight. If she were going to die, she'd take her killer with her. Stealthily, she moved to the fireplace and toyed with one of the heavy andirons nearby, watching Monika's movements out of the corner of her eye. If Monika dared to lay hands on her, she'd find herself clubbed with a fire iron for her troubles.

"That certainly doesn't sound like the words of courtly love I would have expected from a suitor," she said with a tinge of disapproval, hoping to keep Monika unaware.

Monika shivered. "I must admit there were times when he frightened me with his knowledge. But Oleg always insisted it was just as important for him to know how to take a life as how to save one."

"But what could you possibly find to love in a man with such ghoulish interests?"

Monika reached for the pillow atop Zarek's bed and fluffed it with rapidly beating hands. "He had a well turned leg and a handsome face," she admitted.

As Chesna watched Monika's blush rise up in her apple cheeks, she smiled and released her grasp on the handle of the makeshift weapon. Replacing the poker, she sighed in relief. She was being foolish! Monika was only doing what Chesna had asked her to do, telling her about Oleg.

Just because Oleg knew a great deal about poisonous plants didn't mean Monika was the villain trying to kill her. She let her thoughts drift off as she watched a white flower petal waft downward from the pillow and onto the floor.

"What's this?" Monika picked up the petal and toyed with the bloom between her fingers. Suddenly, her eyes grew wide, and her face paled. "Chess? Where did this come from?"

Closing the gap between them, Chesna reached for the

flower scrap in Monika's hand. "I don't know. It doesn't resemble anything that grows in the meadow."

"I should hope not," Monika's voice came out a harsh whisper. "This is jimson weed."

"Jimson weed?"

Monika nodded solemnly. "Oleg once called it the perfect killer. The flowers are so beautiful that many people can't resist the urge to smell their perfume, especially children. But their fragrance is poisonous when inhaled."

Terror snaked through Chesna's veins. "H-how does it work? I m-mean, if a child were to smell the flowers, how would you know if he or she was in danger? Are there warning signs?"

"Let me think for a moment." Monika paced with the petal in in her hand. "The first symptom that the poison has been inhaled by its victim is a headache."

Mama, my head hurts...

Dear God, no!

With shaking hands, Chesna reached for Zarek's pillow. Placing her hands on either side, she pulled with all her might. The case tore open and hundreds of the same pretty white petals floated onto the newly made bed.

Her knees collapsed, and she sank to the floor where the world went dark.

30

When Chesna opened her eyes, two faces loomed over her. On a cry, she covered her face with an upraised arm.

"Chess." Karol's voice reached through her fears. "It's me. Are you all right?"

Slowly, carefully, she lowered her arm. Karol and Monika stood at her bedside. Concern etched their brows and crinkled the corners of their eyes.

Hold.

She was in her bed, in her chamber.

"Easy, Chess," Karol reached out a hand toward her.

"Stay away from me." She shrank back and curled into a tight ball against the headboard. "Don't touch me."

"Calm yourself," he soothed in a tone more fitting for a frightened kitten. "No one's going to hurt you."

"Good. Then get out. I don't know how I got here, but—"

"You swooned when you saw the flower petals in Zarek's pillow," Karol said.

"The pillow." Memory pierced the fog like a dagger to the heart. Those horrid petals, each one a whisper of death, and enough of them to destroy a dozen children.

"Monika came to fetch me to help," Karol continued. "I carried you to your bed."

But if Zarek's pillow hid those deadly blooms...

She scrambled up, sought her own pillow behind her, only to find a bare headbard. Eyes narrowed in suspicion, she glanced back at Karol.

"The petals were in your pillow, as well," he answered her unasked question. "To be safe, we disposed of all the pillows and then inspected the entire quarters. There are no other flowers or poisons anywhere in the nursery or this bedchamber."

She relaxed her stance only slightly, still uncertain whether or not to trust these two. "Where did you dispose of the pillows?"

"Well, I might have liked to exchange your pillows with those of General de Valmiere, but..." He cast a grin at Monika, "...we thought better of it and tossed them on the trash heap outside the walls of the palace. I told two of the kitchen boys to be certain to pour the contents of the residents' chamber pots atop the petals to keep any unsuspecting vagabonds from stealing death."

"Very clever, Karol," Chesna murmured. "I never realized before how clever you are."

His grin flipped to a dark frown. "I'm still the same man I was yesterday. Don't let your imagination run away with you."

"I'd like to believe you," Chesna retorted, "but yesterday was a rather difficult day for me. And thus far, today seems to bode no better."

Karol's round face reddened brighter than his hair. "I have never given you reason to distrust me. I love Zarek well. You know that." He cast another glance toward Monika, this one more furtive than the first, and then turned back to Chesna.

Chesna didn't miss the exchange between the two. She desperately wanted to believe him, but something niggled at the back of her brain. Pietor had made his point well yesterday when he'd remarked how strange it was that Karol had been in both places when attempts were made on her life. But there was more.

Karol had access to the royal nursery. Very few others did.

And no attempts had been made on her life until after Monika's arrival at the Majestic Palace. Was that mere coincidence? Or was it possible Karol and Monika were involved in this intrigue together?

Had Monika developed the poisons based on information from her former betrothed and given the items to Karol to administer? Was there really an Oleg? Or was he just a means to an end? Was he a phantom Monika had devised to gain entrance into the Opal Palace?

And if Karol and Monika were the villains trying to kill her, Chesna had just made a serious error. They knew now she suspected them. They'd be twice as careful, yet more determined to be rid of her before she could confirm her suspicions.

"Before you jump to any conclusions," Karol said, his tone edged with ice, "be aware that, although your pillow and Zarek's were both stuffed full with the offending blooms, your husband's pillow was packed with nothing but goose feathers."

Her spine snapped to rigid. "Are you claiming Pietor had something to do with this?"

"I don't know if he did or didn't," he admitted. "But I do know you're quick to assign blame to me, and I've done nothing to arouse such enmity from you. Don't forget, I've been your confidant since the beginning. Do you remember the plans we made together at the Church of St. Ambrose? We vowed then to trust no one but ourselves."

Chesna's brain swam in an ocean of suspicion. Pietor's voice resonated in her head. *Trust no one.*

"Get out, Karol," she said in a soft voice as she pointed at the door. "Take Monika with you and get out of my chamber. Now."

Karol's shoulders slumped, and he shook his head as he turned, Monika behind him. "God help you, Chesna. I pray you haven't made a grave mistake."

Chesna waited until she was alone before she spoke again. "So do I," she whispered to the empty room. "So do I."

She cried for nearly an hour. But when the tears subsided into little hiccoughs, she wiped her eyes and washed her face with water from the ewer and basin on her bedside table. She stared at her reflection in her hand mirror for a long moment. Her ministrations weren't enough to clear the misery from her face. With her puffy eyes and her ashen cheeks, she looked as if she'd wept for days.

A scuffling noise from the doorway had her whirling, fists at the ready, poised for battle.

The steely-haired woman screeched and backed away.

"Irina. Is something wrong?"

Zarek. Had something happened to Zarek?

"I was going to ask you the same thing," she said with a worried frown. "Monika and Karol returned to the kitchens quite some time ago, but you never came back downstairs. You look so pale. Is everything all right?"

Chesna nodded. "Everything is fine."

"It's your marriage, isn't it?" she pressed as she rushed closer. "Oh, Chess. I'm so sorry for the things I said to you earlier. You're right, you know. I don't know what it's like to be forced into a marriage with a man I don't love. I don't know what it's like to be married at all."

"I understand, Irina," she said.

"No, you don't." Irina's eyes brimmed with unshed tears. "I can see how miserable you are. And I feel so responsible. It's my fault you were trapped into marrying that odious man in the first place. How you must hate me."

"I don't hate you," Chesna told her with a sigh. "Don't blame yourself for what's happened to me."

"But I do blame myself. If I hadn't lied to the French general about your relationship with King Jarek, he wouldn't have insisted on marrying you to one of his officers. I only wanted to help. I wanted to protect Mik— Zarek, but I made the situation worse. Can you ever forgive me?"

"What's done is done." Chesna waved a hand in dismissal. "It's forgotten, Irina. Don't think of it any longer."

Irina smiled. "I promise to make it up to you somehow," she said solemnly.

But Chesna shook her head. "That's not necessary."

"Of course it is. Somehow, I'll help you escape this marriage that has been enforced on you."

Chesna stifled a laugh. She didn't wish to escape her marriage. She loved Pietor. But she dared not tell Irina. "It doesn't matter. Pietor will be leaving with the French in three days' time. I doubt he'll return."

She doubted he'd survive. To hide her fears, she looked out the double set of windows. Off in the distance, the Carpathian Mountains sprayed vibrant colors across the graying sky. Their lush lawns lay covered in widespread beds of snowy lily-of-the-valley; bright pink mossy saxafrage and rhododendron; pale purple birdseye and the more vibrant purple of the alpine snowbell; as well as the tall, slender yellow gentian. Guarding over these vivid wildflowers stood the towering silver fir trees. So peaceful, so lovely. Such a deceiving palette for death.

Gentle hands landed on her shoulder and slowly turned her around. "Come. It's time for the evening meal."

She allowed Irina to lead her from her bedchamber to the staircase. Her gaze strayed upward to the fat cherubs, their baby faces beaming with smiles that only made Chesna more bereft. On trembling legs, she took her first steps down.

"You've missed far too many meals lately," Irina said from behind her. "And we can't have you weak from hunger."

Chesna, still focused on the cherubs, chewed on her lip to keep her thoughts inside as she descended to the main floor.

Three days. No. Today was nearly over. She had two days and a few hours to discover who would want to kill her and Zarek, who committed treason against the royal family, who would secretly plot with Napoleon Bonaparte...

"Chess!"

On the last step, Chesna and Irina both turned. A breathless Karol raced forward, his face gleaming with sweat and his breath heavy from exertion. He pushed past the two guards who stood like bookends in front of the outer doors. Bent at the waist, hands on his thighs, he struggled to speak. "Zarek."

Zarek. Panic roared through her, a hurricane of terror. "Where? What's happened? Where's my boy?"

"In the woods. Hurt."

Oh, God, no. She didn't wait to hear more. Skirts bundled in her fists, she fled. Apparently her expression showed enough dread or determination that the guards didn't attempt to waylay her. They quickly stepped aside, and she pushed through the heavy doors on a shout. "Zarek!"

Crickets buzzed in the twilight. An occasional firefly glowed green then melted back into the darkness. In the background, shadowy soldiers milled around even lines of tents.

She kept running, kept calling. "Zarek! Where are you?"

Tears clouded her vision, streamed down her cheeks. Every footfall thundered in her ears as she raced through the meadow of crushed wildflowers, their colors bleeding gray in the last vestiges of daylight. "Zarek!"

The Amatian Forest loomed, its jagged wall of fir and ash trees piercing the deep mauve sky. She plunged past the spiny branches, over the uneven ground and scattered rocks. Her soft shoe skidded on the slippery moss, trapping her foot in the crevice between two large stones.

In an attempt to free herself and keep moving, she yanked her leg, wrenching her ankle. Pain shot from foot to thigh, and she cried out as she pitched forward. Hands outstretched to break her fall, she collided with the damp forest floor. The metallic taste of loamy soil filled her mouth, and she sputtered. Braced on her arms, she lifted her face off the ground and struggled against the fiery stars zipping up her right leg. She managed to raise herself up on all fours when a voice sneered from behind her.

"Well, this is a timely misfortune."

She turned to confront the voice, but an explosion rocked her head, and her vision went black.

31

Pietor knelt at Zarek's side. A strip of his shirt, soaked in the clear water of the lake, staunched the flow of blood from the slash in the boy's thigh. A knife wound. Nothing accidental about a knife wound on the edge of a lake.

How could he have been so short-sighted? He should have heeded his own advice: *Trust no one.* Why hadn't he ever considered that, although Chess was a threat to the traitors in the palace, Zarek was the greater threat? Why had he let down his guard once he'd walked outside with the boy?

He, Karol, and Zarek had been playing Hunt the Quarry, a favorite childhood game where one person, the Hunter, turned his back and counted to ten. Meanwhile, all the other players, the Quarry, hid. At the end of the counting, the Hunter sought out his hiding Quarry.

Zarek, as one of the Quarry, had chosen a hiding spot within the middle of a thick pine copse at the edge of the forest. He would have been successful in eluding Pietor's notice if he hadn't cried out and stumbled into the open. Pietor, searching behind the nearby boulders, spotted the boy, prone and screeching. At first, he thought a bee might have stung the child. Or perhaps he'd wandered into a swarm of mosquitoes. Until the blood began to stain the ground beneath him.

By the time he realized Zarek had been attacked, the villain had disappeared. Now, the child paid the price for Pietor's folly.

"Chesna," the boy murmured, his eyes glazed. "I want

Chesna."

Although they were alone, Pietor shushed him with a finger on his royal lips. Apparently, Zarek was in too much pain to remember his subterfuge. Still, he couldn't take the chance someone might be close enough to hear the child's ramblings and wonder why he called his "mama" by her given name.

Pietor dared a glance around the lake. Darkness had already settled. Where the hell *was* Chesna anyway? He'd sent Karol off to fetch her, a decision he'd had cause to regret with every second that elapsed without her arrival.

Something was wrong. Dread settled in his bones. If Karol had already located Chess and told her the boy was injured, nothing less than death would have kept her from Zarek's side.

Something was definitely wrong. Pietor's conscience tore in half. Obligation demanded he couldn't abandon his king. But dammit, his heart insisted he find his wife.

Gently, he scooped up the whimpering sovereign and cradled him against his chest. "Hold tight, Zarek. If Chesna won't come to us, we'll have to go to Chesna."

As he strode away from the lake, he prayed he'd find her tearing through the meadows toward them. But the ball of ice in his stomach already knew he'd lost her.

♥

Despite the thunder and lightning brewing inside her skull, Chesna opened her eyes. To total darkness. Touching a finger to her temple, she groaned.

"Excellent. You're awake." The husky voice came from a shadowy figure nearby.

"Who's there?" In this inky place, with her head pounding and her vision murky, she discerned nothing familiar.

"All in good time," the voice replied.

An odd smell stung her nostrils, like moldy straw. The fog slowly lifted from her brain, and she struggled to regain her bearings. She lay on her side, the ground beneath her rough and uneven, with sharp pebbles that dug into her hips through her gown.

No need to assess her situation. She already knew she'd fallen into a trap. But if she lost her head, gave in to the panic swirling inside her, Zarek would suffer.

She could very well die in this dank, dark place. A lump of regrets rose in her throat, the loss of all she might never experience. Pietor's face swam in her memory, the words *I love you, Chess. I never stopped loving you...* an echo she might carry into the hereafter.

The last Dubrow, however, would protect her king with her dying breath. Of course, crafting a plan of attack required her to know her companion's identity—and any compatriots he might have.

Keep talking, her father's voice spoke in her head. *The more you can get the villain to reveal, the more weapons you can use against him.*

"Where are we?"

No reply came. The only sound she heard was a distant scratching, erratic and under normal circumstances, mildly alarming. But these were hardly normal circumstances.

She rose on shaky legs, fisted her hands at her sides. "Where are we?" she repeated, this time with more force.

"Don't take that tone with me," the figure retorted. "In this place, you will finally give me the respect I deserve."

Passion obviously overrode the villain's need for secrecy. The voice lost its husky quality, revealing a distinctive feminine pitch and a hesitant accent that conveyed the speaker's native language was *not* Amatian.

Chesna, eyes slowly growing accustomed to the darkness, managed to discern brick walls and a stone floor covered in...grain? Lice? She didn't know. Fighting shivers of revulsion, she scanned the area. Her captor stood in the farthest corner, a dark silhouette in this unlit cage.

"Respect? For treason?" At the last second, Chesna bit back confirmation of the villain's identity. *Irina.*

Irina's cackle, edged with hysteria, smacked the walls and tightened Chesna's spine. "You're the treasonous one. In time, everyone will know how much I sacrificed for the good of Amatia. I even eliminated the woman I'd served from infancy to pave the way for the new ruler."

Chesna's blood froze. Her skin grew clammy, from both the surroundings and the horror of what Irina intimated.

"Jasia? You killed Jasia?"

"She brought her death upon herself," Irina spat. "She shouldn't have insisted upon giving Jarek a son. I had to protect the true heir to the throne."

"By killing his mother?" Despite her intention to stay strong, the shudders racking her from head to toe escaped through her mouth.

"Not Mikhail, you fool. Mikhail should have died like his siblings. Whenever Jasia would announce she was carrying another brat, I fed her small amounts of tansy for months to cause her to miscarry. But she kept trying. And she finally succeeded in delivering Mikhail safely. At first, I wasn't perturbed. I thought an infant would be easy to dispose of. He might die in his sleep or carelessly fall down the stairs and break his neck. But Jasia named *you* as the child's governess. I was never allowed near the boy. And worse, she insisted on giving Jarek more children." She sighed dramatically. "I had no choice. I had to keep her from bringing any more sons into this world. Luckily, the years of poisoning had weakened her so much she couldn't survive her last labor. I really didn't kill her, you know. The birthing of her daughter is what killed her."

Chesna didn't try to stem her horror. The woman was mad! "I thought you loved Jasia."

"I did love Jasia. But I loved Milos more."

"Prince Milos?" Scattered pieces in her head clicked together to form a perfect picture. Irina in the kitchens, confessing how she'd loved a man once, but because of who he was and who she was, they could never marry. Pietor's confession regarding his father's treasonous activities. If Irina was Prince Milos's lover...

"He wanted the throne for his son." Irina's statement drew her back to the dark hidey-hole. "When Napoleon began conquering countries in his quest for power, Milos made a pact with the emperor. In exchange for a smooth conquest in Amatia, Pietor would be placed on the throne as grand duke. You understand, don't you? They all had to die: Jasia, Jarek, and Bela first. Now you and Mikhail will be next."

The white petals of death rose in Chesna's mind. "I-I n-never realized you had such a penchant for poisons."

"I didn't start with poison. Not right away. First, I told General de Valmiere that you were the king's mistress."

On that horrible morning...

Chesna's knees weakened, but she rooted her feet to the filthy floor. "You weren't protecting Zarek. You wanted de Valmiere to kill us both."

"Yes. But that certainly backfired on me, didn't it? Instead of killing you, he married you off. To Pietor!" She laughed again, a maniacal sound that raised hackles on Chesna's nape. "Milos is no doubt spinning in his grave to see you married to his son. He purposely sent Pietor to St. Petersburg to remove him from your influence. You aren't fit to be Grand Duchess of Amatia. If not for your father's influence with the throne, you'd have merely been some pretty peasant wench, long married and fat after birthing a dozen children for your farmer husband."

How would Irina react if she knew Pietor had always wanted to be a simple farmer with Chess as his wife? Best not to divulge that information. "Who poisoned my wine? Did Monika help you with that?"

"God, no. Although that simpleton appeared at just the right time. If you had died that day, suspicion would have automatically fallen on her. *I* wanted you dead. No one else. Poison seemed to be the easiest way. It always worked for Jasia. But you were just too smart, too strong, and too lucky."

The evil spilling from Irina's twisted brain terrified her, but she had to keep the woman talking, discover as much about the plotters in the palace as possible. "But you couldn't have tried to drown me in Lake Matya. Not without help."

"Of course, I did. And I almost succeeded, until Pietor and that fool Karol began calling for you. I had to run back to the palace before anyone discovered me there. I was surprised you didn't ask me why I was on the third floor when you returned to the nursery yesterday. I had just replaced the devil's trumpet petals in your pillows when we ran into each other on the staircase. Once again, you were lucky enough to escape what I had planned for you. I heard Karol order the boys to destroy the pillows so no one would mistakenly steal them. But now, your luck has finally run out. *This* time I will succeed."

Chesna fought to remain calm, swallowing hard against the fear that threatened to engulf her. "You don't have to do this, Irina. Please? Pietor can have the throne and anything else he wants."

"You don't understand. Pietor is besotted with you. He has no interest in the throne. You're all he ever wanted. But when you're gone, he'll feel differently. Didn't I promise I'd find a way for you to escape your marriage? Unfortunately, the only way out is death. Your death."

Chesna's mouth went dry, and her heartbeat sped up. She wouldn't beg for her life. But she'd disgrace herself a thousand times over to save the prince.

"Please, Irina?" She entwined her hands in prayer. "Don't do this. Let me take Mikhail away from Amatia. No one need ever know he's really Prince Mikhail. I would continue to raise him as my own Zarek. Please don't harm him. He's only a little boy. You can't kill an innocent child."

"Don't tell me what I can or can't do, Chesna. I gave my dear Milos a solemn vow. I will ensure that his son, Pietor, sits upon Amatia's throne. Where he belongs. Amatia must be ruled by a competent man and not some weak, snot-nosed brat."

Irina shoved Chesna so hard, she fell to her knees in the dirt. While she struggled to rise, Irina grabbed her by the hair of her scalp and forced her head up. The coldness of a steel blade pressed against her throat.

Svarila, abide with me. Lend me your power. Share your courage. Help me protect my child.

Chesna clutched Irina's wrist, fingernails digging into flesh, until the woman cried out in pain and released her. Immediately, she scrambled out of reach and assumed a fighting stance. "You would kill the rightful heir to install a reluctant pretender on the throne?"

"Pietor is only reluctant because of you. You nearly ruined everything!" Irina whirled to slap Chesna, but she easily blocked the blow. "When you and your precious Mikhail or Zarek or whatever you call that boy are dead, Pietor will accept his responsibility to the people of this country. How unfortunate that you promised your father you would protect Mikhail's hold on the throne. We're on opposite sides of the very same issue, Chess. I want the prince dead, you want him to live. Which of us will win in the end, do you think?"

"The one who leaves this hole alive," Chesna replied.

She lunged at Irina, ready to battle to the death.

32

Every step that brought Pietor closer to the palace splintered off another piece of his heart. Terror ratcheted up his spine. By the time he pulled open the heavy door leading into the hall, hope had fairly well abandoned him.

Inside, he came to a stop near the staircase where Karol paced, fingers raking frantically through his red hair. "I ordered the servants to bring hot water and linen strips to the nursery," he said, loud enough for the guards positioned at the doors to hear and digest. "Told them how Zarek took a tumble." Karol leaned to the side to look around Pietor's solid form. "Where's Chess?"

"You saw her? When? How long ago?" How much of a start did the villains have? Perhaps hope would lend a hand after all.

"She was here in the hall when I reached the palace," Karol replied. "She took off before I caught my breath. She didn't find you?"

"She never came."

Karol swore—loudly and quite colorfully. "She's in trouble."

"Mama?" Zarek murmured against Pietor's chest.

Now what? How could he tear himself in half? His heart screamed for Chesna. But Zarek need his injury tended. He stole a glance at the soldiers, then at Karol. Jackals surrounded him on all sides.

"Give me the boy," Karol urged and thrust out his arms. "Find Chess."

Pietor hesitated.

"For heaven's sake, Pietor. Go!"

Instead, he cradled the boy closer. How could he know what truly lurked in Karol's mind?

"You still don't trust me?"

"I trust no one right now." He glared at Karol, as if by the power of staring he might discern the servant's motives. Time ticked from the ornate clock behind him.

"Pietor." Zarek's voice, whisper-soft but firm, broke the resentful silence. "Find your wife. I will go with Karol."

"I don't—"

"Be careful you don't speak treason, Pietor." The child's statement, barely audible, held enough royal command that Pietor bowed his head in supplication.

"Yes, sire." On a sigh, he surrendered his hold. While he transferred the boy into Karol's care, he asked, "Did anyone go with Chess when she left here?"

"No," Karol replied. "She fled too fast to wait for an escort. Not that I think she would have trusted anyone to accompany her even if I had insisted."

No, she wouldn't. *Trust no one.*

Someone must have waylaid her after she left the safety of the hall. The same monster who'd lain in wait to attack Zarek? Most likely.

Someone with a very sharp knife in his possession.

♥

Chesna collided with Irina, the impact sending them both to their knees. Fire seared her ribs. The knife. She sucked in a breath so dusty she choked. Irina seized the opportunity to knock her flat into the ground. Chesna rolled away a moment before Irina brought the knife down again.

Somehow she had to get that blade. Once more, she clamped her hands on Irina's wrists, this time strong enough to crush the delicate bones.

Growling like a rabid animal, Irina struggled to pull free. Each jerk of her hand pierced the knife into the fleshy part of Chesna's left side. The world slid sideways, and Chesna's vision blackened at the edges. Her arms ached. Still, she held on.

Irina wriggled and shook, until she positioned the knife into a more lethal position. With her strength waning, Chesna yanked up her skirts and brought her knee into the woman's chest. On a wheezing gasp, Irina staggered back, dropping the blade. Chesna balled her fist and slammed the woman in the throat.

While Irina howled her outrage, Chesna scrambled across the floor. Irina dove forward, pinning her by the hem of her skirt. Chesna stretched and managed to put an index finger on the edge of the blade. Gently, gingerly, inch by excruciating inch, she dragged the knife into her possession.

Irina lunged. One arm upraised to shield her, Chesna grasped the hilt. Eyes squeezed shut, she thrust forward. The blade slid into soft human flesh. A gurgle erupted from Irina's mouth as the warmth of fresh blood sprayed Chesna's face. And then...

...Silence.

Awareness shone on her. She'd taken a life. For Zarek. Mikhail. Her king.

Once Irina's body thudded to the ground, Chesna backed against the wall and sank to her knees. When she grasped her left side, her fingers came away slippery with her own blood. Again, she became aware of that odd scratching sound, this time closer and recognizable. A sound from her childhood. A sound she'd never forget.

Rats.

Shivers racked her, and she curled into a tight ball.

Get up, my girl. We'll get you out of here. Her father's voice called to her from a long ago memory. *Come, Chess. Come to Papa...*

The rats, of course, had followed her to the top of the ladder that day. Rats in the root cellar. Eyes glowing in the darkness, skinny tails whipping across her bare legs. Now they'd found her here.

They flooded toward her in a wave, tumbling over each other and Irina's fallen body in a frenzy of blood lust. The smell of the women's injuries must have drawn them. Every muscle froze, leaving Chesna too stiff to move. Sheer terror paralyzed her. As a child, she'd worn heavy black shoes, shoes that could crack a few rat skulls. But now she wore slippers of softest kid, useless against the surging horde.

She would die here, if not from the blood seeping through her blouse, from rat bites. But at least she'd saved Zarek. The last of the Dubrows had given her life for her sovereign. He would live to ascend the throne, to rule Amatia with wisdom and judiciousness. Thanks, in some small part, to her.

Did I make you proud, Papa?

Closing her eyes, she surrendered to the blackness waiting to claim her.

♥

Lantern in hand to illuminate the dark night, Pietor scanned the ground as he tried to retrace Chesna's steps. She would have run through the meadows, skirted the army camp in favor of the forest edge. Yet, he found nothing. No sign of Chesna, no clue as to what might have happened to her.

Staring up at the starlit sky, he beseeched the heavens for help. *Please don't let her die.*

He thought back to her words to Zarek in the nursery. *I'm a Dubrow. We don't die easily.* An outlandish boast, but he'd cling to it until he found her. Chesna Dubrow Gabris dead? Not possible. She'd survived Napoleon's invasion, an enforced marriage, a poisoning attempt, and an aborted drowning. Surely, God wouldn't be that cruel, to allow them to rekindle their love only to take her away before the sun set.

Was it only this morning when she'd smiled at him and he'd felt as if she'd touched his very soul? How many hours since he'd told her, "I love you, Chesna. I never stopped loving you."? How many lifetimes had elapsed since he'd heard her voice? Her laughter? Not enough. He needed more. At last he fully understood how she'd suffered when he'd disappeared from her life all those years ago. A half-life, she'd called this feeling.

When he finally found her, he'd sink to his knees, beg her forgiveness for every moment she'd spent mourning him. Then he'd find a way to leave the French army before the trek to Russia. He'd convince her to sail to America with him. To create their own dynasty. Children who'd inherit their mother's courage, her wisdom, her deep well of love. Lucky, lucky children. But first, he had to find her.

He plunged past the forest's edge, his heart thudding her name in a tattoo of love. *Chesna, Chesna, Chesna.* Moonlight, reflecting off the lake, danced silver on the pine boughs. And on the ground, a rut of disturbed loam and leaves created a strange path through the woods. As if someone had dragged something along the forest floor.

Chess!

Hope renewed, he followed the line nature had drawn to help him find his wife. The rut wended beneath heavy branches of pine, through thicket bushes, around rocks the size of Zarek. While he stayed on the trail, Pietor silently screamed her name.

She couldn't be dead. If Chesna were truly dead, he would know. Somehow, he believed, he would sense it. He would feel her loss as strongly as he would if he suddenly lost a limb or an eye. He would know she was gone. And he didn't feel her loss now. So she had to be alive.

The burned out shell of an old building seemed to pop up from nowhere. The grain silo had caught fire decades ago. No one had bothered to rebuild, its location too far from the palace for convenience. Instead, a new grain silo had been erected closer to the rear entrance of the kitchens. Thus, this black husk sat empty. Or was it?

Once again, his heart split: half elated he might have found her, the other half dreading what he'd see inside. He placed his lantern on the ground and moved to the entrance. His hands trembled as he touched the handle. On a deep breath, he yanked the door open.

Dark and silent. *Oh, God. No.* A shout welled inside him, rage in all its impotence. He raced inside, prepared to fight an army to save his wife. Instead, he found two shadowy lumps on the floor, a battalion of rats zipping between them.

"Oh, God, Chess, no!"

The lump closer to the wall moved.

"Chess?"

"Pietor." Her drained voice sang more strongly than a choir of angels.

He raced forward, crouched beside her, and gathered her against his chest. "Chess. Let's get you out of here."

Light suddenly spilled into the darkness.

"Pietor," she repeated in that same harsh, tired whisper. "Behind you."

He whirled.

Major Montfort stood in the doorway, a pistol aimed at Pietor. "Sorry, Gabris."

The bang and puff of smoke barely registered before the bullet slammed into him. A scream rent the air as he sank to the stone floor beside Chesna.

33

When Chesna opened her eyes again, she found her bare-chested husband lying beside her. In their bed. In the governess's chamber of the palace.

"Welcome back, my dove."

She stared at him in awe. How on earth...? "Are we dead?"

A broad smile broke out on his face. "No, Chess. We're both very much alive."

She sighed at his reassurance, but just as quickly, her relief turned to terror. "Irina?"

Pietor shook his head, took her hands and kissed them one at a time. "Irina is dead. The knife went right through her cold, black heart."

"She killed Queen Jasia, and she tried to kill Zarek." Fear rocketed through her, and she jerked upright. "Zarek!"

He gently pushed her down against her pillows. "Zarek is fine," he assured her. "You, however, need your rest. You lost a lot of blood. I'm not sure you're fully recovered yet."

Propping the pillows against the headboard, she arched a brow. "How long have I been recovering?"

"Five days now." The grin left his face, and lines of worry etched his forehead. "You nearly scared me to death. The blood, the rats, the mud."

"Mud?" She blinked. What mud?

"Apparently, Irina dragged you from where she first waylaid you to the old grain silo. By your feet. You were covered in mud, leaves, and pine needles from chin to knees. I thought I'd lose you before we could get you back here to the palace."

"H-how did we get here?"

"Major Montfort carried you." He leaned over her and nuzzled her neck with his whiskered cheek. "But I was able to walk up here on my own."

"Major Montfort?" She pulled away to stare at him. Surely he was mistaken. "He *shot* you. I saw him shoot you."

"In the shoulder. He also cut Zarek's thigh that night." Pietor exhaled his warm breath just behind her ear, sending pleasant shivers rippling from her neck to her toes. "Funny thing about Major Montfort. Seems he was under direct orders to be certain Zarek and I didn't leave for Moscow. Unfortunately, his commander didn't specify how he was to keep us here. Montfort came up with his own solution." He sat up higher in the bed, revealing the strips of bandage that covered his left side from his neck to the top of his elbow. "I'm not very useful to de Valmiere with half of me swaddled in bandages."

The more Pietor told her, the more her brain swam in muck, and she shook her head to clear it. "You mean that horrid Major Montfort is on our side?"

Pietor chuckled. "I know. I couldn't believe it myself, but it's true. Major Montfort is one of Amatia's best spies. When your father learned I was being sent to General de Valmiere's command, he told Montfort who I really was and ordered him to stay by my side and keep me out of trouble. It was Montfort, by the way, who convinced de Valmiere you and I should be married."

"Then, perhaps, we should thank him."

"We'll have to write him. He and the rest of de Valmiere's soldiers left three days ago for Moscow." He wrapped his right arm around her waist and hauled her up against his side. "You'll be happy to know, however, it's only my upper half that's useless right now. My lower half is still in proper working order."

Chesna squirmed out from under Pietor's embrace. "Three days ago? You mean the French are gone?"

"Temporarily," he reminded her, placing a finger upon

her lips and softly tracing a line. "Unless of course your father is correct and they meet their defeat in Russia."

"Of course I'm correct," Bela announced as he strode inside the bedchamber with a broad smile. "I'm never wrong. My daughter knows that."

"Papa!" She blinked, rubbed her eyes. When his image still stood in her doorway, her heart danced. "You're alive?"

"As alive as I ever was," Bela told her with a chuckle. He approached and leaned to kiss her forehead before turning his attention to the bed's other occupant. He frowned. "Pietor, I realize you two are married now, but do you think you can keep your hands off my daughter until I'm no longer in the room?"

Pietor immediately leaned back against the headboard, but his expression showed no shame at his father-in-law's rebuke. "I can try. Don't stay too long."

Chesna's cheeks burned hot enough to set the bedcovers on fire. Quickly, she changed the subject. "Where have you been for the last six weeks? Do you have any idea what I've gone through?"

Bela beamed proudly. "I know everything, my clever girl. Major Montfort kept me well informed of the happenings here. By God, you not only outmaneuvered my spies, you showed resourcefulness and valor, as well. And you kept His Majesty safe. A father couldn't be prouder of any child than I am of you. You're a Dubrow through and through."

"She's a Gabris now, Bela," Pietor reminded him.

"Thanks to me," Bela grinned.

Pietor frowned. "I'd like to think I had something to do with my own marriage."

"You showed up and said 'I do' when Father Grigory asked you," Bela retorted. "The rest was *my* doing, Pietor. Never forget it."

"You still haven't answered my question, Papa," Chesna interjected. "Where have you been?"

"I've resided as a guest of Father Grigory in the Church of St. Ambrose since the day after the invasion."

"But I don't understand. Why didn't anyone tell me you were alive?"

"Only Major Montfort and Father Grigory knew the

truth," Bela explained. "If de Valmiere had discovered I was alive, he would have stormed the church to reach me. Major Montfort reported to the general he had buried me beside the royal family. de Valmiere believed him. I only returned to the palace when I was certain the French army was long gone."

"But what happens if the French defeat Tsar Alexander's troops in Russia?" she asked. "They'll return here and we'll all be forced to flee from Amatia."

Bela shot a meaningful glance at Pietor who nodded solemnly. "I must flee from Amatia regardless of the outcome in Moscow, my dove," Pietor told her.

For a long moment, Chesna said nothing. Finally she sighed. "Because of your link to the throne. As long as we remain in Amatia, someone might attempt to overthrow Prince Mikhail and set you in his place."

"King Mikhail," Pietor amended. "But yes. The longer I remain in Amatia, the more tenuous Mikhail's rule becomes."

She took a deep breath for fortitude. "So, where are we going to live?"

Pietor shook his head. "You don't have to go with me if you don't wish to, Chess," he reminded her. "Your father will remain with the king."

"The Dubrows always remain with their sovereign," Bela added.

"But I'm a Gabris now. My obligation is to my husband and, God willing, our children." She took Pietor's hands between her own. "Where you go, I go."

He smiled and traced a finger gently down her jawline. "I was thinking we should settle in America, my dove. What say you to that?"

Her eyes never left his face. "I say yes."

"An excellent choice," Bela replied. "Though not unexpected. And so, in gratitude for your loyalty and service to the crown, His Majesty has deeded four hundred acres of fertile farmland in a place called Cow Harbor, New York to Pietor and Chesna Gabris."

Four hundred...? Chesna's jaw dropped. "We're overwhelmed by His Majesty's generosity."

"Don't be. You earned it."

"One last gift His Majesty has provided for you," Pietor said as he lifted her left hand from the bedclothes. The royal signet ring she'd worn since her wedding day had been replaced with a simple circlet of gold. "He ordered the royal jeweler to create this out of the pieces from your mother's earrings."

Emotions tumbled inside her: surprise, gratitude, relief, excitement at the coming journey, and wonder. "His Highness thought to do this for me?"

Her husband shrugged. "I might have suggested you'd appreciate the sentiment."

She threw her arms around his neck and kissed him with the happiness her heart could no longer hold. Pietor nuzzled her neck again. Sparks ignited in her bloodstream, and she melted into the featherbed. "Mmmm..."

"Chesna looks quite tired, Bela." Pietor's hands roamed over her skin. She licked her lips, pulled him closer. "I believe she and I need to rest for awhile. If you'll excuse us..."

On a sigh of surrender, Bela strode to the door. "You held out longer than I thought you would, Pietor," he noted with a grin. "You and Chesna take all the time you need. His Majesty and I will attend to other business until you are no longer...indisposed."

He closed the door firmly behind him, but Chesna barely registered his exit. "I love you, Pietor."

"I love you, Chess. Didn't I promise I'd come back for you?" He kissed her forehead, her cheeks, and finally, her lips. "I would never wish to disappoint you, my dove."

EPILOGUE

Dear Bela,

You are a grandfather now. Danica Arabella Jasia Gabris was born on the third of May. She and Chesna are strong and healthy. And for that, I must give praises to God.

As its name would lead one to believe, Cow Harbor is a port city on the coast of Long Island Sound with acres of rich and fertile farmland. We have begun building an expansive home on forty acres of this farmland, which Chesna still intends to fill with our dozen children.

Although Chesna is taken with America's natural beauty and the warmth of this country's residents, I do worry about our vulnerability to British occupation. Chesna finds it amusing that we left Amatia to avert a war only to arrive in America in time for their current battle with England. Perhaps she is correct when she tells me that intrigue seems to follow us, whether we wish it to or not. Or perhaps I am correct when I say that your daughter is drawn to intrigue, whether she will admit to it or not.

Whatever the case, we are blissfully happy, Bela, and eternally grateful to King Mikhail for his generosity in providing us with all that we need for a prosperous life in our new land. Our daughter may be an American by birth, but she and her parents will always be loyal Amatian citizens.

Until we meet again in another time and place, may God watch over us all and keep us in His grace...

—Excerpt from letter dated June 1814

ABOUT THE AUTHOR

Gina Ardito is the award-winning author of more than twenty romances in contemporary, historical, and paranormal sub-genres. In 2012, she launched her freelance editing business, Excellence in Editing. She's hosted workshops around the world for writing conferences, author organization meetings, and library events.

To her everlasting shame, despite all her accomplishments, she'll never be more famous than her dog, who starred in commercials for 2015's Puppy Bowl. For more information, to sign up for her newsletter, and to learn about all things Gina, visit her website at https://ginaardito.com.

BOOKS BY GINA ARDITO

THE MONEY SERIES
The Bonds of Matri-money
A Run for the Money
◆
That's Amore!
◆
THE NOBODY SERIES
Nobody's Darling
Nobody's Business
Nobody's Perfect
◆
Chasing Adonis
Duping Cupid
◆
THE AFTERLIFE SERIES
Eternally Yours
In Your Dreams
Waiting in the Wings
◆
THE CALENDAR GIRLS SERIES
Charming for Mother's Day
Duet in September
Reunion in October
Homecoming in November
Memories in December
◆
Even Now
A Love to Keep Me Warm
Lightning in a Bottle
Echoes of Love
◆
ANTHOLOGIES
Kaleidoscope Hearts 2

www.ingramcontent.com/pod-product-compliance
Lightning Source LLC
Chambersburg PA
CBHW060404180626
46817CB00007B/2506